**SEEING IS BELIEVING**

Sarah frantically explained to the motorcycle policeman who pulled her over. "Scott Corbin," she said, still breathing hard. "The Chameleon. He's right back there and he has murdered six women. He's a convicted serial killer."

She blinked back her tears and groaned aloud, aware of how vulnerable she really was. Why had she ever been so foolish as to testify at that man's trial? Now he would track her down and kill her.

The main question Sarah had, however, was, How could she possibly have seen Corbin today?

He had been executed by lethal injection six months earlier at the state prison in Huntsville, Texas. . . .

**Praise for *Without Sin***

"Riveting. . . . The twists and turns will keep readers guessing until the very end. A most entertaining read." —*Romantic Times*

"Authentic and enticing. . . . You won't predict the ending—never in a million years."

—Leonard Goldberg

# DEAD RINGER

Charles Smithdeal

AN ONYX BOOK

ONYX
Published by New American Library, a division of
Penguin Putnam Inc., 375 Hudson Street,
New York, New York 10014, U.S.A.
Penguin Books Ltd, 80 Strand,
London WC2R 0RL, England
Penguin Books Australia Ltd, Ringwood,
Victoria, Australia
Penguin Books Canada Ltd, 10 Alcorn Avenue,
Toronto, Ontario, Canada M4V 3B2
Penguin Books (N.Z.) Ltd, 182–190 Wairau Road,
Auckland 10, New Zealand

Penguin Books Ltd, Registered Offices:
Harmondsworth, Middlesex, England

First published by Onyx, an imprint of New American Library,
a division of Penguin Putnam Inc.

First Printing, September 2002
10 9 8 7 6 5 4 3 2 1

Printed in the United States of America

*For Debbie*

## Acknowledgments

For Death Row information, thank you to Mary Anne Weaver, technical writer, Executive Services at Texas Department of Criminal Justice's BOT Complex (Administration) in Huntsville, Texas.

Thank you, Melissa McGrath, detective, Homicide Division and Crimes Against Persons, Austin Police Department, Austin, Texas, for sharing meaningful details about how homicide investigations are carried out. And congratulations to the entire division for their near-perfect conviction record in recent years.

Thank you to Steve Shepherd, founder and president of Regency Voice Systems Inc. in Dallas, Texas, for sharing valuable details about banking-software systems and businesses.

Thank you, Tiffany Yates, for an outstanding job of copyediting.

Thank you, John Paine, for your exceptional story sense and your ability to create order and a natural flow from my sometimes erratic ideas.

Continuing thanks to my esteemed editor, Hilary Ross, for her invaluable insights, ideas, suggestions, and guidance.

Thank you once again to Phyllis Westberg, of Harold Ober Associates in New York—a shining example of what literary agents should aspire to be.

Most of all, I thank God for giving me the desire and ability first to read, and then to write. And for allowing me to live in these wonderful United States of America.

# CHAPTER ONE

"Oh, my God."

Sarah had stopped for a downtown Austin traffic light when an unexpected movement drew her attention to the edge of the crosswalk. She almost screamed.

She gawked through her windshield, stunned, at a face from her worst nightmare.

The man stood amid a group of sweltering pedestrians in the Texas July heat, his eyes fixed on the traffic signal above Congress Avenue. He wiped his sweaty brow on one arm and rotated his head once again in a circle above his shoulders, then quickly replaced his baseball cap and sunglasses.

Sarah's fingers cramped from gripping her steering wheel so tightly. It couldn't be. What she saw wasn't possible. Yet there he was, straightening now and starting directly toward her.

She jammed her foot against the accelerator and shot across the intersection, oblivious to right-of-way concerns, screeching tires, and blaring automobile horns. Her only impulse was to escape. She had traveled less than thirty feet when she slammed on her brakes to avoid a scruffy, bent-eared dog that darted across the street. The instant the animal was safely across, Sarah sped away, her heart hammering against her ribs. She was too frightened to risk a glance in her rearview mirror.

Moments later Sarah frantically explained to the motorcycle policeman who pulled her over.

"Scott Corbin," she said, still breathing hard. "The Chameleon. He's right back there and he has murdered six women. He's a convicted serial killer."

Back at the intersection minutes later with the patrol officer, Sarah anxiously scanned a horde of office workers scurrying to and from lunch-hour errands. No Scott Corbin.

The young officer took a quick inventory of Sarah Hill—brunette, about thirty-two, five-five, no wedding band, driving a well-tended dark blue '98 Honda Accord. She could be attractive if she made herself up and displayed her figure more, he thought. Even as upset as she was, she had kind eyes that sparkled a startling green.

The policeman not only questioned what Sarah had said; he cited her for running a red light and reckless driving.

Sarah's hands trembled as she drove off, frustrated, angry, and still frightened. She was suddenly overwhelmed with an awareness of being all alone in the world. Other than coworkers at the office and acquaintances at the animal shelter, she had no one to turn to. Even Phyllis, her one close friend, had moved away three months earlier. Sarah's entire family consisted of herself and Margot—her beautiful little cat.

She blinked back her tears and groaned aloud, aware of how vulnerable she really was. Why had she ever been so foolish as to testify at that man's trial? Now he would track her down and kill her.

The main question Sarah had, however, was, How could she possibly have seen Corbin today? He was dead.

Scott Corbin had been executed by lethal injection six months earlier at the state prison in Huntsville, Texas.

Still shaky when she arrived at Integrated Systems Inc., Sarah hurried to her desk and sat, clasping her hands tightly in her lap to control their trembling.

Amanda Stowe came into Sarah's office almost immediately. Blessed with bouncy blond hair, an enviable figure, and a friendly disposition, twenty-six-year-old Amanda carried a perpetually surprised expression on her face.

"Are you all right, Sarah?"

"Oh, I . . . I suppose so. I've just had a very frightening experience."

Amanda's expression went from surprise to concern. "I knew something was wrong when you didn't stop at the front desk. It's the first time since I started here that you haven't said something nice to me on your way in. What happened?"

"Well, I . . ." Sarah didn't care to go into the details just now. She really needed to phone the police. "A little dog ran out in front of my car and I almost had an accident. Plus, I got a traffic ticket."

"No wonder you're so upset. I know how much you love animals. Is it all right?"

Sarah assured the receptionist that the dog was safe. The instant Amanda left, Sarah phoned the Austin Police Department. She forced herself to sound collected when she asked for Det. Robert Garding.

"Sorry, ma'am," she was told. "Detective Garding retired almost a year ago. Can someone else help you?"

Sarah tried to hide her disappointment. She had come to know and trust Detective Garding five years earlier. She eventually gave a description of the man she'd seen to Det. Harry Wilkes.

"He's thirty-four years old," she began, "six feet tall, medium build with broad shoulders and a narrow waist. Approximately a hundred and seventy-five pounds, perhaps a little less now. Black hair combed straight back, with a widow's peak. Brown eyes so pale they're almost yellow, and always moving . . . like they're constantly watching for something or somebody. Strong cheekbones and chin. A straight nose with a high bridge and sculpted tip."

As she spoke, Sarah flashed on Scott Corbin sitting across from her in a crowded Mexican restaurant nearly six years ago. Their first date. Well, it wasn't really a date—she had met him for lunch one day. She recalled how she had delighted in studying his strong features each time he'd looked away that afternoon. Less than a month later she had discovered what a monster he was.

Sarah shuddered, then continued her description to the policeman. "He had a neatly trimmed short brown mustache today," she said, "but didn't used to. He has this strange habit of rolling his head around over his shoulders sometimes, as though he's held his head in one position too long and his neck is stiff. He wore blue jeans and black work boots and a short-sleeved blue work shirt. Aviator-type dark sunglasses. A tan baseball cap with a brown-and-green emblem and writing on the front. I couldn't read what it said. Oh, yes, he carried his left arm at a funny angle as he started toward me."

"Was he carrying something under the arm?"

"It was more like he'd slept on it wrong or something. He might have been wearing a shoulder holster, with a gun under that arm. He always carries a gun. And a knife. Usually more than one knife."

"How do you know that?"

"It came out at the trial."

A significant silence followed; then Detective Wilkes asked, "Ma'am, are you talking about the same Scott Corbin who killed all those women a few years back? The serial killer?" The officer's voice had gone rigid. He was familiar with the man Sarah described.

"Of course that's who I'm talking about," Sarah responded, struggling to contain her frustration. "The Chameleon. How many Scott Corbins are there?"

Silence. Then, cautiously, "Ms. Hill, you must be aware that Scott Corbin is dead."

"That's what I thought . . . until today."

"Oh, no, ma'am, there's no doubt about the Chameleon's being dead . . . the state executed him last January." The officer's voice had become totally flat. "You did not see Scott Corbin today. You saw somebody who looked like him."

"I know what I saw, Detective Wilkes. He may have lost weight and grown a mustache, but he's very much alive."

Unable to convince the officer over the next several minutes, Sarah asked again how she might locate Det. Robert Garding.

Detective Wilkes didn't have that information.

Sarah's office at ISI was one of several ten-by-ten-foot cubicles within a high-ceilinged room. Sound-dampening gray partitions provided ample privacy in the cubicles, both for sound and sight, yet the cubicles remained bright and airy.

Her desk sat near a north-facing window, and was metal with a manufactured mahogany top housing her computer station. Sarah saw to it that her office remained organized and uncluttered, as it was today. Virtually all her work was performed via telephone or computer, and all records stored on the computer's hard drive, backed up on floppy disks.

ISI created and sold software systems for banks. Their systems not only expedited internal banking procedures and data storage, but enabled bank customers to interact via telephone or computer with information about their account balances, auto loans, home mortgages, and so forth. On-line-banking customers could also pay monthly bills and transfer funds securely between their accounts from anyplace in the world where they had access to the Internet. Sarah's job as support manager entailed troubleshooting company installations, a task she generally accomplished without leaving her chair. She was, in fact, generally acknowledged as one of the top troubleshooters in the industry.

Sarah queried Southwestern Bell's information service for Austin and surrounding areas. Two Robert Gardings were listed, but neither turned out to be the retired detective. She sat silently at her desk for several minutes after the second call, organizing her thoughts. Then she instituted a nationwide computer search.

The bucolic scenes along Highway 290 between Stonewall, Texas, and the historic German farming community of Fredericksburg made Sarah feel that she had entered another world. Far removed from the hot, flat terrain of her childhood outside Abilene, this was the Texas Hill Country. Rolling green hills, lazy rivers, and lush pastures were interspersed with immaculately manicured peach orchards. White-tailed deer seemed to roam wherever they liked. The idyllic setting almost relegated her concern about a malignant serial killer to fantasy. Almost.

After driving past the George Bush Gallery, the Admiral Nimitz Museum, and the Marketplatz in Fredericksburg, she followed Highway 16 and eventually parked in a gravel drive under a giant white oak.

Retired detective Robert Louis Garding came around the side of the old stone farmhouse. He wore faded jeans and mud-crusted work boots instead of a detective's suit and tie, but he hadn't really changed at all. Tall and rangy, in his late fifties, Garding had iridescent blue eyes beneath thinning white hair, a quick smile, and an easy manner that belied the carbon-fiber core Sarah had come to respect when they had worked together to put Scott Corbin away.

Inside, Sarah commented on how inviting his living room was, with its stone walls and rough-hewn beams. The furniture was hand-carved and gnarly, but comfortable, not unlike its owner. She shuddered at two heavily antlered heads mounted over a stone fireplace. How could people do that to such magnificent animals? She chose a leather-backed chair facing away from their pleading eyes, tugged her skirt down over her knees, and crossed her ankles. At least there were no guns in sight.

"Notice how cool it is in here?" asked Garding. His voice was masculine, but carried a slight nasal intonation, and one side of his mouth opened wider than the other when he spoke, as if talking around an imaginary cigarette. A hint of a drawl suggested an East Texas or Louisiana upbringing. He took a seat opposite Sarah on a worn leather sofa.

"The room feels marvelous," Sarah replied. "It must still be ninety outside. It was over a hundred in Austin today."

"And this is with no air-conditioning. These walls are fourteen inches thick and as airtight as a nun's alibi. Seamless metal roof. I'll tell you, those old Germans knew how to build. Their sheep pens are better constructed than most houses today." He studied Sarah's face. "How you doing, young lady? You sounded worried over the phone. Somebody hassling you?"

Sarah took in a breath, then told him what she had seen. She hoped he wouldn't think her hysterical, or overreacting. She had promised herself never to be like her mother in that regard.

Garding listened patiently, then fished around in a shirt pocket as though searching for something. Sarah knew he had quit smoking five years earlier, right after the trial ended. Rummaging through his pockets probably gave him something to do while he mulled over what she'd told him. Perhaps he was absently checking for the spiral notepad he'd carried for so many years.

He finally responded. "Sarah, I drove through the damnedest rainstorm you've ever seen to make it down to Huntsville that night. I wasn't about to be late. And you'd better believe I kept my eyes glued to that observation window once I got there." Garding screwed up his craggy face. "I personally watched the lethal injection flow into that sick bastard's veins. My only regret was, I couldn't push the plunger myself."

# Chapter Two

Sarah was drawn back to that Congress Avenue intersection the next noon like iron filings to a magnet. Not that she expected to see him again. Not really. She went back to reassure herself that the remainder of what she recalled had been real.

The traffic signal was the same. The buildings. The hordes crowding the crosswalks. She had considered picking up a salad from Town Lake Deli, but her stomach had been a bit grumbly all morning, probably from the chocolate she'd been unable to resist the night before. It couldn't have been the wine, she told herself.

Sarah stopped suddenly, her breath caught in her throat. A man coming out of the delicatessen rolled his head over his shoulders exactly the way Scott Corbin had. But this man didn't look anything like Corbin. She craned her neck for a better look.

*My God, could it be?* Yes, it was him! But he looked entirely different today in bun-hugging black jeans and pointy black boots. He wore a tight Corona Cerveza T-shirt over a chest and arms more muscular than she remembered. A straw hat and black handlebar mustache made him appear Hispanic. His skin appeared deeply tanned—but it was unquestionably him. She watched the way his incongruous pale eyes searched the street, his walk, even the strange way he carried his left arm. Any lingering doubt was dispelled when the man suddenly rotated his head in a circle again. Corbin had once told her how good it felt to "pop" a neck stiff from hours of reading or typing. Said he had a touch of arthritis in his cervical vertebrae from a high school football injury.

Sarah's heart thrashed like flushed quail. She willed herself to disappear, and instantly ducked behind a portly gentleman in a business suit. A split second later she dared to peer around to watch where Corbin might go. With similar-appearing Hispanic men on the sidewalk, she had to search to find her quarry. But there he was. She struggled with an impulse to shout a warning to somebody. In the end she was too frightened to make a sound. When the man providing her cover abruptly turned into a doorway, she fell in behind two others. Corbin walked several paces ahead, the macho swagger of his gait matching others in view. Blending. A chameleon.

*The* Chameleon.

Sarah frantically searched the sidewalk and streets with her eyes. No policeman in sight. Her tongue seemed stuck to the roof of her mouth. She was roasting all over except for her forehead, which was surprisingly cool. A heel caught on something for an instant and she fought for balance, both eyes glued to the macho figure quickening his steps around the corner.

Had he seen her? Why was he hurrying? She tried

to swallow an enormous lump in her throat, but it wouldn't budge.

She rounded the corner and shielded her face with her purse just as Corbin bounded through the open door of a bus. The bus roared away.

As she stood in a noxious cloud of exhaust, Sarah's mind raced. While confused and frightened, she was reassured somehow that she had confirmed what she had seen before.

Scott Corbin was very much alive.

Det. Harry Wilkes listened patiently to Sarah's second report. He interrupted when she began her description of Scott Corbin.

"I have that right here, ma'am. A neatly trimmed short brown mustache—"

"No, it was long and black. The twirly kind villains in old movies wear."

"Of course. Were you able to read what it said on his baseball cap with the brown-and-green emblem today?"

Sarah was too upset to be dissuaded by his insinuation. She almost shouted into the phone, "He wasn't wearing a baseball cap." She immediately contained herself, however, reverting to her businesslike tone.

"He had on one of those straw hats that farmworkers wear. He's made himself up to look Mexican; don't you understand?"

"Of course . . . that's exactly what the Chameleon would do."

"Precisely."

Detective Wilkes condescendingly agreed to dispatch a car to the area, despite Sarah's protests that Corbin had escaped more than five minutes earlier on a transit-system bus and would be widening his lead each minute they spoke. She strongly recommended that the police search all blue-and-white Number 13 Capital-Metro buses traveling south on Congress Avenue. She was chagrined that she'd been too agitated to record the license number.

The detective asked her to please be sure and let him know the next time she saw this dead man—particularly what type of mustache he might have grown.

Sarah fought back tears of anguish as she hung up. She had certainly expected a different response. Interest, at a minimum, or concern. She dialed the number for retired detective Garding and told him what she'd seen.

"Sarah, I remember how accurate you always were about things, but we both know you couldn't have seen Scott Corbin. You obviously saw somebody who looks an awful lot like him . . . I don't doubt that."

"It was him, Detective. I know it was. Both times."

Garding didn't speak for a moment. Finally he asked, "Has anything upset you lately? You been having those nightmares again?"

"I was not dreaming, I am not being hysterical, and I am not mistaken. I saw Scott Corbin. I worked beside the man for a year, Detective Garding. I went out with him once."

After unsuccessfully trying to convince Sarah of her error, Garding finally agreed to check into what she thought she had seen. "I got my private investigator's license about three months ago," he said, "so this will be my first chance to use it."

"I'll gladly pay you."

"Don't worry about that for now . . . let's wait and see what I find. Now, tell me again exactly where you thought you saw him. Both times."

Shortly after finishing her conversation with Detective Garding, Sarah punched in the phone number for the *Austin American-Statesman.*

During a break that afternoon Sarah told a small collection of coworkers about her second sighting. Integrated Systems had over thirty in-house employees, apart from salespeople in the field. For those who hadn't been close to the situation, she shared details of Scott Corbin's arrest more than five years earlier.

First to crowd into her office was ISI's thirty-six-year-old purchasing agent, Marvin Jamison, who had sandy hair, a perpetual tan, and huge, brown, sleepy eyes. Marv was a glad-hander and aging jock who'd be at home in any country-club bar. He wore an open-necked flowered sports shirt. Like Sarah, Jamison had worked with Corbin at their old company, Electronic Business Systems, before they were bought out by ISI, so he added colorful bits of information from his own recollections.

Their receptionist, Amanda Stowe—whom Marvin Jamison often referred to as "the new blond girl with the teeth and tits"—was also present. Amanda stood next to Jamison, mesmerized by what she was hearing. Since Amanda had been hired only three months earlier, this intrigue was entirely new to her.

Tad Roman quietly listened, expressionless. Tad had always reminded Sarah of a freshly scrubbed Boy Scout. He was the only thirty-one-year-old man she knew who still slicked his hair back with oil. Tad wore heavy black-framed glasses and seemed to have a perpetually drippy nose, due to allergies. Sarah had been training Tad Roman six years earlier, when Scott Corbin first reported for work at EBS, so Roman was familiar with many details as well.

Bringing Amanda up to speed, Sarah said, "When Scott Corbin was hired to work at Electronic Business Systems—EBS, as we called it—we had no way of knowing he had already killed four women. Mr. Shapiro was president of the company then, and he asked me to break Corbin in, then train him as a troubleshooter."

Software programmer Clarence "Cosmo" Rivers, twenty-five, paused on his way past the gathering just long enough to peek in and razz Sarah. Long and lean with sunken eyes surrounded by dark circles, Cosmo was as weird as he appeared. ISI's number one software programmer and creative genius, Cosmo had an IQ rivaling the national debt and a black ponytail halfway down his back. He lived in sandals and shorts or motorcycle attire, and spoke in a cant intelligible only to other programmers. People like Cosmo were a necessary evil that electronic businesses clamor for, then hide away in back rooms. He worked in an enclosed office with a solid door, affectionately termed "the rubber room." Today he wore black jeans, motorcycle boots, tiny, oval, wire-framed sunglasses, and a black T-shirt. The shirt depicted a man attempting to cut a hangman's noose from his own neck with a blood-dripping saber.

"Hey, Sarah," Cosmo said, "how many rapists and serial murderers have accosted you so far today?" He made a ghoulish, trilling "Wooo-ooo-ooo-ooo" sound, laughed demonically, and hurried away. Rivers had also worked with Scott Corbin.

Ignoring Cosmo, Sarah continued, surprised at the interest being shown. Normally people came to her only when they needed help solving some software or logistical problem, or to offer obligatory congratulations after the company's annual awards banquet.

Her hope was that sharing her frightening experience might make it less ominous somehow. She really needed somebody to listen. Somebody who'd believe what she said.

"As I was saying," Sarah said, "I trained Scott Corbin, then worked alongside him for a year." She did not mention that she had been romantically interested in Corbin until the evening before his arrest. "And you know how they say you can never tell a serial killer? That they're the person next door who everybody thinks is so normal? Believe me, they're right. I never suspected a thing until that night."

"What night?"

The question came from a new arrival to the assemblage, Marissa Young. About thirty-three, five-seven, auburn-haired, and soft-spoken, Marissa was a divorcée from California with an attractive face and figure. She had been hired as operations manager for ISI a year ago, and was doing an outstanding job. Behind her back Marissa was known as "Miss Perfect," for she often dressed and behaved like a schoolteacher.

"I was talking about the night Rhonda Talbot was killed," Sarah replied.

Marissa asked, "Who's Rhonda Talbot?"

"The Chameleon's last victim before he was arrested." Sarah explained, "I was just saying how Scott Corbin—the Chameleon's real name—had killed four women before he came to work here, and a fifth during the time he was here. Actually, at EBS. He worked right beside me and I never suspected a thing. Then he murdered Rhonda Talbot . . . a horribly vicious attack. He taped her to a dining room chair and cut her into ribbons."

The senior vice president's secretary, Tracy Leigon, approached and interrupted from outside the cubicle. Tracy was twenty-nine years old, built like a fire hydrant, and spoke the way people sound after breathing helium.

"I'm good friends with the wife of a policeman who worked on that case," Tracy said. "My friend said the Chameleon slashed his victims into pieces, then removed their eyes."

A collective groan went through the room. Tracy continued, enjoying her moment, "Nobody knows what he did with the eyes because they never found them."

"Excuse me." With a sudden greenish cast to her complexion, Amanda Stowe quickly wove her way between the others and left. Marvin Jamison locked his gaze on Amanda's sizable breasts and let out a sigh when her tight bottom brushed against him on the way out.

Sarah continued, "Marissa, I know you didn't move to Texas till last year, but it was really scary living here back then. This man terrorized Austin for over three years. His victims were brunette women in their early thirties, between five-three and five-six. All had been tortured and their bodies severely mutilated. And, to answer your question, Rhonda Talbot worked for ISI before the rest of us came over from EBS. She was ISI's operations manager."

Tracy Leigon added gravely, "The very position you hold today, Marissa."

Marissa lowered her head for a moment, but didn't speak. One manicured hand toyed with the formal collar of her gray pin-striped suit. "Oh, my," she finally replied.

Sarah said, "I'm not sure exactly how they met, but Scott Corbin had dinner with Rhonda Talbot the night I was referring to." Sarah recalled the painful sense of betrayal she had felt that evening when she saw those two together. A feeling that had later turned to relief. She added, "Rhonda was short and brunette, like all the others."

"Exactly like you are, Sarah," said Tracy Leigon.

Sarah tried to ignore her comment, continuing, "I had attended a fund-raising dinner for the animal shelter that night, and was walking back to my car when I ran into Scott Corbin with a very pretty woman. I stopped to say hello and he introduced me.

They were both nicely dressed, and said they had just had dinner at Basil's Restaurant over on West Tenth. Actually I had met Rhonda briefly when she and some others toured our offices at EBS once, but I didn't recall her name."

Marvin Jamison interrupted, "Anybody who believes that Sarah actually forgot something, raise one hand." Nobody did. He laughed heartily.

ISI's thirty-five-year-old senior vice president, Anthony Shapiro, interrupted from the entrance to Sarah's office. He was a decent-looking man, trim and neat, who bubbled over with sexual energy and drive. He had coifed light brown hair that never seemed to need cutting, and professionally manicured nails. He was immaculately dressed in a tan suit and tie and wore thick eyeglasses. Shapiro suggested that it was time to return to work.

As they dispersed, Marissa Young softly said, "Perhaps you'll finish your story for us later, Sarah? And we want to hear what the police are doing about the man you saw at that intersection."

Sarah received a faxed document from the *Austin American-Statesman* minutes after she returned to her desk. The Chameleon had remained so newsworthy four-plus years after his arrest, the report took up half a page. Sarah zeroed in on the details she sought.

> *. . . following his execution by lethal injection, Scott Corbin was pronounced dead at the Texas Department of Criminal Justice's Death House in Huntsville, Texas, at 6:17* P.M. *on January 12.*

"If not Corbin, who?" Sarah asked herself. "How could I be so wrong?"

Sarah jumped when she heard a noise outside her apartment window that evening, but saw nothing unusual when she peeked through the venetian blinds. She checked the locks and security chains on both the front door and kitchen door for the third time, drained the last of a bottle of chardonnay into her glass, and returned to the sofa. Every light in her apartment was on. Her uneaten dinner of green salad and steamed vegetables with chunks of tofu rested on a TV table beside her.

Her living room was pristine and as uncluttered as her office, done in a pink-flowered gray and white fabric on the sofa, armchair, and drapes. Framed botanical prints hung on one wall. A Susan Rios print adorned another, depicting an inviting sun porch.

A glass-top dining table and four chrome-and-leather chairs near Sarah matched the coffee table in front of the sofa. She consulted her typewritten TV schedule, and selected the next program she would watch while she ate. In the kitchen Dame Margot, a lissome white longhaired cat with Dresden-blue eyes, jumped down from the top of the refrigerator and investigated a bowl of cat food.

Sarah toyed with her own food and attempted to concentrate on the TV show. At length she laid her fork and napkin down and picked up the article she had received that afternoon from the *Austin American-Statesman.*

She finished her third glass of wine as she reread

the account of Scott Corbin's execution, resisting the urge to open another bottle. She had resolved to limit her drinking to one or two glasses each evening, no matter how lonely or how bored she might feel. Certainly never more than three.

She scanned the article again and thought of the man at that intersection. The man she had now seen twice. In her heart she knew exactly who she had seen, no matter what anybody said—Detective Garding, that policeman at Austin Police Headquarters, or the author of this newspaper article. Every fiber of Sarah's body screamed out that she wasn't mistaken.

She sat shaking her head, thinking, remembering. Feeling. This report was wrong. Dead wrong, somehow. She was certain of it.

Though slightly tipsy when she stood to check her door locks once again, Sarah walked carefully to the refrigerator and opened a new bottle of wine.

# Chapter Three

Noisily shaking 20N Rancher's Cubes in a plastic bucket, retired detective Robert Garding enticed his bleating sheep into a fenced enclosure behind the barn and closed the gate. He hurriedly spread the pellets into widely separated piles to avoid having his feet trampled. Hungry sheep were aggressive, pushing and shoving far more than he would've thought before retiring from police work. And strong. But dumber than dirt.

He reflected on Sarah Hill's visit as he walked to the house—what she thought she had seen. A nice young woman, but too intense. Stiff. Needed a husband and children to worry over, if you asked him.

Yes, Sarah had been a help during the investigation. She was the only eyewitness who had seen Scott Corbin with Rhonda Talbot the night Talbot was murdered. At least, the only one to come forward and testify.

Garding knocked caked mud and sheep dung from his boots before going inside the house, as if anybody cared. Living alone for the three years since Mary Beth died, he neglected many of the things he had adjusted to at her insistence. Things like not tossing his dirty clothes into a corner in the bedroom, or leaving dishes piled in the kitchen sink for days at a time. What difference did it make, really? He had cleaned things up a bit when Sarah called and asked if she could drive down to speak with him. Washed the dishes, stuffed his dirty clothes inside a closet, and made the bed. He'd even swept the floor in the living room and mopped the kitchen. Oh, yes, and cleaned the front bathroom and put the toilet seat down.

He let out a long breath. He'd gladly do all those things and more to have his beloved wife back.

God, he missed Mary Beth.

Garding tossed his straw Stetson on the table he used as a makeshift desk in the kitchen. He opened a drawer and removed a file, then tilted his ladder-back chair up on two legs and thumbed through newspaper clippings and pages of personal notes.

The Chameleon. What sort of twisted SOB would do those things to another human being? Especially to a defenseless woman? A coward is what he was. He'd never try that shit with a man.

Garding dropped his front chair legs back to the floor and scratched one ear. Even the memory of that pervert was giving Sarah Hill nightmares. Poor girl. Sarah had never done anybody any harm.

Garding stood and went to the sink counter. He clapped his hands into a cloud of gnats above the peaches he'd picked two days before. He rinsed a peach and walked into the living room, savoring the ripe, sweet fruit from his own orchard.

Minutes later he spoke with a clerk in the Classification and Records office for Huntsville State Prison. "I need to get copies of some documents on an inmate who was executed there last January the twelfth," Garding began. "His name was Scott Corbin."

"Are you with TDCJ, sir?"

"I was the arresting officer . . . Austin Police Department, Homicide Unit. Now I'm private."

Sarah's phone call to Austin PD the next morning confirmed that Detective Wilkes had asked a car to patrol the area where she reported spotting the "suspicious" man. So far nobody had identified anything out of the ordinary.

Sarah was returning from the ladies' room when she saw Marvin Jamison leaning over the reception counter, giving Amanda Stowe his most seductive smile. Marvin had the obnoxious habit of talking to a woman's face while staring at her breasts, which he was doing at the moment. As Sarah approached, he was saying something to Amanda about slipping out early for a long lunch.

"Sorry to interrupt," Sarah said. "Amanda, I'm expecting a call from Det. Robert Garding. Please put him through straightaway."

"Sure thing, Sarah."

Jamison hitched up his trousers and grinned, saying, "You're looking especially nice today, Sarah."

"Thank you, Marv. By the way, how's Mrs. Jamison feeling? Did she get over her cold?"

Jamison nearly stuttered his answer. "Oh, yeah . . . sure . . . she's fine."

Sarah glanced knowingly at Amanda before continuing toward her office. Marvin had always been quite personable, but Sarah had no respect for his morals. Morals, hell—his overt lechery. He apparently had some irrepressible need to seduce every woman he encountered. She really disliked that.

Several women from the office had invited Sarah to join them for lunch. She and her officemates sat on the grass beneath a shade tree alongside Town Lake. Similar to New York's Central Park, the greenbelt was an oasis in the middle of a bustling city, serene and inviting, separating modern high-rises from the shore of the tranquil lake. It was slightly cooler today, fresh breezes off the water offering scents of honeysuckle and gardenias. Above the distant traffic noises floated birdsong and the hum of bees. Squirrels scampered nearby. No sooner were the women seated than they asked Sarah to continue the story she had begun the day before.

"There isn't much more," Sarah said, pleased to have been asked. She usually brown-bagged lunch at the office or ran errands during the noon hour and snacked on a piece of fruit. Having someone to eat with was a welcome change.

"Rhonda's murder hit the news the next day," Sarah began, "and Scott Corbin didn't show up for work. I didn't know at the time, but he told detectives he had heard about her death and went to the police station to see if he could be of help. What he was really doing was trying to divert suspicion from himself. Anyway, two detectives came to the office and asked if any of us knew anything that might help find the murderer. They knew that Corbin worked there and they considered him a suspect, but they didn't come out and say that till later. So I told Detective Garding and his partner, Detective Jared, about seeing Rhonda with Scott Corbin the night before. They got a search warrant the next morning and found all sorts of evidence in his apartment . . . things from the other murders as well. They even found Rhonda's bloodstained panties under the front seat of his car. I had watched her get into that car the very night she was killed." Sarah had to stop for a moment to collect herself. The memory remained terribly unsettling.

Marissa Young asked softly, "Did he rape her in the car?"

Before Sarah could respond Tracy Leigon answered in her little Martian voice, "The police didn't think so." Hunkered down on the ground, Tracy resembled a fire hydrant even more than when standing. She added, "But you don't want to imagine the things he did once he got her inside the house."

Everybody except Tracy stopped eating. Sarah cleared her throat and continued. "They asked me to testify at his trial. I tell you, I was scared to death, knowing he'd be right there in the courtroom no more than fifteen feet away, glaring at me the entire time I was on the stand. But I did it. I testified. I drove down to Kerrville and stayed at the Y. O. Ranch Resort for the full week. Kerrville is where they had moved the trial to . . . a change of venue because of all the publicity in Austin. It took the jury less than eight hours to convict him of three murders, although everybody knew he had committed all six." Sarah paused again. "Poor Rhonda Talbot was his sixth victim, the one that finally put him away. And I was the last person known to see her alive." She thought for a second, then added, "Besides Scott Corbin, of course."

"Oh, Sarah, you poor thing," Amanda Stowe said, pinching a corner of her lip between her teeth. "I can just imagine what you must have gone through."

"I didn't sleep very well for a long time afterward, that's for sure." Sarah flashed on a recurring nightmare that had soaked her gowns with perspiration for months after the trial. The dream always began with Scott Corbin working pleasantly alongside Sarah in the office. Next they would be holding hands and looking into each other's eyes across a candlelit table. He would take her into his arms as if to kiss her, but instead he would suddenly point an accusing finger and begin slashing her to pieces with a butcher knife—and her wide-awake all the while.

Tracy asked, "Does everybody know why they called him the Chameleon?" She didn't wait for a response. She rarely did. "He blended in so well that no two witnesses ever gave similar descriptions of him. A real master of disguise. My friend who's married to the policeman says he could be standing right beside you and you wouldn't even notice he was there."

"That's spooky," Amanda said, shivering as if from a sudden chill. Pensive for a moment she then asked very softly, "Why did he pluck out their eyes?"

Tracy answered, "That was some deep psychological thing about his victims never identifying him, even after they were dead. Like if police were to call in a psychic or something."

An extended silence followed while all but Tracy merely toyed with their food.

Amanda broke the silence. "Sarah, I'm impressed. I really am. If you hadn't come forth they never would've arrested him in the first place. They certainly wouldn't have found all that evidence. You're a hero, girl."

"Heroine," Tracy corrected with the faintest hint of jealousy.

"And then they . . . killed him?" asked Amanda.

Sarah replied, "I was also in the courtroom the day he was sentenced, five years ago. He was executed by lethal injection this past January the twelfth at the state prison in Huntsville." She straightened, stuffed her container of uneaten salad into a paper bag, then added, "Or so they said."

Later that afternoon Sarah Hill looked up from her computer monitor to see Cosmo Rivers leaning into her office. Today he wore a black leather motorcycle jacket and boots, with tan Bermuda shorts. A weird smile distorted Cosmo's face.

"Enjoying the attention, Sarah?" As he spoke he removed a rawhide tie from around his ponytail, then shook his long hair out over his shoulders.

Sarah asked what he meant.

"Oh, come on," Cosmo chided, "isn't that why you resurrected the big, bad monster? Nobody paying enough attention to little Sarah lately?"

Sarah was at once shocked and wounded. When she could respond she said, "I didn't resurrect anything, Cosmo . . . Scott Corbin was standing not three feet from my car alongside Congress Avenue." Garding's words about watching the lethal injection flow into Corbin's veins echoed in Sarah's mind, releasing a modicum of self-doubt. "I saw either him or his clone. Why would you think I'd make that up?"

"Are you saying you didn't enjoy the notoriety when the Chameleon was arrested? All those policemen and reporters hovering around you? The DA personally asking you to testify?"

"I certainly did not."

"Or getting your picture in the paper? When have you ever been on television except for when you fingered"—two fingers of each hand simulated quotation marks around his words—"the Chameleon monster?"

"If you think I enjoyed that, you're very mistaken. It was a horrible experience."

"Was it?" Cosmo tossed his hair and smiled knowingly. "Somehow I don't think so." He left.

Sarah was livid. How could anybody make such an accusation when all she had ever done was her civic duty? She prided herself on making the fewest errors humanly possible. And she knew what she had seen. She forced herself to count way beyond ten. In an effort to calm her emotions she turned her attention to a problem at a Frost Bank branch office. Someone at the bank had improperly reset their computer after a power outage, and the bank's phone lines were swamped with customer complaints.

Sarah went on-line and activated the bank's reset button right from her desk. She smiled, pleased with her precision. Traffic on that particular information highway unclogged instantly.

Sarah suddenly smacked the desk beside her keyboard with her open palm. "How dare that creep accuse me of such a thing." She sat staring at her monitor's screen for several moments, seething with anger.

Her instincts had never failed her before. Those instincts told her that the man she had seen was not a look-alike. Not a double. Scott Corbin was very much alive. And, God willing, she intended to prove it. She quickly swallowed an ibuprofen tablet with a sip of water, then phoned Robert Garding. Her head was really beginning to ache.

"I did some checking after the last time we spoke," Garding said through the phone. "In fact, I have a couple of things you ought to see. What's your fax number?"

Moments later Sarah read what Garding sent. Scott Corbin's name was at the top of a document, and the signature of the Texas Department of Criminal Justice's institutional-division director appeared at the bottom. The official "return of death warrant" affirmed that Corbin's execution by lethal injection had been carried out precisely as ordered by the Kerrville judge.

Long seconds later a chill snaked up Sarah's spine when she read Scott Corbin's faxed death certificate. Cause of death was listed as "Homicide; court-ordered lethal injection." The time was exactly as the newspaper had reported: 9:17 P.M. on January 12—almost exactly six months earlier.

Sarah searched her memory. Where had she been the night before she saw the man at that intersection on Congress? Of course, at the opening of *A Texas Romance* at the Live Oak Theater. She'd had only one glass of wine at intermission—all she ever allowed herself in public. Another glass when she returned home. Definitely no more than two. Besides, a couple of glasses of wine at night wouldn't have clouded her judgment the following day. It never had before. And what about the second time she saw him? She had felt perfectly fine then, too.

She studied the documents again, uncertain whether to be dismayed or reassured. She was unquestionably relieved that Scott Corbin wasn't loose on the streets to violate and murder again; however, she was greatly distressed that she could have been so badly mistaken.

Her. Sarah Hill. About anything, let alone something so vital. But she was convinced: Scott Corbin was indeed dead.

Then who had she seen that day on the street? Both days?

She sat shaking her head. On the rare occasions when she was unable to solve a problem in her job, she became obsessed. In this instance, however, she would have to force herself to accept that she'd very likely never know the answer.

Two men who were exact duplicates of the Chameleon, spotted within days of each other, at the exact same location.

What were the odds?

Sarah dialed Robert Garding's home number. What would it hurt to have him ask a few questions at the Huntsville prison? Maybe Scott Corbin did have a twin. A twin who'd want revenge on anybody who had helped send his brother to the execution chamber. Garding had said he was a private investigator now. So let him investigate.

The attractive woman glanced up and down the motel's hallway before putting the keycard into the slot. She was blond, tanned, athletic, and fashionably dressed in skirt, blouse, and heels. About thirty-five. When the small light on the door blinked green, she hurried inside.

"If you know what's good for you, you won't touch that light switch."

The woman froze where she stood, unmoving. The door latched behind her. A harsh male voice had come out of the darkness somewhere to her right. Faint strips of daylight were visible around the outside edges of drapes closed over a single window.

"Get over here. Now!" the man commanded.

"Where? I can't see anything."

"Straight ahead five steps, then left."

She did as she was told, then stopped when her leg touched the edge of the bed. Her pulse was racing, her mouth dry.

"Take off your blouse."

"No. I don't want to."

"Dammit, do as you're told."

She did. She dropped the blouse beside her feet.

"Now the brassiere."

She undid her brassiere and dropped it as well. Hands came out of the darkness to cup her breasts roughly; then his mouth was on one nipple, eagerly sucking.

The sound of a zipper being lowered was unmistakable, and the man abruptly turned her to one side. "On your knees, bitch."

She kicked off her shoes and knelt. Strong hands guided her head. Something firm yet velvety poked her in the cheek. She encircled his throbbing member with one hand, then took him fully into her mouth. He groaned aloud from above her.

Minutes later the man commanded, "Take off your skirt and panties."

Without a word, she rose up off her knees and did as she was told.

"Put these on. Hurry!"

Her eyes were adjusted to the darkness enough that she could make out his outline in front of her. She felt for the garments he held out, then slipped them on. She could hear him removing his shoes, then his trousers and undershorts.

"Get over here. Now!"

She watched a silhouette lie back on the bed. She found his hairy chest first, then his throbbing penis. She sat astride him and slowly took him inside. This time she groaned along with him.

"Wait," he commanded. "I want to watch your tits jiggle." He extended an arm and switched on a bedside lamp. "That's better."

Her skin was golden except where a skimpy bikini

had been, and her breasts firm and full. Anthony Shapiro pulled the woman's well-toned white buttocks against his every thrust.

Nude except for the black garter belt and black stockings, the woman rocked against Shapiro in a frenzy until their grunts and pants crescendoed to an excitement neither could contain. She yelled aloud; then the sound shut off at the exact moment when Shapiro clenched his teeth and groaned aloud. They both laughed softly and she collapsed against his chest.

When she could speak she said, "Oh, God, Tony . . . that was wonderful." Her voice was low, slightly husky.

"You were dynamite, Lil." He stroked her bare back, slowly working up to the back of her neck. "When I saw you in that garter belt and those stockings, I couldn't hold back another second."

She made a sound the way a contented cat purrs.

After a brief silence, he asked, "Sure you weren't followed?"

"Of course I'm sure."

"How can you be so certain?"

She pushed up on her hands to look at him. "I circled the block three times before I pulled into the parking lot. Don't be paranoid."

"I'm not paranoid. You know my wife's lawyers."

"Ex-wife, Tony."

"Not *ex* enough to suit me. She filed another suit Monday. The greedy bitch wants everything I'll ever have."

The woman smiled knowingly. "You must have a

stash somewhere. Either that or you've found a new source. You seem to have plenty whenever I see you."

Without responding he rolled her aside and sat up.

She said, "What? Where are you going?"

"I need to get back to the office. They think I'm having lunch with George Eiche, the general manager of First Federal." He put on his thick glasses, then picked up the phone and dialed.

"Amanda, this is Mr. Shapiro. Any calls for me?" He listened patiently, then said, "I'm leaving the restaurant now. Should be there in about fifteen minutes." He hung up and disappeared into the bathroom.

The woman got off the bed, removed the garter belt and black stockings, and began getting dressed. A minute or two later Shapiro returned and pulled on his shorts and trousers. "Do you like being tied up?"

"I've never tried it."

"You're kidding. I figured your husband was into everything."

"Ha! Variety to him means doing it every other Wednesday instead of alternate Fridays."

"I'll bring some handcuffs and rope next time. It's an incredible way to get off." He hesitated. "How about coke? Have you ever had sex after snorting a couple of lines? You get so wound up you can go all night. Really. You don't ever want to stop."

Late that night a figure wearing jeans, a dark windbreaker, sunglasses, and a baseball cap emerged from the shadows behind a Castle Hill apartment building. His excitement mounted as he watched, motionless, through a ground-floor window.

A young woman with long dark hair laughed inside with a young man above blaring country-western music. The young man wore a short-sleeved shirt, jeans, and western boots, and drank from a long-neck bottle of beer. The woman had on red western boots and a short red-and-white-checked skirt that exposed good thighs and the edge of pink panties whenever she twirled around fast.

She clearly wasn't wearing a bra, and the man watched her ample breasts bounce as she danced. Even through the window, he could see her nipples straining against the thin cotton blouse. Aware of a delicious sensation of heaviness in his genitals, he touched himself, feeling his penis stir, then stiffen and grow.

When the boyfriend left nearly a half hour later, the dark figure outside moved quietly to the bedroom window. The young woman sat on a bench by the foot of her bed. Unaware she was being watched, she swung one ankle at a time up over the opposite knee, removing her boots.

He could see the dark outline of pubic hair through thin panties each time she opened her legs. Oh, God, now she was taking off her blouse. He thought he would surely explode in his pants when she paused in front of a mirror and idly cupped her pert breasts in her hands. Pink nipples pointed up and out, and he could almost feel their turgor against his tongue. His breath caught when the woman stripped off her skirt and panties. And he *had* seen black pubic hair through her panties. Her bush was full and dark, exactly the way it should be.

With country-western music still blaring, the nude young woman padded to her bathroom and turned on the shower.

Blending into dark shadows the man outside deftly popped the window screen loose with a screwdriver, donned a stocking mask and latex gloves, and slipped inside.

His pulse pounded and his fingers trembled from the thrill of anticipation. He had waited so long for the soul fix of bloodcurdling screams. He could almost feel the softness of alabaster skin beneath his fingertips; could smell the unmistakable aroma of shampooed hair and cleaved flesh; and felt the excitement of watching and feeling the flow of pulsing crimson blood. His mouth watered at the anticipated sweetness of her most delicate organs, and his erection was throbbing now, straining against the dark fabric of his trousers even before he rubbed himself.

He carefully lowered the window behind him and shut the blinds. Midway across the bedroom he picked up the young woman's freshly discarded panties and held them to his nose, inhaling the musky scent he had craved for so very long. Quickly raising the volume even higher on her stereo, he hurried into the bathroom.

The woman's eyes froze wide with fear the instant he swept back the shower curtain, and her mouth opened to scream even before he raised the knife. Seconds later the man laughed aloud through his stocking mask as blood spurted and splattered on white bathroom tile.

He shuddered with a satisfaction long overdue as the woman's agonizing screams clung to his body and nourished his very being. He hardly noticed the spreading wetness in his undershorts.

"Please, God, no," she pleaded again.

Her attacker aimed a stout knife with a tarnished, round-tipped blade toward her face.

"Why?" she shrieked, fighting furiously against his superior strength. "Why are you doing this to me?" Her dark hair spilled onto her shoulders when her shower cap fell into a pool of red foam swirling around her feet.

She kicked and screamed till her legs flew out from beneath her and her head banged against cold porcelain with a terrible thud. Hanging on the edge of a desperate consciousness, she felt every slice and tug as this madman forced her head under the bloody water and scooped out her eyes. One at a time.

The woman gagged and coughed and threw up on herself while the man carefully positioned both of her intact orbs in a plastic sandwich bag—hazel-colored irises with large and unmoving black pupils, preserved now on a bed of crushed ice.

The woman's second-best feature would stare into space for eternity. Unblinking. Forever horrified.

She was too weak to struggle when the man grabbed her feet and dragged her through her living room, but her nails dug into cheap carpet on an uneven floor. Though she was blind now, the optic centers in her brain witnessed a kaleidoscope of vibrant colors. A separate set of sensory receptors recorded the searing hot pain where her eyes had been, and her throat released the most awful sound.

Her shrieks of agony sang to the man while he taped her to a chrome-and-vinyl dining chair. He quickly switched the stereo to a classical FM station and raised the volume again. It was only after he disemboweled her with a ten-inch butcher knife that the woman escaped, mercifully, into a serene release that was both silent and black.

The figure in the stocking mask emitted heavy breathing and orgasmic moans as he worked, one hand rapidly caressing his erect penis, the other carving his victim into pieces.

# Chapter Four

Two Homicide detectives flashed ID at a patrolman behind yellow crime-scene tape. The apartment building looked run-down for a middle-class neighborhood. The outside was brick, two-story, with dingy white paint flaking from window frames and metal downspouts. Inside they found the mutilated carcass of a woman, her head and limbs grotesquely bound to a dining chair with silver duct tape. The woman appeared to have been in her early thirties, with long dark hair matted to her skin by dried blood. Sightless bloody sockets remained where her eyes had been, and her chest and abdomen were laid open like a side of beef.

Det. Jack Barnaby, the taller of the two detectives, spoke with the medical examiner's investigator and directed a crime-scene photographer to take more pictures of the woman's organs. Barnaby was forty-five, with a fleshy nose and cheeks and narrow, nervous eyes. A twenty-year veteran, Barnaby had worked his way up through Austin PD's ranks from patrol officer to Homicide detective, and consistently maintained the number one conviction record in the department. He seemed to have been born with an instinct about crime and criminals. Especially murders.

Despite his tendency toward the rotund, Detective Barnaby was invariably tailored and immaculate in a sport coat, dress shirt, and tie. His legs, though camouflaged by stylishly creased trousers, appeared to be thin.

Barnaby surveyed the scene again while his associate, Det. Jim Moyers, busied himself first in the bedroom, then in the hallway outside, interviewing neighbors.

Their report would say this woman's body had been eviscerated—a euphemism, in this instance, for the carnage they witnessed.

Detective Barnaby noted coagulated blood gone stiff nearly every place crime-scene technicians indicated it was permissible to walk. His shoe covers made tacky pulling sounds each time their soles ripped free of dingy carpet or blood-smeared vinyl tile.

Ann Garmany, the medical examiner's investigator, was an attractive brunette woman of thirty-two. Ann directed Detective Barnaby's attention to a nearby wet bar.

"He laid it out like a meat-market display case," Garmany said. "I'm surprised he didn't insert some of those little plastic price markers advertising today's special."

Barnaby viewed the victim's kidneys, spleen, and one reddish brown lobe of her liver artfully sliced and stacked atop the wet bar alongside an intact heart and pancreas.

Garmany added, "Both eyes seem to be missing."

"Damn," Barnaby said. He shook his head sadly, then willed his features not to reveal the repulsion he felt inside. "You're doing a great job, Ann. You always do. Thank you."

"Sure, no problem. I just hope you catch this bastard before he can do this again."

Barnaby nodded, forcing a confident smile. "We'll get him." He turned to the photo tech and said, "That's terrific, Fred. A couple more shots in here, then let's move into the bathroom, okay?"

Det. Jim Moyers returned from the hallway and set his laptop computer on a table already dusted and cleared by technicians. A head shorter than Barnaby, Moyers was thin and wiry. Blond hair, baby-smooth skin, and a certain innocence of manner made him look like a man of twenty-five. In fact he was in his mid-thirties, with over fourteen years of exemplary service with APD, the last six spent in Homicide. Precise and detailed in his work, Moyers personally managed to always look rumpled somehow, as if wearing a larger person's clothes.

Moyers's fingers danced across the keyboard for several minutes, recording pertinent details he had learned. The victim's name was Betty Lynne Archer, though that would be confirmed by positive visual ID and either fingerprints or dental records. She had been a licensed vocational nurse, according to her neighbors, and was said to be friendly and outgoing. The building superintendent had voiced a strong opinion about Betty Lynn's poor taste in music, which he said she had played entirely too loud. Moyers had also questioned a retired schoolteacher who lived down the hall. The teacher had seen a young man wearing jeans, boots, a short-sleeved green shirt, and a brown western hat leave the building a few minutes after eleven o'clock the night before. The schoolteacher had assumed that the young man was Betty Lynne's new boyfriend.

While Moyers recorded responses to his questions, Jack Barnaby walked about the scene looking, touching, and sniffing. Though they rarely admitted it openly, each detective was pleased whenever the rotating duty roster placed them on the same case. They made a good team.

Detective Barnaby often joked about Moyers's ever-present laptop, which he called "Jim's ectopic brain," and Detective Moyers sometimes referred to Barnaby as the Count. Moyers had first tagged his coinvestigator with that nickname when he saw Barnaby stick an index finger into, then taste, a splatter of blood at a crime scene. Barnaby said he had needed to know quickly if the blood might have come from a particular suspect. He had spotted a bottle of insulin in the suspect's refrigerator during a preliminary investigation. Sure enough, the spattered blood did taste sweet. The diabetic suspect, verified by DNA testing, had not only been at the scene, he eventually confessed to that murder.

Jack Barnaby made one final pass through the apartment. Among other things he noted details of blood drops versus splatters; location and condition of towels and damp washcloths; cost and condition of the victim's clothing, shoes, handbags, undergarments, and fixtures and furnishings. The victim had obviously been killed in the apartment, not elsewhere and then dumped here. Because of the ritualistic mutilation, the murderer must have spent considerable time in the apartment, so Barnaby had technicians search trash cans and ashtrays for discarded items such as cigarette butts and chewing-gum wrappers—modern technology could derive DNA evidence from dried saliva on a cigarette butt, or fingerprints from a gum wrapper. They dusted for latent prints everywhere, including handles of spotless-appearing kitchen knives, and the underside of the toilet seat and toilet-paper holder. They searched for stray hairs of any color, caliber, or origin, either head, body, or pubic. The scene did not appear to be "staged." The apartment had not been ransacked. Money and credit cards remained in the victim's purse. The only sign of a struggle was in the bathroom, where the victim appeared to have been "blitzed" and overpowered in the bathtub. Judging from the torn shower curtain and blood and water patterns on walls and ceiling, she was very likely taking a shower at the time the mutilation began. Barnaby didn't want to think about how long it probably went on.

After the roof, hallways, front door, and windows had been checked, Det. Jim Moyers confirmed a crime-scene technician's opinion of forced entry through a bedroom window. The perpetrator had most likely used a screwdriver or heavy knife that he brought to the scene. The ground outside the window was dry. They located a branch pulled from a nearby bush, which the intruder had apparently used to erase any shoe imprints in the soft soil. They bagged the broken branch. Everybody there knew they could never regain anything missed, damaged, or lost at a crime scene, so they took everything that remotely looked like evidence.

After conferring with all technicians again the detectives released the body to Ann Garmany, the ME's investigator. She and two assistants wrapped the remains in a sheet very carefully, to preserve any evidence while it was being transported to the morgue.

On the way out Barnaby said to Detective Moyers, "If I didn't know the son of a bitch was dead, I'd swear this was the work of the Chameleon."

Amanda Stowe entered Sarah's office around 10 A.M. the following day, obviously upset. "Is what Marvin Jamison said true?"

"It's highly unlikely," Sarah replied, convinced that Marvin would utter whatever might bring him within touching distance of Amanda's bountiful breasts. "What did he say?"

"Well, that . . . Oh, I don't want you to be angry with me. Or him. Just forget that I asked."

"What? I've known Marvin for years . . . I'm beyond getting angry at anything he says." Sarah reflected on the man's early attempts to take her out. Being targeted by Marvin would hardly make any woman feel special. Certainly not unique. Apparently magnetized by above-average breast volume, he had also been drawn to Marissa Young since the day she arrived from California. Amanda appeared to be his current prey.

The young receptionist forced her lips closed for an instant, then blurted out, "He said that with you making it up about seeing the Chameleon the other day, somebody else should get the office award for accuracy this year."

Sarah felt the heat rising in her face. How could he? Why would . . . ? Either Cosmo or Tracy had obviously said something to Marvin. Most likely Tracy. Sarah wanted to shout that Tracy was merely jealous of her. "Fireplug woman," Marvin called Tracy, "with the little toy feet and windup voice." Marvin said that Tracy could never stand still on a sidewalk for fear that dogs might pee on her.

Instead of lashing out Sarah calmly said, "I suggest that Marvin not get his hopes up, Amanda. I don't recall him ever being considered for that particular award, or any other."

Amanda nodded, hesitant. She sucked in her lower lip for an instant. "Did you really see him? That Chameleon person?"

"You mean recently?"

"Yes."

"I saw either Scott Corbin or his clone . . . somebody who looks exactly like him." Sarah reflected on the overwhelming evidence that she had been mistaken. She *had* seen somebody. "Do you believe I'd make up a story like that? Report anything that wasn't true?"

"I didn't think so. No. No, you wouldn't."

"I not only wouldn't, I didn't. Okay?" Sarah was shocked at the unintended edge in her voice.

"Sure. Hey, I'm sorry. I didn't mean to upset you."

"You didn't upset me. I have a slight headache today, that's all." She looked directly at the young woman and added, "Amanda, you're very sweet . . . watch out for Marvin Jamison. You know he's married. He has a lovely wife."

From the expression on Amanda's face Sarah realized she'd made a mistake the instant the words left her lips. What others did was none of her business, and she never interfered in the personal lives of others. If she hadn't been so upset, she would never have said anything like that, even though it was true.

Amanda nodded, started to say something, but didn't. She smiled meekly and left, gazing in the general direction of her shoes.

Flooded with guilt Sarah quickly went after Amanda to apologize. She'd had no intention of hurting the young woman.

When she caught up with Amanda, Sarah apologized, then declined an invitation to join the girls for lunch. The thought of eating caused something foul to well up in her throat. Besides, she had other plans. What Amanda had said only reinforced Sarah's determination to prove them all wrong.

Sarah drove her Accord over to Congress and up toward the gold-domed State Capitol. Near the deli where she'd seen Scott Corbin's Hispanic double, she pulled to the curb and lowered both front windows to avoid reflections. Even with the noonday heat the fresh air and open spaces were welcome.

She opened a Cordura-nylon bag on the console beside her and removed her video camera. She had charged the batteries that morning and inserted a fresh film cartridge. She'd show Tracy Leigon and Marvin Jamison and Cosmo Rivers all a thing or two. If necessary, she would spend every lunch hour for the next six months at this intersection to prove that the man she saw was a dead ringer for Scott Corbin.

Sarah checked her viewing angle from both sides of the car and in all mirrors. *Good.* She could film from either the driver or passenger-side window, depending from which direction he might come.

She reflected on her mother's telling her as a child that everybody has a duplicate somewhere in the world. She couldn't help wondering if this man, whoever he was, realized how cursed he was to resemble the quintessential monster of his time. Surely not. She fleetingly wondered if she should warn him—after she had carefully recorded his likeness on film, of course.

Almost an hour later Sarah had scanned the faces of hundreds of people who bore no resemblance to Scott Corbin. She glanced at her wristwatch, aware that she should return to her office. From her vantage point in the car she quickly surveyed people on both sides of the street once more. Though disappointed, she wasn't altogether discouraged, well aware that people tend to establish routines where they're comfortable. They go to the same dry cleaners, buy groceries at the same market, because it's safer than risking the turmoil of change. One of the two men would show eventually, unless being here had been a total fluke for both. That seemed highly unlikely.

Sarah opened the camera bag, preparing to leave. She pressed the red button to kill the camera's power.

Suddenly he was there—blink of an eye—coming out of a computer-rental shop on the corner and heading straight toward her car.

Clean-shaven today, the man wore a tan business suit and tie and carried a leather briefcase. His walk was confident and purposeful, that of a successful executive. But it was him. She'd never mistake those pale, restless eyes.

Sarah frantically juggled her video camera, toppling the bag over and spilling its contents across the car's floor. A strange moan rose out of her throat. She fumbled to turn on the camera's power, then broke a nail struggling with the lens cap. An eternity flew past before she somehow scrambled over into the passenger seat and centered the man's face in the viewfinder.

He had advanced faster than she realized, and she zoomed in too close on his nose and one eye, jerky and distorted because her hands shook so badly—a Picasso portrait of a serial killer.

But there'd be no question about her veracity now. The camera was recording. She fought to hold her breath and backed off on the zoom rocker, almost subliminally noticing the odd carriage of his left arm. Her heart pounded unmercifully against her ribs.

*Oh, my God!*

The man stopped abruptly and stared straight into Sarah's camera. His startled expression left no doubt that he'd realized he was being filmed.

His face changed again when Sarah lowered the camera for a better look. Her breath caught when, to her amazement, he was standing directly in front of her.

Even worse, the man clearly recognized her, too.

# Chapter Five

Sarah's heart nearly jumped out of her chest. A split second after recognition had distorted his face, the look-alike Chameleon grabbed for her video camera. Breathlessly grappling with him through the passenger window of her car, she thought her fingers would surely break, trapped as they were in the twisted strap atop the camera. Suddenly he gave a mighty tug and her chest slammed against the door frame. She held on fiercely. No way would she give up her precious evidence. Before she could call out for help or otherwise attract attention, the man forced his way into her car. If anyone had witnessed what was happening she never saw them.

The man shoved her into the driver's seat, roughly untangling her fingers from the camera strap. He switched on the ignition, then reached across and rolled up the windows.

"Drive!" he ordered. "Now!"

More terrified than she could ever recall, Sarah started the engine and slammed into the car behind them. She tried to see if he had pulled a gun or knife, but couldn't be certain.

"Not reverse, dammit . . . forward!" He was opening his briefcase.

She managed to shift into drive and careened into a traffic lane, certain she would be shot or stabbed at any moment. Tires squealed and a horn sounded somewhere behind her.

"Look where you're going. Slow down; do you want to get us arrested?" He was terribly agitated.

*Oh yes,* she thought, *won't somebody please arrest me?* Where was that motorcycle policeman now? There wasn't even a meter maid in sight. She shifted her eyes ahead and slammed on the brakes just in time to avoid rear-ending a red Suburban sporting a trailer hitch.

"Go around him," the man ordered gruffly. "Turn left at the corner." Perspiration poured down his flushed face. He began pulling yard after yard of videotape from its cassette, destroying her precious evidence. He was definitely angry enough to kill her.

She turned as directed.

"Slow down."

Frozen with fear, Sarah had no idea how fast she was driving or where he was directing her.

Several blocks up Lamar Boulevard, Sarah managed to ask, in a voice not her own, "Who are you?" But she already knew, unless Scott Corbin had an identical twin.

"Shut up and drive." His face was locked in a frightful scowl. He wiped his brow with a sleeve of his suit coat.

After a lengthy silence the man said, "Do you still live alone?"

*Oh, God,* Sarah thought. How could he know that? This was no twin.

"Answer me, dammit."

She tried to swallow, but her throat wouldn't work. "No, I don't."

"You're lying."

She tried again. "I live with a football player. For the Cowboys. From Dallas."

"What position?"

She hesitated. "What?"

"What position?"

Her mind raced. "That's private . . . none of your business."

"Dammit, what position does he play?"

"Oh, I thought you . . ." What an inane time to blush. She searched her memory banks. What would the biggest, meanest man on the team be called? She tried to recall one of those beer commercials they were always running on TV. She shook her head and said, "Uh . . . quarterback."

"Take me to your apartment."

Sarah sank deeper in her seat, her heart fluttering wildly. She finally mustered enough courage to clear her throat and ask, "What makes you think I live in an apartment?"

"Just drive, and no more bullshit, okay? Go straight to your place and keep it under the speed limit." The man added, shouting furiously, "Do it, Sarah!"

PI Robert Garding had watched shimmering waves of heat dance above I-45's flat pavement for mile after endless mile, and his pickup truck's temperature gauge hovered near the red zone. Huntsville, Texas, was as hot and dry as a blast furnace when he finally pulled up to the gatehouse outside the BOT complex. The heat nearly blistered his face when he rolled down his window and showed his photo ID to a uniformed corrections officer. Garding said he had called ahead, and was expected. He added that it had taken a lot longer than he'd expected to drive down.

As he waited for clearance, Garding reflected on why he was here. He had been reluctant to come all the way to Huntsville, but Sarah seemed to need the reassurance of his personal visit. She had even insisted on paying him for his time and expenses. And she wasn't the hysterical type—she had obviously seen somebody who looked like Scott Corbin. Also, she had raised one question Garding hadn't considered before, about the possibility of Corbin's having an identical-twin brother. Garding remembered doing the usual checking when he had arrested Corbin six years earlier. He recalled that Corbin had no parents alive or any siblings, but it was possible that something could have been missed. Perhaps he'd find some piece of information in the prison records that he hadn't been aware of before. Besides, he liked Sarah Hill. It would be very satisfying to know that she felt better after his visit. To tell the truth, it felt good to be working again.

Garding stared through the windshield past a twelve-foot chain-link-and-barbed-wire fence toward a massive metal warehouse. Two smaller buildings nestled beneath a cluster of pine trees. A sign still identified the compound as Brown Oil & Tool, from the days before the state had purchased it from the oil company. It was now the administrative section for the Texas Department of Criminal Justice's area prisons. Garding reflected on the last time he was in Huntsville—the night he had watched Scott Corbin die.

On a tour that night following the execution, Garding had learned that the TDCJ had located Death Row for the entire state in the east building of the Huntsville Unit from 1928 to 1952, then over by the east wall. Death Row inmates were moved to the Ellis Unit in 1965. As the numbers of capital murders escalated right along with the state's population, TDCJ moved Death Row again in 1999, to the Terrell Unit, forty-five minutes away over in Polk County—in a town with the incongruous name of Livingston, Texas. Executions always had been performed in the Death House at the Huntsville Unit. Starting in 1995 close relatives and friends of deceased victims were allowed to witness executions, in addition to the usual law-enforcement officers and news reporters. The execution chamber could be viewed through large glass windows from two separate observation rooms—one for friends and family of the offender, the other for close relatives and friends of the victims. Corrections officers made damn certain to keep those two groups apart.

Garding could vouch for the fact that lethal injection was quick—the one he saw took less than seven minutes from the time IV lines were hooked up in each of Corbin's arms. The warden had told Garding personally that the cost for drugs used, per man or woman executed, was $86.08. For some reason that figure had stuck in his mind.

The corrections officer interrupted Garding's musings when he raised the wooden arm of the entry gate. "Okay, sir, drive on through."

In the Classification and Records office Garding reviewed Scott Corbin's death warrant and return-of-death-warrant document, again confirming the time and date the execution had been carried out. The heavyset female clerk who assisted him appeared to be in her late forties, and was either Hispanic or American Indian. She had raven-black hair and shiny dark skin showing signs of recent acne. She had just returned from lunch.

Garding asked, "Was Corbin buried or cremated?"

The clerk shuffled through some papers. "I don't have that information in here, but most of them get buried." Her rhythm of speaking suggested that she had been raised in Mexico.

"Who makes that decision?"

"Each inmate signs a form saying who's to claim his body, after he's dead and all. The Huntsville Funeral Home prepares the body for burial; then the family picks it up. What they do with them after that is up to each family. If the family don't claim them, they get buried at state expense in the Captain Joe Byrd Cemetery here in Huntsville." The clerk slowly shook her head. "A lot of the graves don't even have markers . . . just a simple white cross."

Garding listened patiently, then nodded. "Hmmm. Very interesting." He thought for a moment. "Does anything in that record indicate whether Corbin might have had a brother? For instance, a twin brother?"

The clerk narrowed her eyes. "If he did have a twin, do you suppose the brother would be a murderer, too? I mean, if he was identical, that might make sense."

"I wouldn't know."

The clerk searched the records again. "No, sir, I don't see anything about no brother, but inmates don't always tell the truth. A man who'll murder all them women don't worry much about telling a lie. He might've wanted to protect his brother, if he had one." She looked up from the records. "There's been six sets of brothers executed in Texas that I know of. I always figured that must be real hard on their mamas, you know? But none of them was twins that I know of."

Garding nodded. "You've been very helpful, Officer. Would you mind telling me who claimed Scott Corbin's body?"

"Sure, it's right here. A Dr. Darvid King."

Garding wrote the name in his spiral notepad. "Is he a relative?"

"Probably."

"Do you happen to show an address or phone number for Dr. King?"

"It's right here if you want to copy it down."

Ann Garmany directed detectives Jack Barnaby and Jim Moyers to an autopsy room in the morgue. The ME, Dr. Harriet McGrath, had just completed the gross examination of their murder victim.

McGrath looked up when they approached the stainless-steel table where she worked. "This is a bad one, guys."

"Tell me about it," Barnaby said. He stared down at the young woman's mutilated body and shook his head. "Have you pinned down the time of death?"

"Between two and six A.M., but she suffered terribly before she finally died."

Moyers found available counter space for his laptop and turned it on.

Turning away from the remains on the autopsy table, McGrath stripped off her latex gloves and the plastic apron covering her scrub suit. She lowered her surgical mask. Aquamarine eyes sparked with intelligence, and her angular face was both pretty and intense, framed by dark red hair worn short. She moved like the athlete they knew her to be. Dr. McGrath's idea of a relaxing weekend was to fly to Boston or New York, run a marathon, then fly home. She walked to a nearby sink and washed her hands, then blew her nose into a tissue. "Let's go into my office, where we can talk."

McGrath's desk was cluttered with medical records and typewritten reports. Her walls were adorned with photographs of long-distance runners, both male and female. A binocular microscope sat on the counter of a wall-unit bookshelf behind a green leather chair. Dr. McGrath took her seat, saying, "Let me guess what's going through your minds, gentlemen. You're thinking that whoever did this has studied the smallest details of the Chameleon murders."

Barnaby replied, "I've seen copycats before. This guy's a friggin' clone."

Moyers agreed.

"He is good," McGrath said, "but not perfect." She swiveled her chair around and flipped on the lamp beneath the microscope's stage. "Tell me what you see."

Barnaby had to adjust the interocular distance and focus knob to see what lay in the center of the circular field. "What?" he asked.

Detective Moyers eased into position and had a look, then raised his head quizzically. "They're not squiggling around, but are those sperm?"

"Good eye, Jim. It's dried ejaculate."

"So she was raped," Barnaby said.

"I don't think so," McGrath replied. "This was in her abdominal cavity . . . on the front of her descending aorta and about where her spleen used to be." She paused. "The bastard cut her open, then masturbated inside her. The Chameleon never did that."

"That sick son of a bitch," Barnaby said, grimacing.

Moyers quickly added, "Yeah, but he just handed us his calling card. We'll have his DNA now. Right, Doc?"

"Absolutely. Plus we found three pubic hairs that don't match with the victim's." She turned off the microscope lamp. "Whoever did this had an opportunity to study the Chameleon's MO, but isn't as thorough as the original was. He screwed up on one very important detail." She paused, then asked, "Did you arrest the boyfriend?"

"No," Barnaby replied. "He swears she was fine

when he left around eleven last night. He works midnight to eight in a convenience market, so at least half a dozen people saw him at different hours during the night. Three already confirmed that he was at work. And the perpetrator got in by forced entry through a bedroom window."

Moyers asked, "Any way to speed up DPS on this one, Doc? My last DNA report took two months."

"You can go to a private lab, but it'll cost major bucks. You know APD won't authorize the expenditure. Even then you're talking two weeks minimum, if everything goes perfectly, which it rarely does. I'd plan on three or four weeks even there. The Department of Public Safety lab is good, and it's free to us, but it's first come, first served. How long it takes depends on how backlogged they are."

"Did you confirm her ID yet?" asked Moyers.

Dr. McGrath nodded. "Her mother came in straightaway, poor thing . . . nobody should have to see their child like that. We also submitted fingerprints to AFIS for backup confirmation, and her mother gave us the name of her dentist. If she's not in AFIS's database, we'll compare dental X rays."

Barnaby let out a long sigh. "Let's hope CODIS has this bastard's DNA on file."

"If he's been picked up on a sex-related offense in this country in recent years, it'll be there," McGrath said. "Federal law. From the looks of this poor woman, I'd say this guy has done this before. Probably several times."

# Chapter Six

Sarah's apartment was a one-bedroom on the ground floor of a building faced with gray stone and white wood, surrounded by low shrubs. The complex sat on a knoll just off Seventeenth Street, with covered parking in the rear. Her captor insisted that she park in her usual slot, then forced her inside through the kitchen entrance. He kept one hand in his partially opened briefcase all the while.

Each time the man unexpectedly moved Sarah recoiled from the anticipated appearance of a knife or pistol. He quickly closed the venetian blinds and forced her to take a seat on her living room sofa.

Sarah's voice trembled when she whispered, "You're really him, aren't you?"

"Shut up."

"Otherwise how would you know my name?" A vision of Scott Corbin's death certificate swirled through her mind. What was she saying? Of course he wasn't Scott Corbin. This man absolutely could not be him. Yet she knew he was. For God's sake, she had worked alongside Corbin for a year. She *knew* him.

The man walked restless circles around the small

room. As if suddenly remembering something, he quickly looked in the bedroom and bath, watching her with one eye all the while.

Sarah eased over toward the telephone when she heard a hall-closet door open.

"Don't even think about it," he barked. He came back from the hallway still carrying the briefcase.

Sarah was certain that was where he carried his weapons. This man *was* Scott Corbin. There were differences, sure, but none that couldn't be explained by five years in prison. The realization that she was sitting in the same room with a serial killer virtually paralyzed her. Yet she knew absolutely that the Chameleon was dead. Either that, or he had pulled the ultimate switch and had somebody else executed in his place.

Sarah's pulse pounded in her head till she thought she would black out. Tiny black spots swirled before her eyes, and her ears sang with a high-pitched keening sound.

She stifled a sob as he approached; then she shouted, "How did you get away? What do you want with me?" She hated losing control, but seemed incapable of stopping herself. She had never before imagined this level of fear.

"I told you to shut up!"

"I'm going to die anyway, so what difference does it make if I talk? And don't shout at me. I have to know."

"I need to think, dammit."

"So think, but answer my questions. How can you be alive? Why aren't you dead?" Not knowing was almost as bad as learning the horrible truth. He looked like Corbin. Sounded like Corbin. But was this really the Chameleon? She wanted proof. Some piece of information that would crystallize what she believed to be true. "How do you know my name?"

He set the briefcase on the floor and ignored her questions, pressing his fingers against his temples and massaging hard. The collar of his white shirt was unbuttoned and his tie pulled down.

"Only Scott Corbin would know I lived alone."

The man sat heavily in a chair opposite her and squeezed his eyes shut.

"Was that you dressed like a workman last week? Then a Mexican farmworker?"

He didn't respond. He slowly held both hands in front of him in the strangest fashion. Palms up, thumb and first two fingers pressed tightly together, and his eyes squeezed tightly shut. As Sarah watched he began to hum, so quietly at first that she had to strain to hear it. Then, gradually, louder. And louder.

Sarah glanced toward the front door. Could she make it before he could respond? What was he doing anyway, some sort of demonic ritual before he disemboweled her?

Just then the man opened one pale eye and glared at her. He stood abruptly. "Where would you keep a length of rope?"

"What makes you . . . I don't have any rope." She swallowed hard. "What do you want with rope?" Sarah jerked back when, without warning, the man ran one hand into his pocket. She held her breath. He went to the front window, opened a pocketknife, and cut the cords from her venetian blinds. She had expected the knife to be bigger.

He returned quickly and spun her around on the sofa, then tied her hands behind her back. "If you don't shut up, I'll tape your mouth closed."

"How do you expect me to keep quiet when you won't tell me who you are or how you got away?"

"I'm warning you, Sarah."

"Why are you trying to make me think you're the Chameleon? And how do you know my name?"

"Did you hear what I said?"

"I heard, but I have to know. It's been driving me crazy all week. How can you possibly be alive?"

"Shut up! I can't think with you firing incessant questions at me."

"Then answer me. Why did you accost me? Why did you take my camera? Why bring me here? What are you going to do to me? Don't I have a right to know?"

The man glowered at her, his pulse pounding in his temples. He looked as though he might have a stroke. Between gritted teeth he growled, "Dammit, Sarah, what makes you think a man convicted of killing three women would care if he adds one more to the list? Shut your flapping mouth before I stuff a shoe in it!"

Sarah went rigid.

And completely silent.

A Lincolnesque man in his early forties slammed down a telephone receiver, jumped to his feet, and raced from behind his cluttered desk. He removed his white lab coat and tossed it haphazardly on a coat tree as he hurried out of his office. In the main room outside, one male and two female technicians seemed absorbed by their duties at sophisticated laboratory equipment. The man racing through stopped momentarily to inform a technician named Andrew that he had to be away for a few days. A family emergency, he explained tersely. He ran out the door carrying his suit coat and attaché case.

# Chapter Seven

Senior vice president Anthony Shapiro walked swiftly from his office past the reception desk. As though the visit weren't planned he stopped to ask Amanda Stowe a question. He adjusted his thick glasses and stared down the front of her tantalizing neckline while Amanda gave directions over the phone. Shapiro had a perfectly good intercom on his desk, and a perfectly good secretary, but indulged himself with a visit to Amanda's desk at least once each morning and afternoon. This was his early afternoon treat.

Shapiro's personal secretary, Tracy Leigon, had been passed down from the company president, Harrison Hodge. A cousin of Hodge's wife. Shapiro's first act when he took over following Hodge's retirement would be either to can Tracy or to present her to whomever he selected as his vice president. He almost laughed every time he thought of assigning her to Marvin Jamison. Jamison would absolutely die, stuck with a pig like Tracy—but he wouldn't try to screw her, which would be a first. At least he hadn't yet. More likely, however, Tracy would wind up working for Marissa Young—Shapiro's top candidate for senior vice president—and everyone would be happier, which could only help the bottom line. And that, Shapiro reflected, was what business was all about.

"May I help you, Mr. Shapiro?" Amanda completed her call and smiled warmly.

"I was on the way to talk with Mr. Roman, but was wondering if Miss Hill is in yet."

"No, sir, she still hasn't returned from lunch. I'm beginning to get concerned."

Shapiro enjoyed another eyeful, then let out a short sigh. "She hasn't called?"

"No, sir, not yet. I'll be glad to let you know when she returns."

"Thank you. On second thought, let Tracy know. I need to discuss an account with Sarah."

"Of course, Mr. Shapiro."

Amanda watched him walk away. If he'd wear contacts instead of those magnifying-lens glasses, he'd be about a six on her marriageability scale. Being recently divorced, however, might even push him up closer to eight. Definite potential there.

Amanda checked her face in her compact mirror and wiped a smudge of lipstick off one tooth. A short time later someone called for Sarah.

"Sorry, sir, she hasn't come back from lunch yet. Would you like her voice mail?"

Garding hated voice mail, along with those automated systems that asked you to listen carefully to fifty-seven inapplicable options before you pressed 1. "Just tell her that Robert Garding called. I'll be out of town for a couple of days. I'll try to reach her later."

As Amanda was hanging up, Marvin Jamison approached the reception desk and asked, "When would be a good time for us to have lunch?"

"Well, I . . . I suppose next Tuesday or Wednesday would be okay, if you really think we should."

"I don't know if I can wait that long." He smiled and eased around the edge of her desk, moving close. "That sure is a pretty sweater. Is it angora?" He ran the backs of his fingers lightly over the nap of her pink sweater.

"It's some kind of synthetic. It only looks like angora."

Jamison watched her face while he ran his fingers along her collarbone, then down to lightly brush her left breast.

Amanda grasped his hand in hers and moved it away, exaggerating a scolding stance. "Now, now, Mr. Jamison, no touching."

"Marv," he said, grinning. "I was only checking out the merchandise."

"I know exactly what you were doing, Marv . . . you bad boy."

Jamison straightened when Tracy Leigon exited a nearby office and walked down the hall. Then he leaned close to Amanda again and asked, "Have you ever had lunch at the Shoreline Grill?"

"No."

"It has this incredible view right out over Town Lake. Very romantic."

"I thought you were married, Marv."

He winked. "My wife is."

"What does that mean?"

"Let's just say we have an arrangement." He grinned again and whispered, "She understands me."

A door opened down the hall and voices approached. Marvin winked at Amanda and hurried toward his own office.

Besides interviewing neighbors and relatives, detectives Jack Barnaby and Jim Moyers contacted everybody in Betty Lynne Archer's address book. They did this as quickly as possible. Each day that passed without locating the killer lessened their chances of finding him. So far nobody had any idea who might have had a reason to kill the young woman. More important, all interviews were consistent about Betty Lynne's activities, friends, relationships with relatives and coworkers, and so forth. They could find no evidence that she carried life insurance. There seemed to be nobody who would gain from her death. The boyfriend's alibi checked out completely, plus he seemed like a genuinely nice young man. He had been devastated when he learned what had happened.

The detectives asked about Betty Lynne's habits. They visited the hospital where she worked, and spoke with her coworkers. They learned about places she had frequented, such as where she bought groceries, cosmetics or sundries, gasoline, pharmaceuticals, and film. They asked about what fast foods she liked, and where she generally got them. Somebody could have followed her home from one of those locations. They would visit all those places to see if anybody recalled seeing anything suspicious. They had the film in her camera processed, and checked receipts found in a drawer in her kitchen.

They returned from the health club where Betty Lynne had worked out to Austin Police Department headquarters. Still no viable suspects. Barnaby's and Moyers's cubicles faced one another across a narrow hallway in the bustling second-floor Homicide Unit. Barnaby's desktop and a nearby shelf were filled with framed photos of his striking red-haired wife and two children—a mischievous-looking son who resembled his mother, and a girl pretty enough to be an actress. In the most recent photos the boy appeared to be close to six, and his sister around fourteen. The daughter had Jack's olive complexion and dark hair. An assortment of *Motor Trend* and *Popular Mechanics* magazines rested near a photo of Jack standing beside a green Austin Healey. On a wall next to his coatrack were a collage of crayon drawings spanning a period of ten years. Several contained brightly colored printing with messages like *For my daddy*, or *I love Daddy*.

Jim Moyers's desk was spotlessly clean. The only pictures in sight were of his parents, a solemn-faced couple in their sixties, bone-thin, and one of his older sister and her smiling family taken two years earlier at Christmas.

Moyers sat silently at his desk, punching keys on his laptop, rearranging and compacting information.

"Now what are you doing, Sherlock Gates?"

"Comparing our crime-scene data to some I took off the VICAP hookup."

"Not a bad idea." Barnaby admitted enormous respect for the FBI's profiling system—Violent Criminals Apprehension Program. Compiling data from the entire United States gave the Fibbies a huge sampling. In Barnaby's experience serial killers left a signature he could read like a stop sign. With this latest murderer everything smelled like a copycat.

Barnaby impatiently asked his associate, "Find anything?"

Moyers shook his head, still focused on the lighted screen. "It keeps coming up with no viable match."

Barnaby glanced at his watch and stood. "Well, hell, I'd guess it wouldn't be *viable* . . . the Chameleon is dead."

This man certainly appeared to be Scott Corbin, but Sarah was having second thoughts. He didn't act like the man she had known. Then again, would anybody be the same after five years in prison? Or had he even been in prison?

The man rummaged through Sarah's refrigerator, then slammed the door. "Don't you have anything to eat in this house?"

"There's a banana and a couple of oranges on the counter over the dishwasher."

"That's it? That's all you've got?"

"I planned to stop by Whole Foods Market after work today." Mentioning work released a bubble of hope in Sarah's mind. They'd be worried at the office that she hadn't returned. Probably check with local hospitals to see if she'd been in an accident, or notify the police. She was never late in returning to work.

She shifted on the sofa, trying to free her hands from the cords binding her wrists. The bubble was expanding, her hopes growing.

The man stopped short. "Work," he said. He picked up the telephone and ordered, "You're gonna call in sick."

"I can't do that."

"You damn well can and will." He frowned. "What's the number?"

She refused to answer. If somebody at the office didn't alert the police, she'd never get rescued. Nobody else would know she was missing.

"Forget it," he said, exasperated. He pressed 411 on the keypad. Seconds later he calmly said, "Austin . . . the number for Integrated Systems Incorporated. Thank you."

Sarah felt her eyes widen. He even knew where she worked. A thousand new questions whirled through her mind. Just then her beautiful cat pranced into the room and jumped on the sofa beside Sarah.

"What's this?" the man asked.

"My cat . . . Dame Margot."

"How'd she get in?" He hurriedly looked down the hall. "I didn't see her when I searched the rooms."

"She was probably under the bed. She hides there sometimes."

He looked at the cat again and narrowed his eyes. "Whatever." He pressed numbers on the keypad. "Tell them you started feeling sick right after lunch. Throwing up . . . diarrhea . . . had to come home."

"I won't fabricate an illness." Miss Veracity tell a lie? She'd never live it down.

"Oh, I think you will." He extended the receiver toward Sarah and simultaneously scooped up Margot with the other hand. "You don't want to see your cat hurt, do you?"

Sarah inhaled a long breath, then slowly let it out. Would he? Of course, she knew the answer. Anybody who would kill six women wouldn't hesitate to murder a defenseless little cat.

She could hear the buzz of a distant phone ringing. Her eyes went back and forth from his determined face to her innocent pet.

A familiar voice said, "Integrated Systems, this is Amanda . . . how may I help you? Hello . . . hello?"

The man's eyes hardened. He tilted his face slightly so that he was glaring down from even more of an angle. She could see the muscles working along his jaw, almost feel his fingers tightening around Margot's neck.

Sarah's bubble burst in that instant. "Hello," she said toward the phone's mouthpiece.

"Hello?" echoed Amanda.

"Amanda?" The receiver was at her ear now.

"Yes. Oh, Sarah," Amanda said excitedly, "is that you? We've been worried. Where are you?"

"At home."

"Is something wrong? You don't sound like you. What happened? Did your headache get worse?"

"Yes. Yes, it did."

"Is it a migraine? I have a friend with migraines. Do yours make you throw up?"

Sarah was watching Margot's eyes. He hadn't hurt the little cat. Yet. She answered stiffly, "Yes, I have been throwing up. I won't be able to return to work today." Telling that lie went against Sarah's every principle.

"Sure, I understand. Don't worry, I'll explain to everybody. I'm sure you'll feel better by tomorrow."

They thanked each other and hung up. The man showed his first hint of a distorted smile and released Margot. He was obviously pleased that he had forced Sarah to lie. She tried not to imagine other twisted demands yet to come.

He asked, "Do you have a steak in the house?"

"No."

"Some hamburger? Hot dogs?"

"No."

"Damn . . . don't you know how to cook?"

She stiffened. "I'm a very good cook. I don't eat meat."

He stared at her, incredulous, then turned and walked to her kitchen. Opening one set of cupboard doors after another, he stood in the middle of the small kitchen with hands on hips, shaking his head.

"What the hell?" he said.

She started to apologize, but changed her mind. What did she care if he chose to eat like a barbarian? He was a homicidal maniac. The sudden reminder hit hard. Sarah felt her arms and chest begin to shake again. She was suddenly very cold.

He noticed. "What's wrong?"

"It's cold in here."

Perspiration trickled down the man's forehead

and soaked the armpits of his dress shirt. His eyes searched the walls until they settled on the thermostat in the hallway. He grumbled while he adjusted the air-conditioning dial.

"Thank you," Sarah managed. She had to clear her throat to be heard.

The man peeled a banana and sat again. Before taking the first bite, he asked, "Are you hungry?"

"No, thank you. I had some tangerines earlier."

He nodded, then wolfed down the banana. His suit coat and tie lay draped across the coffee table. He rose, searched the refrigerator again, and poured a dollop of fresh carrot juice into a glass. Tentatively tasting it he made a face and replaced the plastic bottle's lid. He filled a fresh glass with water and drank it down. He picked up a neatly typed sheet of paper from the dining table and read it. "What's this?"

"My TV schedule."

He almost laughed. "You type out what you're going to watch two weeks in advance?"

"I like to plan ahead."

"Don't you ever go out?"

"Of course I do. That's just for . . . in case I happen to be home." She felt her face flush. "I go to the ballet, plays. Lots of places. I took Mrs. Widener to the ballet last Saturday night."

"Who's Mrs. Widener?"

"A woman who lives across the street. She had a stroke last Christmas, so she's confined to a wheelchair." What business was that of his, anyway? Sarah wouldn't dare admit that except for the night she had mentioned and one other, she hadn't been out since her friend Phyllis had moved to New Orleans, three months ago. Going places by yourself just wasn't the same.

Moments later the man found two potatoes in a pantry bin. "How long does it take to bake these?"

"A few minutes in the microwave." Sarah let out a sharp breath. "Just who are you, anyway?"

"You know."

"No, I don't. I thought I did, but you aren't. I mean, you can't be who I thought."

"Do I have to wrap them in aluminum foil first?"

"Absolutely not. Not in the microwave, not ever."

Searching the refrigerator again he asked, "Where's the butter?"

"I use olive oil. Cold-pressed virgin oil." She suddenly wished she hadn't used that word. He didn't seem to have noticed.

"Not even margarine?"

"There's soy cheese in the bin on the right, under the middle shelf. Who are you, really?"

He slammed the potato down on the counter beside the refrigerator. "Dammit, Sarah, fix this thing for me. I'm starving."

She straightened, incensed. "Only if you tell me who you are. You are not Scott Corbin, because he would have killed me by now."

The man stared at her for several moments. He wiped his mouth with the sleeve of his shirt. "If I tell you, will you bake this damned potato? Both of them?"

She swallowed. "All right."

After a lengthy silence he said, "I'm exactly who you think . . . who you know I am."

"You're not Scott Corbin. That much I do know."

"Yes, I am, Sarah. That's exactly who I am."

# Chapter Eight

The gaunt man from the laboratory finally found a vacant parking space on San Ysidro Street in Austin. He fed quarters into the meter, then walked three blocks to an address scribbled on a piece of paper. As he approached the building where ISI had their offices, an Austin PD patrol car rounded the corner and rolled to a stop nearby. The man turned abruptly and headed off in another direction. The expression on his face broadcast a high level of anxiety, but nobody on the streets seemed to notice. Or care.

"This tastes awful."

"Don't eat it then," Sarah quipped. She turned from the kitchen sink to glare at Scott Corbin—or whoever this man really was. He sat shirtless at her dining table adding far too much salt and pepper to the potatoes while staring at the TV screen. He had forced her to wash his white dress shirt and undershirt by hand. She had thought such work menial and degrading on the occasions when she had watched her mother do it for her father years before. She still did.

Corbin mashed everything together with a fork,

soy cheese melting into the steaming potato. It had looked quite appetizing to Sarah before the deluge of salt and pepper. Had this madman not kidnapped her, she might have baked a potato for her dinner.

Drying her hands first she removed a place mat from a drawer and arranged it beneath his plate. "If you are Scott Corbin, how can you be alive?"

"Off-limits." He crammed a forkful into his mouth.

She watched silently for a moment, then returned to the sink and resumed scrubbing the armpits of his shirt. She was surprised at how muscular this man was—more so than she remembered Scott Corbin. This man's chest had a mat of curly black hair. She had never seen Corbin's bare chest.

Sarah broke her own silence moments later. "I don't understand. You look and sound exactly like Scott Corbin, and you're pretending to be him for some reason, but why would anybody do something so ludicrous? I mean, why mimic a convicted murderer?"

Instead of answering he merely stared at her from where he sat, chewing, eating the steaming potatoes she had prepared. He returned his attention to the TV.

The man explained nothing despite her repeated attempts. After eating he said he needed time to think. He tied Sarah to her bed using drapery cords and began to tape her mouth shut.

"Please," she begged, "don't tape my mouth. I can't stand being confined. I'll suffocate if you do." The possibility was horribly oppressive, already making it hard to breathe.

"It's your choice. Will you keep quiet?"

She nodded eagerly.

"Say it. Give me your word."

"I'll be quiet."

He left her there, mouth not taped, and returned to the front of the apartment and his precious TV.

Even if Sarah could get loose she couldn't go anywhere. The bedroom windows were locked shut, the keys in a kitchen drawer. There was no window in the bathroom, and both doors to the outside were at the other end of the apartment. She prayed that somebody might phone or come by to check on her, perhaps become worried that she didn't answer, and call the paramedics. Or the police.

Nobody called. Nobody came by. Hours passed.

Silent tears ran down Sarah's cheeks and into her ears. She muffled her cries, certain this man would murder her if she made a single, audible sound. He might not be Scott Corbin, but he was just as crazy. Maybe crazier.

At least Corbin had known who he was.

Just before quitting time Amanda received another call from Robert Garding. She told him Sarah had called in sick.

"I had a couple of questions I wanted to ask, that's all."

"Would you like to leave a number where she can reach you tomorrow, Mr. Garding?"

"I won't be where she can find me. Tell her if I don't speak with her tomorrow, I'll be at home over the weekend. She has that number."

Garding hung up the phone in his motel room near Huntsville. He had wanted to ask Sarah for more details about the person she saw. For instance, exactly how the man had resembled Scott Corbin.

Was it possible that the man was related to Corbin? A brother Corbin denied having? A twin?

Garding checked to be certain the air conditioner was on high, then lay back on the bed and unbuttoned his shirt. In the morning he would go see the person who had claimed Corbin's body, Dr. Darvid King. He wondered if King was a relative of Corbin's. Could be, even though he had a different name.

Sarah jumped, startled and disoriented. She was astounded that she had somehow fallen asleep. Light was fading outside and the man was in her bedroom, wearing the T-shirt she had washed. Without a word he began loosening the cords that strapped her to the bed.

She asked in a tremulous voice, "What are you going to do?"

"You're gonna iron my shirt; then I'm going out."

Her spirits soared. He was going to leave? Without killing her?

She sat up and rubbed circulation back into her hands. A momentary dizziness came and went, and she had a terrible taste in her mouth. She was almost too embarrassed to ask, but no longer had the option. She had held back for hours.

"I need to go to the bathroom."

He glared at her. "Just for a minute."

After washing her hands Sarah rinsed her face and

gargled. She looked terrible in the medicine-chest mirror, her green eyes red-rimmed and puffy, her face drawn. She needed a glass of wine. To her accusing reflection she whispered, "Who wouldn't need a glass with a serial killer in the house?"

Outside the bathroom Sarah thanked the man for granting her privacy while she had freshened up.

He grunted a response.

Once she had ironed his shirt he again tied her to the bed, still refusing any explanation. She felt used and angry.

"I have to tape your mouth this time. I can't take the chance that somebody might hear you scream."

She almost fainted. What did he mean by that?

Her efforts to resist were no match for his strength. He sealed her mouth with mailing tape from the hall closet, then took her car keys and left.

Sarah tried every possible maneuver to get loose, but it was useless. Her struggles only made her wrists and arms ache, her ankles burn. She fought the overwhelming desire to cry, for it made her nose stuffy and she would surely suffocate. She held back looming dark waves of claustrophobia by forcing her mind to view only light and air and open spaces. Saw herself running through midmorning pastures in the Texas Hill Country. She beamed telepathic messages toward Detective Garding, praying that he might find a sudden compelling reason to visit her.

Nobody could hear her through well-insulated walls. They probably wouldn't hear even if he hadn't taped her mouth shut. Except possibly the apartment manager, Mrs. Whitstone. That busybody heard and saw everything. Whitstone's only redeeming quality was that she loved cats. Sarah prayed, "Please let her find me now."

Her plea came out as a muffled cry.

He returned hours later with no explanation of where he had gone, but he appeared to be exhausted. He offered Sarah something to eat, either double-meat cheeseburgers and fries or bean burritos. He had also bought two six-packs of Dr Pepper.

She wasn't hungry.

He ate in front of the TV during the local news, then forced Sarah back to the bedroom. She was horrified when he began stripping down to T-shirt and shorts.

"Don't work yourself into a snit," he said gruffly. "I need to shut my eyes. What do you sleep in? Pajamas, a gown?"

"What I have on is fine." She would've loved to change out of her dress and remove her panty hose, but wasn't about to suggest that.

He took a wide belt from her closet and joined it together with his own, then forced Sarah onto the bed and lay behind her. He snugged her tightly against him with the belts, with her protesting all the while.

All he said was, "If you try to escape, I'll wake up. If you yell, I'll tape your mouth closed. Now be quiet and let me sleep."

His breath was hot on the back of her neck, one arm heavy across her upper body and chest.

Sarah lay terrified, joined at the waist to a homicidal maniac. But she didn't cry out. And she didn't try to escape. She was almost too weak from her hours of relentless terror to breathe.

# Chapter Nine

The man was hostile again by nine o'clock the next morning. He'd been in a far better mood earlier. In fact, she had thought he was gone at first when she awoke to find herself not bound. That was before she discovered him sitting cross-legged on the living room floor with his forearms resting on his knees and his palms skyward in front of him. His thumbs and fingers were pressed together in that funny fashion again, and he'd been humming some mantra. She had never before thought of a serial murderer meditating.

Now he was trying to force her to call her office and tell them she was still sick. This being Friday, she wouldn't be in till Monday.

"I cannot lie to them again. I won't."

"You want to know something, Sarah? You're a royal pain in the ass. What are you, my private angel of doom? Did somebody elect you to follow me around just to screw up my life?"

Sarah had been asking herself the same thing, but in reverse. "I've already told one lie for you."

"I'm getting sick of your attitude. My life is at

stake and you're whining about taking a sick day from work."

"*Your* life?"

"Yes, *my* life."

"You're a psychopath. It's my life that's in danger."

"It may be if you don't do what I say." He began stabbing numbers on the phone's keypad. "Dammit, tell them you're not coming in or I'll go find your . . . Margot. I'll hurt her, Sarah; you know I will." He glared at her. "Your choice."

Sarah studied his face, the intensity in his eyes. He was desperate. In the end she had no option.

Amanda answered and told Sarah about Robert Garding's calls the afternoon before. Sarah frantically tried to think of a way to get a message to Garding, but couldn't. She thanked Amanda, then asked to speak with their operations manager, Marissa Young.

"My stomach's still queasy," Sarah said weakly into the phone. "I probably have the flu, and I wouldn't want to spread it around the office."

"Is there anything I can do?" asked Marissa.

"No, nothing. I'll be fine, but thank you for asking." Sarah prayed that she would be all right. She prayed she would be alive when Monday rolled around.

When she hung up the man stood staring at her, a pained expression on his face. Finally he said, "Sit over here at the table. I need to tell you something."

Sarah sat across from him. He really did resemble Corbin.

"First I want you to know that I forgive you," he began.

"For what?"

"For testifying against me."

"Scott Corbin murdered six women . . . of course I testified against him. Who wouldn't, for God's sake?"

"Calm down. I want you just to listen. Don't say anything until I finish. Okay?"

She didn't reply, but glared at him. What did he expect? She suddenly felt exhausted. She had lain awake all night staring into darkness, lashed to some sociopath. Her adrenaline had been running rampant for nearly twenty-four hours. She was pretty near drained.

"I can't tell you how many hours I've spent going over things in my mind," he said. "My arrest, the trial. I was furious with you in the beginning. I thought you were my friend, but the first time you came around was to testify about seeing me with Rhonda the night of her murder. I hadn't kept that a secret, but I felt betrayed. You assumed, like everybody else, that I was guilty. I had hoped you might say I was honest and respectable, or that you'd never seen anything to suggest I was capable of murder."

He silenced her with a gesture. "Please, just listen. I did not kill Rhonda Talbot. No, don't speak. I had dinner with Rhonda that night because I needed to tell her some very important things that I'd uncovered at EBS. I knew ISI was planning a buyout of EBS, but some shenanigans were going on that could greatly affect the price . . . maybe even the decision to buy it at all. Since she was operations manager for ISI, Rhonda was in the ideal position to understand what I had to say. Unfortunately, somebody killed her before she could pass the information along."

"Not just somebody . . . Scott Corbin."

"No, not me, but I believe I know who it was."

Sarah almost came out of her chair. She shouted, "Her blood was all over the panties in your car. *His* car. Rhonda's panties."

"Somebody put them there, Sarah."

"Don't insult my intelligence. What about things the police found in your . . . his apartment? Do you really expect me to believe anything else? They found a knife with blood on it, women's blouses, panty hose. Half a dozen pieces of proof, and the DNA matched the victims perfectly."

"All planted by a very desperate man who knew I was meeting with Rhonda, and why. The person I was about to expose."

Sarah countered everything he said with arguments she had either heard in court or read in the newspapers. Of course he'd say he was innocent. Didn't they all? But she knew her facts.

This man was equally adamant about what he said.

Sarah was better prepared than he knew, and in more ways than one. She knew that sincere act, those pleading eyes. A scene suddenly flashed before her eyes—her freshly scrubbed twenty-year-old fiancé at the door telling her he had joined the navy and was shipping out that very day. Sarah forced the painful memory from her mind, as she'd had to do so many times before.

"I don't believe a word you're saying," she declared when he finished.

He banged the table angrily with one fist and stood. "Believe what you will, then. I've told you the way it was."

Sarah thought for several moments. Lowering her voice she asked, "What are you planning to do to me?"

"Keep you tied up if I have to."

"If you're not a murderer, why don't you just leave?"

"I wouldn't be out the front door before you called the police."

"What do you care? Nobody's looking for Scott Corbin . . . he's dead. You're just somebody who happens to look like him. I don't even know your name."

From the outside it resembled every other single-story commercial cinder-block building in the Houston neighborhood, except this one was painted light blue instead of beige or white.

Inside was another story. Glassed-in cubicles around the laboratory's perimeter housed expensive automated machines. PI Robert Garding saw active digital displays and protruding thermometers and trays filled with test tubes and glass beakers, specimens apparently being analyzed or counted or something.

Garding spoke with a technician named Andrew,

who quickly summoned the director of the laboratory, Dr. B. J. Stratford.

Garding asked about the man named to receive Scott Corbin's remains—a Dr. Darvid King, at this address.

Dr. Stratford was a man of about fifty, short and stocky with a Nero fringe of brown hair on an otherwise bald head. He was built like a wrestler. He invited Garding into his private office, which was small and neat.

"Dr. King is away for a couple of days," Stratford said. "A family emergency."

Garding asked if Dr. King was a relative of the executed prisoner, Scott Corbin.

"No, he's not."

"You're sure?"

"Well, I'm certain Dr. King would have told me something like that. It was never discussed."

"Did you know about his claiming Corbin's body from the prison?"

"Of course."

"Could you tell me how that happened?"

Stratford said, "First, would you mind telling me what this is all about, Mr. Garding?"

"Certainly. I represent a client who saw somebody recently who bears an uncanny resemblance to Corbin. I need to know if there might be any connection to the man who was executed."

Stratford nodded. "I see." He explained first that his own Ph.D. degree was in biology. His laboratory, South Coast Biologics, was primarily engaged in genetic-engineering projects, such as development of drought-resistant soybeans, tomato plants that self-pollinated in cold temperatures, and bacteria that consumed heavy petroleum right out of seawater. He had initially hired Dr. Darvid King, a medical doctor, to perform human genealogy studies, long since abandoned. He explained that genetic engineering of plants was much more profitable.

The scientist consulted his computerized files, then continued. "Scott Corbin was part of one human study—or his cells were. Before his execution Corbin donated his body to medical science. Dr. King claimed Corbin's remains, then took hormone and chromosome samplings and testicular biopsies. On January thirteenth he performed an autopsy on Corbin's body, including sections of the brain for microscopic study. What then remained was disposed of that same day, according to Dr. King's records."

"How would that have been done? Was he buried somewhere?"

"No, his remains were cremated."

"Where was that performed?"

"Here at the lab."

"Were you present when Corbin's body was cremated, Doctor?"

"No."

"Why not?"

"Human studies were Dr. King's domain. My studies are concerned with plant life."

"Were you present during the autopsy?"

"No, I was not. Frankly, Mr. Garding, I preferred not to be involved with human studies at all, which is the other reason my laboratory gave them up."

"Was Scott Corbin the only human you studied?"

"There were two others."

"Before or after Corbin?"

Stratford consulted another file on his computer. "Before."

"Were the other two also executed prisoners?"

"One had been executed. The other died while on Death Row. Cancer, I believe."

"You believe? Didn't the autopsy show how he died?"

"There was no autopsy on that man."

"Why not?"

"It wasn't necessary for the study."

"What about the third man? Besides Corbin?"

Stratford checked. "No. No autopsy. You don't need a complete autopsy to obtain hormone or chromosome samplings or to do a testicular biopsy, Mr. Garding."

"Then why do one on Corbin?"

"I asked that question. Dr. King said he had wondered if Mr. Corbin might have had a brain tumor, so he performed a complete autopsy, including the brain. He told me there was no tumor."

"I see." Garding hesitated. "You said Dr. King was hired to perform human studies. What does he do now?"

"Assists with genealogy experiments and genetic engineering. He's an excellent researcher."

Garding asked when he might speak with Dr. King.

"I should think he'll be returning by the first of the

week, though I don't know exactly what the family emergency was. He left quite abruptly."

"Would you mind giving me his home address and phone number?"

Stratford hesitated. "Well, I . . . I'd rather not give out his address, but I suppose he wouldn't mind if you telephoned him, under the circumstances." He read off the phone number from a file on his desk.

"I really shouldn't have a drink before returning to work," Amanda Stowe said.

"A glass of wine, then. Do you prefer chardonnay? Sauvignon blanc?" Marvin Jamison signaled the waiter. "Bring her a glass of Kendall-Jackson chardonnay."

They faced each other across a romantic table on the outside deck of the Shoreline Bar & Grill. The table was set for lunch with gray linen, pink china, crystal wineglasses, and fresh pink roses.

Amanda admired the view of the park and skyline across Town Lake. "It really is beautiful."

"I told you. Right? Would I steer you wrong? This is my favorite spot in town." Jamison motioned for the waiter again. "Another vodka tonic, please." He lowered his upper lids ever so slightly, then crinkled his eyes. His voice dropped half an octave. "You know, you're a very sexy woman, Amanda. What do you do for fun?" His gaze moved from one jutting breast to the other, back again, and finally up to her young face. "You have an incredible smile."

"Why, thank you, Mr. Jamison." She widened her smile even more.

"Marv," he said, allowing his own teeth to peek through parted lips. "Call me Marv, please." He moistened his lips with his tongue. "We'd better eat up; I want to show you another place before we go back. It's up the lake a ways, and very romantic. If you like it, I'll take you there for a real drink one day after work." He leaned forward and whispered, "The view alone is enough to make you wet."

Perhaps it was her lack of sleep, her exhaustion, both mental and physical. But late Friday afternoon Sarah began to seriously entertain the possibility that this man was who he claimed to be. Details he recounted about when she had trained Scott Corbin at EBS began to penetrate her defenses.

"You were voted Volunteer of the Year for the Central Texas SPCA that June."

How could this man know that unless he was Corbin?

Before she could resolve that question he asked, "Do you remember the day the Round Rock branch of Compass Bank shut down because their system failed?"

Sarah recalled the incident very well, but almost anybody could have heard of it. She asked, "What caused the failure?"

"A secretary left a floppy disk in the A drive when they shut down the night before, so the system wouldn't boot up the next morning. I took the support call and tried everything I knew before I came to you for help. You simply had them remove the disk, then logged on on-line and booted up their computer right from your desk. Had them up and running in less than two minutes."

Sarah searched his face. Nobody would know those details except a handful of people in her office and one or two people at the bank. She looked this man over with renewed interest. The evidence was compelling, but might still be a trick. She had always felt she could tell when a man was lying.

"Look, give me a break," he went on. "I know how methodically you assemble facts. Let me ask you something. How did you conclude that I murdered Rhonda in the first place? You only saw us together on the street after dinner. Did you see her die? Did you hear her scream out for help, or see who ran away after she was dead? Do you absolutely know who plunged the knife into her? Do you, Sarah? Were you there?"

Sarah sat back in her chair and looked away from him.

He continued, "Did you ever see me do anything to suggest that I might be capable of murder? Did you ask what time I left Rhonda after dinner that night? What time I got home? If there might've been time for somebody to plant evidence in my apartment or put her panties in my car while the police interrogated me most of the next day and night? We worked together for an entire year, Sarah. I thought we were friends. Did you once write to me in prison to ask if you might've been wrong? To consider my side of the story? Five years, Sarah. I was on Death Row for five very long years."

The man stopped speaking. He looked directly

into her eyes and studied her face. His expression softened. He said, "I really liked you, Sarah. I respected you. You taught me whatever I know about software systems. Of all the people I knew, I especially wanted *you* to believe the truth."

Sarah suddenly recalled watching this same handsome face when she had trained Corbin at work—the curve of his lips, that dimple in his chin. She even remembered that wild sensation that had raced up her arm, like an electric shock, when their hands would accidentally touch. She swallowed hard, but didn't speak.

"What about now?" he asked. "You have a logical mind. We used to call you Miss Foolproof behind your back." He paused for breath, extending and clenching his fingers in frustration; then he abruptly rolled his head around over his shoulders. His neck popped audibly when he did.

"You're wrong this time, Sarah. Miss Foolproof didn't check her facts. Your information sources were faulty and you failed to double-check them. Is any of this ringing a bell? I *am* Scott Corbin. I did *not* kill Rhonda Talbot or anybody else. I have one shot at proving I'm not a murderer, and that's only if I find whoever set me up."

Sarah was both angered and disturbed by the criticism leveled at her. She had jumped to some conclusions when he'd been arrested, yet the evidence had been overwhelming. Her limbs suddenly felt limp. She managed to ask, "Then why did you attack me in my car?"

"Because you would've done me in again. When I

saw you with that video camera, it was déjà vu . . . Sarah Hill pointing her righteous finger. Putting one hand on the Bible and swearing that she saw me alive. Your videotape would've been playing in every police department and on every TV screen across Texas before midnight." He paused, breathing rapidly. "I have a plan I've dreamed about for five years. Believe me, anybody who's never slept on Death Row has no idea how long five years can be.

"Just as I set my plan into action, lo and behold, there you are again, and you're like a terrier with a rope. I knew you'd never let it go once you saw me. I went after the camera but you wouldn't turn loose. Next thing I knew we were here. Now what am I supposed to do? I can't let you go and I won't kill you." He shook his head. "As close as I can figure, you have two choices: You can either help me find the real murderer, or stay tied up in bed till I do. At least that way you won't interfere."

Sarah was warmed by his statement that he wouldn't kill her. "Yesterday wasn't the first time I saw you. Why do you keep changing your appearance?"

"I need to be as invisible as the man who set me up."

# Chapter Ten

"Ouch, that hurts."

Sitting astraddle the nude blonde bound to the corners of the motel bed, Anthony Shapiro leaned forward to glare menacingly into her face.

"I'll bite your damned nipple off," he growled. He lowered his mouth to her breast again.

"I'm serious . . . that's too hard."

"You like hard things."

"Not teeth. You're scaring me, Tony."

"Enough of your whining, bitch! And I'm not Tony, I'm Ivan the Terrible." He quickly slid to the foot of the bed, then buried his head between her thighs. "I'm going to rape and pillage and devour you from the inside out."

She moaned softly as he began with his tongue. "Ooh . . . that's better, Ivan."

Minutes later Shapiro thrust and nipped and groaned in orgasmic spasms atop her as the woman yelled out, climaxing for the third time. Shapiro collapsed on her, then rolled to one side, gasping for air. The woman slowly shook her head from side to side, still tethered to the bed.

When he untied her and returned from the bathroom, she asked, "When will you get the rest of the money, Tony?"

Shapiro was already getting dressed. "I told you, it has to stay offshore for a while."

"It's been over six months."

"You don't understand. Myra and her lawyers watch every move I make. They're convinced I have millions hidden somewhere."

"Don't you?"

"I have enough to live on."

"You don't have to be so evasive. I'm on your side, remember?" She put her arms around his neck and kissed him full on the lips.

"I'm just being cautious, Lil. If certain people ever find out what I did, it'll be all over for me. Don't think that bitch wouldn't tell them, either, if she had proof."

"People like who? The IRS?"

He didn't reply. He tucked his shirt inside his trousers. "I have a little money here. I'll buy you something nice. Some jewelry."

"I was hoping we could go somewhere together. Acapulco, maybe, or Cancún."

"Too risky."

"I'll say I'm going to a board meeting for the theater company. He'll never know the difference."

"I'm talking about Myra's lawyers. They hired somebody to follow me right after the divorce. He's probably still out there . . . they could easily find out if I left the country." He slipped his feet into alligator-hide loafers. "Give me a while longer. Just a few more months; then we'll be set for life. Okay?"

Sarah awoke from a greatly appreciated late-afternoon nap to find the bedroom dark, the apartment silent. She didn't even hear the sound of the TV for nearly the first time since he had arrived. She hated how he sat there with the remote all the time, constantly flipping channels. Whiplash television. It made her dizzy.

Curiously, she almost missed the sound now.

Margot awoke and stretched on the bed beside her, purring softly.

Sarah whispered, "Has he left?" She eased into her mauve slippers and nylon robe and tiptoed into the hallway, tightening the robe over her gown. Corbin had allowed her to take a much-needed shower before her nap. She actually felt good, considering the emotional trauma she'd suffered.

Corbin sat at the dining table in T-shirt and trousers, staring at her computer's screen. He had obviously removed the computer from her bedroom while she slept.

The thought of him in her bedroom, watching her sleep, was most unsettling. She asked what he was doing.

"Welcome back," he said. "You look refreshed. Love your hair that way, Woodstock." He drank from a can of Dr Pepper.

Sarah's hands immediately flew to her head, flattening the hair that had sprung up while she slept.

"I'm trying to find something on the Internet," he said, "but I'm not very good at it."

"You didn't have computers in prison?"

"Not the Internet. We weren't even allowed TV on Death Row." He attempted to key in some commands, oblivious to the mouse control at his right hand. "That's what I was doing over on Congress all week—you can rent Internet time by the hour at a cyber café there. I need to identify the suppliers EBS used. I remember some, but there's hundreds in town now that didn't used to be. I can't visit them all."

Sarah almost offered to help but caught herself. She still didn't believe this man. Not completely. Maybe he *was* Scott Corbin—everything pointed to it. But he was lying about not being a killer. Firmly convinced for more than five years that Corbin was a psychotic murderer, she wasn't about to discard her belief simply because he asked her to. She had never doubted that he was clever. He was merely using her as a shield while he hid out. The police would certainly know he had escaped. They must be searching for him. But how had they kept it so quiet? There hadn't been one thing about his escape on the news.

Sarah asked, "Why didn't they execute you like they were supposed to?"

"I don't discuss that."

"I saw a death certificate with your name on it. How do you explain that?"

"I don't."

When he didn't offer more, she said, "Obviously somebody got executed in your place that night. Who was it?"

"That subject is not open for discussion. You can ask anything else."

"How did you escape from prison?"

"Same subject, different tack. *No comprendo.*"

Sarah thought she'd surely explode. "How the hell do you expect me to reach a conclusion if you won't answer my questions?"

"I've told you what you need to know."

"No, you've told me what you *want* me to know. There's a huge difference."

He looked at her for a long moment before quietly saying, "I'm sorry, Sarah, but I simply cannot discuss certain things. You'll have to trust me."

Trust him? A convicted murderer? *Sure, that'll be the day.* She didn't reply, but racked her brain as her anger slowly subsided. She did not believe much of what he'd said. But she had also not believed that Scott Corbin was alive, and here he sat at her dining table. At this point she didn't know what to believe.

Late that afternoon Clarence "Cosmo" Rivers chained his motorcycle to a post outside a building on South Lamar Boulevard. He secured his helmet to the bike and went inside. He paid the ten-dollar cover charge and passed through a blackout curtain, then stood waiting for his eyes to adjust to dim light. Hard-rock music blared from huge speakers overhead. Lithe dancers, male and female, wearing black leather and red vinyl and chains, gyrated on mini-stages throughout the smoke-filled club. Customers who appeared either half-stoned or half-drunk sat on low stools surrounding each stage, drinking beer and smoking. The majority of the customers were men, some young, some old.

A surprisingly tall Asian woman hurried to Cosmo's side and kissed him on the cheek. "Cosmo, baby, where've you been?" She had to shout to be heard above the din.

The woman wore black mesh stockings and high vinyl boots and gloves, and carried a black riding crop. Her dark hair was pulled into a ponytail even longer than Cosmo's. Her small breasts were shapely and bare.

"I've been working, Lea," he shouted. "But it's Friday now and I came to party."

"You came to the right place, wild man. Follow me."

In a back room Cosmo stripped down and put on a black leather hood and a leather cup for his privates. Lea helped him into a chest harness attached to an overhead mechanical pulley, then cranked a winch to raise him several inches off the floor. She began to tap him with her riding crop, lightly at first.

"Harder," Cosmo ordered.

The leather crop smacked loudly against bare skin as the young woman put more force into her efforts. Cosmo winced with each blow, but demanded that she hit him even harder. She did. Without warning, Lea spun Cosmo around, striking him on his back, chest, legs, and bare arms as he rotated in the air.

"I'll get you," he threatened through gritted teeth. "You no-good whore. I'm gonna get even with you."

"You're not gonna do shit, Cosmo, you fucking wimp. I'm in charge here, and don't you forget it."

"I'm warning you, slut. You're going to pay for this."

"Eat me, wimp." Lea smacked the leather crop hard against his exposed buttocks. "Beg me, asshole. You think you can't take any more, huh? You can't make me stop. I want to hear you beg."

Long after Corbin was gone Sarah stared wide-eyed at the ceiling. She tried not to imagine what it must have been like, lying on a cot in a tiny cell day and night.

Already feeling that her walls were closing in after being confined in her apartment for thirty consecutive hours, she tried to imagine the agony he had endured for over five years. Nighttime must have been the worst. The sounds, the smells. Vile creatures stalking about in adjoining cells. Their moans, their threats, their curses. Grown men crying softly into the night. Other things she wouldn't allow herself to consider.

She imagined what an investigative news report on TV might say: *Whispered prayers interrupted by the crazed shrieks of minds stretched past fragile human limits. Brains perhaps genetically imperfect, others damaged beyond recovery by chemicals sold in today's schoolyards.*

*My God,* she thought suddenly. What if he really was innocent? That thought made the horror of her terrible vision even worse.

Sarah swallowed a huge lump in her throat. As frightened as she was of this man, she almost wished he would return. At least turn on the TV. It was so deathly silent with him gone.

She suddenly became filled with a new anxiety. She tried not to imagine what would happen if he did not return. Nobody would miss her until Monday, when she didn't report for work. Sarah bit one edge of her tongue to keep from crying.

What if, as she feared, he was lying about everything he had said, and returned to mutilate her as he had Rhonda? Exactly as the Chameleon had done to all the others.

Would anybody notice, or care, that she was gone?

Her parents were dead. She had no brothers or sisters. The sad truth was, other than her friend in New Orleans, there wasn't a human alive who would really miss her.

When that thought registered fully, Sarah began to cry in earnest. What difference did it make if she suffocated?

Dark clouds obscured the moon as a young woman emerged from an apartment building near the intersection of Oltorf Street and Parker Lane, and hurried to her car. She was pulling out from her parking space when a second car, its headlights off, thudded into her rear bumper. A slow speed accident, but exasperating. She was already late for an appointment.

The woman's anger merged with guilt as she saw a crippled old man with white hair and obscenely distorted limbs emerge from the offending car. She winced, watching his painful struggle to inspect whatever damage he had caused.

She hurried to join the man at their kissing bumpers. "Don't worry about it," she began.

The old man straightened unexpectedly and pressed a handgun into the woman's abdomen.

Waves of ecstasy washed over the man minutes later as Rachmaninoff's "The Isle of the Dead" soared inside the young woman's apartment. The pressure had built inside him so badly tonight, he had thought he would surely explode. As difficult as those long years of abstinence were, it had almost been easier then. Now, like an alcoholic off the wagon, the first woman had whetted a dormant, but voracious, appetite. He hummed with the music, thrilled with his brilliance and good fortune. The exhilarating sensation he needed so desperately was building and building. He would soon peak, then find the blessed release. Until the next time.

He stroked the young woman's skin lightly, and sensuous waves raced up his spine. He rolled her glossy black hair between his fingers, held it to his nose and sniffed. He ran the back of one latex-covered hand lightly over her forehead and eyelashes. He thought he would surely climax from searching the depths of those magnificent eyes. Such a deep, clear brown—wild and frightened now, like a strangled deer the instant before its heart stopped. He ripped the tape from the woman's mouth and inhaled her anguished screams.

"The reward is the blood," he whispered to himself. He traced the point of a butcher knife delicately across her face and along her chest. Thin streams of bright crimson chased the razor-thin edge like a trailing caboose, tracking the knife's erratic path.

"Please," the woman begged hoarsely above the thundering music, "I'll do anything you want."

"Oh, but you are," he whispered in a voice choked with emotion. "Beg some more. Even better, scream for me again."

Thirty minutes later the woman's body sat duct-taped to a dining chair, like a discarded rag doll. Unseeing, unfeeling, unthinking, and no longer breathing or pumping blood, she had been released from her unendurable agony by that merciful god called Death. Her striking eyes had been enucleated and her entrails spilled over pale yellow wall-to-wall carpeting. Except for the presence of two female breasts, her unnatural form in no way resembled the saucy young woman who had left her apartment an hour earlier.

A phone rang incessantly somewhere down the hall as the woman's attacker groaned orgasmically, masturbating yet again into her open body cavity.

A combination of dread mixed with relief flooded Sarah when Corbin returned a few minutes after eleven P.M. He washed his hands first, then untied her, apologizing for taking so long. He said he'd had a flat on the way to the pizza place, and had also picked up his belongings from a motel. He had brought Sarah a salad plus a bag of oranges, a cantaloupe, and some nectarines. And his pizza, of course, along with more Dr Peppers. He said he had tried unsuccessfully to find a friend he needed to help him with something. Said he had searched three of the clubs the man used to frequent.

Sarah washed her tearstained face, brushed her teeth and hair, then proceeded toward the kitchen to ask more questions. She neatened up the living room along the way, overflowing with nervous energy, then set place mats and silverware on the dining table. She poured a glass of chardonnay for herself and, at his request, a Dr Pepper for Corbin. He couldn't seem to get enough of the soft drink.

As they ate, Corbin told Sarah he had taken the job at EBS to follow up a lead early in the Chameleon case. She remembered it coming out in court that he had been an investigative reporter in Dallas after graduating from college. He said he had decided to try his hand at a full-length book, and had been gathering information.

"I remember. You'd broken up with your fiancée in Dallas."

He hesitated. "Actually, it was a divorce."

"Why did you tell me different?"

"I just . . . it was a very painful experience. I really didn't want to talk about it." He shifted topics. "Those photos they found in my apartment, of murdered women, were research for my book. Copies of ones a crime-scene tech had taken."

Sarah also recalled that testimony from the trial—and a similar explanation about newspaper clippings discovered, along with his personal notes about the killings.

"I took the job at EBS when I found out about two

phone calls the police had traced from there to an escort service. One of the victims had worked for that service and I thought there might be a connection. Plus, I needed a job, and EBS had an opening. I was broke after my divorce.

"Nosing around once I was hired, I found several things going on that shouldn't have been. I'd had two years of business before I changed majors, so I know a little about purchasing and outside contract services and so forth. Somebody was stealing big-time from the company."

"Who?"

"I got arrested before I knew for sure, but that's what I told Rhonda about."

Sarah sipped her wine and wiped her mouth on a napkin. "Who do you think it was?" She wanted to see who he blamed for what, to evaluate whether he was just slinging sand.

"I'll tell you what I discovered; then you give me your opinion. Mr. Hale-and-hearty Marv Jamison was enjoying three-martini lunches every other day and played the commodities market like a table in Vegas. You probably knew that he met Helen Hartley at the Econo Lodge every Tuesday."

"I didn't know. She had just gotten a divorce." Helen had been a secretary in the sales department back then, and was long since remarried and gone.

"Yeah, but Terri Jaynes hadn't. He took her to the same motel on Fridays. Marv got very nervous when I started asking how much contract programmers make. Is he still operations manager?"

"No, he's our purchasing agent. We have a woman OM, Marissa Young."

"So Marv took a healthy cut in salary after the buyout?"

"Probably."

Corbin worked on another slice of pizza, then washed it down with his usual. "Anthony Shapiro was living way beyond his reported income. I never found out how."

"He was president of the company."

"Yes, but it wasn't that profitable. He needed to sell to make any real money."

"Who else?"

"Franklyn Russett. On the surface he was a typical twenty-eight-year-old, quiet, hardworking married man. Great at his job, easygoing. But he spent most of what he made buying porno tapes and girlie magazines in sex shops down on South Lamar. I pegged either Russett or Marv Jamison for the calls to the escort services. Or Cosmo. Is he still around?"

"Oh, yes, Mr. Rivers . . . and he is strange." Sarah visualized Cosmo's most recent T-shirt picturing a pack of slathering animals ripping apart the carcass of a child. She shuddered.

"I never could get anything on Rivers, but I know he was doing something. Then there's Tad Roman. Sugar wouldn't melt in Tad's mouth. He seemed too nice for belief. Maybe he is, but sometimes it's the Caspar Milquetoasts who have wild-eyed demons lurking in the recesses of their brains."

Sarah couldn't help being intrigued, despite her

fear. She had wondered about a few people herself. "What exactly did you uncover?"

"Among other things somebody was cooking the books. Overpaying for hardware components, such as two hundred dollars for hundred-dollar chips and nearly double for motherboards. With the numbers they ordered, somebody must've been getting huge kickbacks. One contract programmer would get two hundred fifty an hour while another was paid one twenty-five for the same work. Who knows how many hours they actually worked versus how many got billed?"

"How would that involve Rhonda Talbot?"

"Nearly everybody at EBS had stock options, as you probably did. That's how Shapiro kept such a sharp team, because he sure wasn't paying anybody that well. When I approached a couple of people, including Shapiro, about a few irregularities I had spotted, nobody wanted to know from nothing. So I called Rhonda."

Sarah didn't respond to his comment about her stock options. In fact, she had received options. After making a sizable donation to the animal shelter, paying off her car, and buying a few clothes, she still had a nice little nest egg in CDs at the bank. Her down-payment on a house, someday.

As he spoke Sarah found it harder and harder to believe that this man was insane, or had murdered those women. Still, she couldn't let her guard down. If the Chameleon hadn't been good at manipulating people, he would've been caught long before he was. Sarah wanted this man to relax, to keep talking. He would trip himself up eventually, or give her a chance to escape.

When questioned, Sarah related that ISI was far bigger than EBS had been. Anthony Shapiro was current senior vice president, but had lost some of his luster as potential successor to the corporate throne following a very public divorce six months earlier. His ex had accused Shapiro of cocaine use and physical abuse, and had reportedly taken most everything he had. Sarah doubted the charges were true.

Marvin Jamison remained obsessed with the commodities market and women other than his wife. Sarah didn't know how much he drank at lunch, but she had noticed that he seemed more effective at his job in the mornings.

She said the bit about young Franklyn Russett buying sex tapes seemed to fit. Russett had been robbed and shot to death over four years ago. He hadn't been to work for ten days when his car was fished out of the Colorado River near Marble Falls. Police believed it was a prostitute who shot him.

Sarah couldn't believe anything bad about Tad Roman. Quiet, efficient, he was one of the best support people she had on staff. He even had a new baby.

"And Cosmo Rivers . . . is just Cosmo," Sarah added. "He hasn't changed one iota since you were there."

"Damn," Corbin exclaimed. "I spent five years sorting through people who would've set me up, and you just eliminated my number one suspect."

"Who?"

"Frank Russett . . . I was convinced he was the Chameleon. With him dead how can I prove he committed those murders? I need some kind of proof before they come looking for me."

"Before who comes looking?"

"The police. Maybe certain other people who'll know I've come back to Austin."

Though it was late and she was tired, Sarah wanted to know. "What would they do?"

"The state of Texas would execute me again. The others . . . I'm not sure, but I don't intend to find out."

Just then the phone rang. Marissa Young's voice came through the answering machine, asking how Sarah was feeling. Corbin insisted that Sarah take the call. He quickly rounded up Margot and held her nearby while Sarah told Marissa that she was still under the weather.

"You said *again*," Sarah argued later as she lay on the bed facing the wall.

"No way," Corbin replied.

"Yes, you did. I distinctly heard you say the state of Texas would execute you *again*."

"Get real, Sarah . . . they'd send me back to Death Row and start the execution process all over again."

She turned to watch his face. How could she tell if he was lying?

# Chapter Eleven

"This one's worse than the last one," Detective Moyers said.

Det. Jack Barnaby shook his head. The nude young woman taped to the chair could have been a sister of the first victim. Same five-three or -four height, same general coloring. There was blood everywhere, and a classical music station had been playing on the FM radio when she was found by her landlady at seven-thirty that morning. Slices of human organ meat were neatly stacked on the dining room table, exuding a stench that was downright sickening. It was already over ninety outside. Inside, the apartment was insufferably warm.

Barnaby could almost hear the woman's screams bouncing off blood-smeared walls. Echoes of her painful sobs tugged at his heart, and he could imagine his own blood congealing each time he looked around the room. He ground his teeth so hard that his jaw ached. This young woman had been somebody's daughter.

Ann Garmany approached. "Everything's similar

to before," she said, "right down to the missing eyes."

Barnaby closed his own eyes for a moment. He couldn't begin to imagine a life of total darkness. He hoped the woman had been dead before that happened.

To avoid destroying or contaminating crucial evidence at the scene, Garmany had waited for the go-ahead by crime-scene techs before examining the body. In addition to the techs' dusting for prints and vacuuming for hairs and fibers, each item of potential evidence had already been tagged, numbered, protected by a plastic "tent" marker, and photographed.

Jim Moyers busied himself with details in a back room. The victim's closet was neat, with shoes in a hanging bag, skirts and blouses to the left, dresses to the right, sweaters in clear plastic boxes on an overhead shelf. The woman had picked up two skirts and three blouses the Monday before at Comet One-Hour Cleaners on North Lamar. He could find no crawl space behind or false ceiling above the closet.

A litter box in the bathroom indicated that the victim had a cat, but none had been found. Moyers pictured the massacred and desecrated body of a cat. Serial murderers often enjoyed torturing and killing animals, even though they generally used them as warm-up exercises before moving on to human beings.

Barnaby came into the bedroom. "What's your take, Jim?"

"She lived alone. Valuables and money still here.

She didn't undress voluntarily. Her clothes were ripped off in the living room, and it looks like she put up a pretty good struggle. She was dressed as though she'd been out. Her bed hasn't been slept in."

"Think she might have known him?"

"It's possible. There's no sign of forced entry."

"He might have convinced her to open the door somehow, then forced his way in. Or he could have hooked up with her elsewhere and made her bring him home and unlock the door."

"Did you find something to suggest it was a stranger-to-stranger relationship?"

"Just a guess. The last one appeared to be."

"You think it's the same guy?"

"Don't you?"

Moyers surveyed the room silently before answering. "Sure looks like it, except for the absence of forced entry."

Barnaby nodded. "Did he leave anything? He was here long enough."

"If he did we haven't found it yet."

They walked back toward where crime-scene techs worked the living room.

Barnaby said, "She must've screamed something terrible, Jim. You'd think somebody would have heard her."

"It's a rear corner apartment and the adjacent occupant was away. Everybody had their window air conditioners running. The man across the hall heard loud music playing, but figured she was having friends over. Said she did that sometimes. A lady farther up the hall is nearly deaf, so people in the building are accustomed to a TV playing real loud, with sirens and screams and things. Bottom line . . . nobody heard anything unusual."

Jack Barnaby asked a uniformed policewoman at the front entrance, "Where's the landlady?"

"Outside and to the right . . . the manager's apartment. She's in pretty bad shape, sir."

"'S okay. I'll take it easy on her."

Moyers tossed his gloves into a plastic bag before exiting.

The apartment complex resembled others on the street, with its redbrick facade. Many area tenants were students, the building being only a few blocks from the UT campus. According to the landlady the dead woman had been a graduate student. Divorced. Stephanie Ryan was her name. Barnaby wondered what her friends had called her. Steph? Steffie? Judging from the books inside, she had been studying psychology. The landlady found Stephanie's mother's name and phone number on a rental application.

On the way out Moyers indicated a restless group on the other side of the yellow tape. "What do you want to tell the reporters?"

"Nothing."

"We have to tell them something, Jack . . . otherwise they'll make it up."

"You asked what did I *want* to tell them, not what we *have* to tell them." Barnaby adjusted his tie as he added, "Tell them we haven't determined cause of death. Pending further studies, withholding identity until family can be notified, yada yada yada." He scowled momentarily. "Do not tell them we suspect a serial killer . . . especially not a Chameleon copycat. We don't need that kind of panic in the city."

"Who is this?" Scott Corbin motioned Sarah to the front window early the next morning. The doorbell chimed again. "Hurry."

Sarah lifted a single blind with a finger and peeked out. Whispering, she said, "It's Marissa Young, my operations manager."

"What's she doing here?"

"I don't know . . . she's never been here before."

Corbin closed his eyes for a moment. In a flash he spun around and raced toward the hallway. "Get rid of her," he ordered. "Remember, I'll have Margot and I'll be listening to every syllable you utter. No scribbling notes, either. I can see everything from the bedroom door."

Sarah opened her front door, forcing her breathing to slow.

It being Saturday, Marissa was dressed very differently from her usual office attire. She wore pale green toreador pants and a matching silk top. Her auburn hair was pulled back in a bun and she carried a large thermos.

"I hope I didn't wake you," Marissa said in her usual considerate tone. Her free hand was on the handle of the screen door.

"No, I . . . I've been up quite a while." Sarah suddenly remembered, and coughed, then cleared her throat and covered her abdomen with one hand as if it were sore.

Before Sarah could say more, Marissa eased right past and marched into the kitchen. "I've brought you something guaranteed to knock out a virus. One of my favorite recipes."

"But I . . . how thoughtful, Marissa."

The woman turned and scanned Sarah's apartment. She smiled approvingly. "I love that floral pattern on your drapes, and those pictures." Marissa went to inspect two prints on a living room wall. She stopped momentarily at a Susan Rios print, then meandered past the computer on the dining table and narrowed her eyes at the clutter. "Do you have a guest?"

Sarah thought she would black out from anxiety. Her one chance to let somebody know that her life was in danger, and she couldn't risk saying a word—he had Margot.

"No, no, I was just balancing my checking account." She began to straighten the mess of papers Corbin had scattered on the table, perspiration trickling along one side of her chest.

From Corbin's vantage point in the bedroom Marissa appeared to be half a head taller than Sarah, with coifed hair, good legs and derriere, and nice cleavage. She fussed over Sarah like a mother hen.

Marissa smiled sweetly. "Well, I didn't mean to disturb you, dear. You eat your soup now. Let's hope you feel better by Monday."

"Oh, I'm sure I will." Sarah pressed a tissue to her mouth and coughed again.

Marissa left.

Sarah fell limply onto the sofa.

Margot ran out from beneath Sarah's feet.

* * *

Garding pulled into the driveway of a two-story home in a Houston suburb. It was an unpretentious yellow-brick with gray wood trim, in a middle-class neighborhood. The man who answered the door appeared to be about forty, was thin and pale, and had jet-black hair. He was tall enough to have played basketball in college.

The man extended his hand, "You must be Mr. Garding. I'm Darvid King. Come in, please."

King led Garding into a small but comfortable den that contained a brown plaid sofa and recliner, assorted small tables and lamps, and a TV. King removed a stack of medical journals from the sofa so Garding could sit, and offered him a soft drink or a glass of tea.

Garding accepted the iced tea, and began the interview, using a technique he had polished during twenty years of police work. All Garding had told King over the phone was that Dr. Stratford had suggested they meet so that Garding might ask a few questions about South Coast Biologics' very interesting work. He commented on King's house, asked about the medical journals, how long King had been in Houston, where he went to college, if he had played ball, and whether he had children. He wanted King to loosen up while he studied the man's posture and manner of speaking. The PI expressed interest in framed photos of King on a tennis court with a pretty young woman. The woman was trim and athletic, and had a blond ponytail and huge blue eyes—King's wife, Debbie.

During the entire rapport-building stage, Garding paid close attention to baseline "norms" of the doctor's communication style. Reading people was a survival tactic in police work. King tended to give long, articulate responses. His voice was deep and mellow, relaxed, and his body language open. One hand rested comfortably on an arm of his recliner chair; the other held a can of soda that he casually sipped from time to time. He laughed warmly as they spoke, his eyes moving easily about the room. All in all he was a very pleasant, open, friendly man.

Beginning to close in now, Garding said, "I understand you were away on a family emergency. I hope everything is all right."

King stiffened almost imperceptibly. "Uh, yes, it was . . . turned out to be just a scare. An aunt. She had some chest pain." He waved the question off. "She's fine now."

"I'm glad to hear that." Garding knew that King had returned earlier in the day from wherever he had gone. Wife Debbie had shared that much over the phone. "Does your aunt live in town?"

"Uh, no, in Dallas."

Garding smiled as he watched King change. Almost instantly the man's sentences were shorter, his posture not as relaxed. He was using the word *uh* to stall, buying himself time to think about his responses.

Without warning Garding told the doctor exactly why he had come: that his client had seen a man she believed to be Scott Corbin.

King's pale complexion faded even more. He almost stammered, "Who?"

"Scott Corbin. The man who was executed at the prison in Huntsville."

King shook his head. "Oh, yes . . . umm, wasn't he one of the prisoners in our testosterone study?" His verbal and nonverbal cues were inconsistent. Shaking his head no while simultaneously answering yes suggested a subconscious denial of what he was confirming—a lie. And his voice had gone up half an octave—even the muscles in his larynx had tightened. King set the can of soda on a nearby table, then clasped his hands together and looked straight at Garding. No longer casually surveying the room, he forced a nervous smile.

King's style had changed abruptly, suggesting that he knew exactly who Garding was talking about. It was time to confront him. "According to prison records, you picked up Corbin's remains after the execution, Doctor. What did you do with them?"

"Oh, that one. Yes, I remember now. I took him to the laboratory."

"For what purpose?"

"For our study."

"Could you be a little more specific? What were you studying?"

"Testosterone and serotonin levels. And chromosomes."

"Was there some reason you chose Scott Corbin?"

"He was on Death Row."

"Why him? There are hundreds of people on Death Row."

It was only a split-second delay, but King had to search for his answer. "He was supposed to be a serial killer."

"Supposed to be?"

"Well, he had been convicted. Of three murders."

"And that made him suitable for your study?"

King leaned forward on one elbow, frowning slightly. He absently moved a hand to his mouth—trying to keep the lie inside? His Adam's apple bobbed up and down; then he sought familiar cover in medicalese, saying, "Habitual criminals often exhibit abnormally elevated testosterone levels, Mr. Garding, or diminished serotonin. Some subjects display a supernumerary Y chromosome."

"Did Corbin have those things?"

"No, everything was normal."

"How did you determine that?"

"By serum levels and biopsy."

"A biopsy is when you take a piece of something and look at it under the microscope?"

"Yes." King blinked several times, a mannerism Garding hadn't observed before. Another change.

When Garding didn't speak right away King added, "A person can either be dead or alive when you do a biopsy."

"I see." Garding watched the doctor's face, his eyes.

King's feet seemed restless now, and he shifted in his seat as though physically uncomfortable with this line of inquiry. Was he frightened for himself, or protecting somebody?

"After you determined that all those things were

normal," Garding said, "what did you do with Corbin's body?"

"He was cremated."

"At a funeral home?"

"No, we had a crematorium at the laboratory."

"Had?"

"It's still there . . . we don't use it anymore."

"Why not?"

"We abandoned our human studies."

"Why is that?"

"A similar study was published at the University of Colorado, and they had a much larger sampling. Ours would have been anticlimactic."

"Is that the only reason?"

King frowned. "Frankly, I never cared for the work. It was"—he had to clear his throat to finish his sentence—"very unpleasant."

"What made it so unpleasant?"

"Just . . . I have never liked working with dead people."

Garding paused momentarily, then asked, "Did anybody assist you with these human studies?"

"No."

"Dr. Stratford didn't help?"

"No."

"Were any other studies done on Mr. Corbin, Doctor?"

"Just what I told you."

"You didn't perform an autopsy?"

"Oh. Yes, I did do an autopsy." He shook his head from side to side again, his nonverbal cue totally inconsistent with his answer. "I thought you meant specific studies like testosterone or chromosomes."

"I see." Garding watched Dr. King fold his arms over his chest and cross his legs, closing his body to questioning.

Garding knew that if King shut down, he would never establish the truth. He glanced at his watch and stood. "I had no idea it was getting so late. I've taken far too much of your time, and I appreciate what you told me. I figured my client was mistaken, but I had to do some checking around. She obviously made a mistake about who she thought she saw."

Dr. King also stood, visibly relieved. "I hope I was of some help, Mr. Garding."

"Oh, you were, Doctor. Thank you . . . you helped a great deal." He smiled. "You were probably quite a basketball player, huh?"

"I did all right."

"I'll bet you did. Hey, thanks again. I'll see you around, okay?"

# Chapter Twelve

"Sweetheart, you were magnificent . . . I mean that. Wow." Jamison was still breathing hard.

"Thank you, Mr. . . . er, Marv."

Amanda Stowe leaned forward to position her breasts in her bra, then straightened and adjusted them.

Marvin Jamison watched smugly from the motel bed, completely spent but pleased with himself. He had given this sweet young thing a workout she wasn't likely to forget for a long while. Surprisingly enough she hardly seemed winded.

"I guess I should be getting on home," Amanda said. "I promised my mom I'd cook tonight, so I need to pick up some things from the supermarket."

"What a nice daughter." He propped himself up on a pillow. "How come you still live at home?"

"Apartments are expensive."

"You make pretty good money, don't you?"

"Not that much. I help my mom out since my dad died."

Marv touched himself as he watched her pull on

her skirt. *What a great body.* "What if I helped you get a place of your own?"

"I couldn't ask you to do that."

"You didn't ask; I offered. I'm offering."

"You're talking about a lot of money."

"Don't worry about that. I have money."

"I don't know. What if your wife were to find out?"

"She's not going to find out. I've got money she doesn't know anything about."

"Really? You're being straight with me?"

"Absolutely. Are you interested?"

"What's the catch?"

"No catch. I might want to come over occasionally, you know, watch a movie or something."

"Are you being serious, Mr. Jami . . . Marv?"

"Of course. I mean, do you like movies?"

"I love Julia Roberts and Sandra Bullock. And Mel Gibson."

"How about sexy movies?"

"Name one."

"Oh, maybe something like *Frolicking Nurses* or *Greek Entries.*"

"Have they been on HBO?"

He laughed. "Not likely. There's a lot of nudity, and they get pretty graphic about what they show. But it's exciting. Do you think you'd like to watch them with me?"

"I guess so, if you would."

"I'd like it a lot." He wouldn't mention the asphyxia films till later. He could really get off on those. Then, with a little convincing and maybe a joint or two, she'd try it with him. Him humping away, a plastic bag over her face right up till the very instant when she started coming.

Amanda put on her blouse and began buttoning it. Jamison watched, imagining what he could do to her. Rubbing himself more vigorously now, he felt another erection stirring.

"Hey," he said. "Come over here."

"I really need to be going."

"Not yet, okay? We need to talk about that apartment. And I've got something I think you're gonna love."

"It sure would simplify things if you could trust me, Sarah." Scott Corbin turned the flame down under the bacon he was frying, scrambling three eggs in another pan.

Sarah wrinkled her nose at the offensive aroma. She sat at the dining table with half a cantaloupe, whole-wheat toast, and a glass of freshly squeezed orange juice. "Why should I trust you?"

He transferred bacon to a paper towel to drain. "Do you trust anybody?"

"Of course."

"Who?"

"Well . . . people at work."

"Name some. Who from your office would you trust with your cat for a month?"

She considered the possibilities. *Marvin Jamison? No. Mr. Shapiro? Not really. Amanda? A little too immature. Tad Roman? Possibly. Cosmo Rivers? Forget about it.* Though Sarah wasn't fond of her apartment manager, Letty Whitstone, she would certainly trust her with

Margot. Mrs. Whitstone loved cats more than people. But he had said people at work.

"Marissa Young," she finally said. Marissa would be very responsible.

"Any men?"

"Maybe Tad Roman and his wife."

"That's hedging. What men in your life do you trust absolutely, without question?"

After a lengthy silence, she replied, "None, I guess."

Corbin buttered two slices of toast, then set his plate on the place mat and joined her. He extended his hand across the table.

"What?"

"Give me your hand."

Reluctantly, she did.

He sat looking at her fingers, then caressed her skin lightly. The hairs on her arm stood on end when an electric shock seemed to zigzag up it. It was the same sensation she'd felt whenever he had accidentally touched her during the time they'd worked together. She pulled away.

"What's the matter?"

She rubbed her arm briskly. "That prickles. What are you doing?"

"Our family always joined hands when we said grace together. I was trying to decide where to begin."

Sarah tentatively offered her hand, and he grasped it firmly in his. He closed his eyes and said, "Dear God, thank you for this food we're about to eat. Bless us this day in all our endeavors and forgive our human frailties. Bless our friends and families wherever they may be, and help us find meaning in our lives on Earth. We ask in Jesus' name. Oh, yes, and bless Sarah's cat. Amen."

Sarah sat dumbfounded. A thousand questions filled her mind.

He looked at her quizzically. "Are you all right?"

"I just . . . you surprise me, that's all."

He indicated her cantaloupe. "Eat up. I have things to do in town. As much as I hate to do it, I'm gonna have to tie you back in bed."

"No," she said, recoiling. "I don't want to be tied in bed."

"You don't leave me any choice, Sarah."

"No. Please. Take me with you."

"You don't even know where I'm going."

"It doesn't matter. I want to go."

That same morning at Austin police headquarters, detectives Jack Barnaby and Jim Moyers discussed their number one case with a task force of fellow Homicide detectives at their monthly meeting. Since Det. Melissa McBain had moved over to Homicide from the Sex-Crimes unit only two weeks earlier, much of the basic information discussed was intended for her benefit.

Barnaby pointed to a conclusion he'd written on a white dry-erase board with a green marker. A life-size wall chart of human anatomy hung to one side of the board, for accurately specifying wound locations in their reports. A McDonald's orange plastic pumpkin sat on a shelf above Barnaby, with a teddy bear poking its unlikely head from inside the pumpkin—for frightened children who accompanied witnesses to the Homicide department. Or the offspring of murder suspects.

"When you consider all the evidence," Barnaby said, "there must have been two Chameleon killers all along—Corbin and a copycat." He drew a large green circle around the number 2.

Det. Linda Torres asked, "What about the DNA tests?" Linda was thirty-five, a single parent with early middle-age spread and a don't-mess-with-me attitude.

Moyers explained. "Rhonda Talbot's DNA matched blood on the panties found beneath the front seat of Corbin's car. Blood on the clothing and the knife found in his apartment matched DNA from two additional victims. The copycat must've killed the others . . . the same man who's started leaving semen on later victims."

"But you said Corbin didn't do that. And why didn't the other guy do it from the beginning?"

"Maybe the copycat somehow knew that Corbin didn't leave semen. Or he wore a condom at first. *Cocksafes,* they call them, for obvious reasons. The killer is becoming arrogant now. Thinks he can't be caught."

Det. Melissa McBain spoke up. An athletic woman of twenty-eight whose eyes sparked with warmth and intelligence, she asked, "If there was a second killer, why would he stay dormant all this time?" Except for the Glock 9mm semiautomatic at her side, Melissa looked more like a UT cheerleader than the highly effective Homicide detective she was becoming.

"He was dormant because he's a cluster killer," Barnaby replied. "Murders three or four close together, then hides out for a while. He's probably a clean-cut, pleasant, normal-looking guy most of the time. When his hunger to kill builds up to a certain point, he can't resist it anymore. Killing is a form of sexual release for these psychopaths. Not an uncommon pattern."

"Or," Moyers added, "he may have been out of the country or incarcerated somewhere for a few years. We're taking a hard look at potential suspects recently released from prison."

"Serial killers study up on each other," Barnaby said, "probably to get ideas. So we should study them, too. I've asked Linda to share some information she looked up for us."

Linda Torres stepped to the front, consulted her notes, and told them about historical serial killers. She began with Peter Kurten, the Düsseldorf Vampire, whose violent, drunken father forced his mother to have sex in front of the children. A local dog catcher taught Kurten how to masturbate dogs, then how to torture and kill them. He had practiced bestiality, and described in his diary receiving "intense sexual pleasure from watching blood flow" from women he had raped and murdered, stabbing them twenty or thirty times each

Linda added, "He said it was the *activity,* rather than the specific victim, that created his sexual pleasure . . . though molesting them did enhance his thrill.

When they caught him, they asked if he felt any remorse for his killings. Kurten replied, 'No. In fact, as I think back, I rather enjoyed it.' "

Linda looked up with an expression of disbelief, then looked back at her notes. "Theodore Bundy first witnessed animal cruelty by his grandfather, and liked it immensely. Jeffrey Dahmer deliberately killed animals using his car long before he murdered seventeen men. Henry Lee Lucas killed animals and had sex with their corpses. That was before he killed his mother, his common-law wife, and others."

"Thank you, Linda," Barnaby said. "Melissa, what did your research show?"

Melissa McBain came forward and read aloud from an FBI profiler's statement. " 'There has never been a recorded case of a female performing sadistic mutilation murders. Several studies have been done on habitual criminals, and violent behavior seems to be testosterone-related.' "

Linda Torres interrupted, saying she had no reason to doubt *that* statement. Said it made perfect sense to her. Everybody present knew that Linda's ex-husband was in prison for selling drugs to high school kids. They also knew that he was too frightened of Linda to ever come out.

McBain continued, "Most serial killers are white males in their twenties or thirties. From an early age they learn to observe, assess, and appraise people and situations, including the needs and weaknesses of other people. They are often cunning manipulators, alert and adaptable. It also says there are an estimated five hundred serial killers at large today in the United

States alone, with ninety percent of those committing crimes of a brutal sexual nature." She looked at Detective Barnaby. "Can this number be right?"

"If the truth were known," Barnaby said, "it's probably even more. People move around so easily today, they're harder to catch. One victim in Florida, another in New York, a third in Iowa or somewhere. Nobody associates them unless they've left something containing their DNA at the scene and turn up in the CODIS database." He paused. "Do you know what the letters in CODIS stand for?"

"Combined DNA Index System," Melissa said.

"That's right," Barnaby said. "A few years back the legislature passed a law that requires all sex offenders or persons convicted of sex-related offenses to give a blood sample for DNA. That national file is CODIS, and it was a giant step for law enforcement."

Barnaby asked Jim Moyers if he had anything to add.

"Just that these weirdos often keep souvenirs from their victims as trophies. Our current killer takes their eyes. And, like Peter Kurten did, some of them keep diaries. They enjoy revisiting what they've done over and over. Also, I've studied the original Chameleon case, since our current killer has copied him so thoroughly. I suggest you all familiarize yourselves with it, too. It's filed under Corbin . . . Scott Corbin. There's a perception that copycat killers always do the exact same thing with each killing, but they don't. There are variations depending on how the victim reacts, progressive behavior of the killer, and so forth. This man's leaving semen is a prime example of a difference, and it may be the thing that leads us to him."

"Thanks, Jim." Barnaby paused, then said, "Guys, this bastard is twisted and he's merciless. He preys on women in their early thirties who live alone, and he prefers pretty brunettes. Continue to go through the who, what, where, why, when, and how as you consider possibilities. I just told you about two whos. What was the cause of death? A vicious mutilation with a knife. Why does he always take their eyes? Ask yourselves why each victim was selected. What was her profession? Who had access to her home? Who stands to gain from her death? How or when did the victim and suspect cross paths? For instance, he may work at a supermarket or drugstore or gas station or photo-development booth or fast-food place or health club or anyplace where he crosses paths with his victims. We can't be sure, but we think these recent cases were stranger-to-stranger relationships, that neither victim knew the killer.

"Help us find out what the victim was doing immediately prior to her death. Who saw her last? What was her routine? These are serial killings. Typically the victims are not only similar in appearance, but have similar jobs or hobbies, live in the same area, shop at the same mall—something that puts them in contact with the killer. We need to find that common thread." Barnaby let out a long breath and lowered his voice almost to a whisper. "I want that sick bastard and I want him now. I'd like to power-nail his ass to an oak cross in front of the State Capitol building."

# Chapter Thirteen

Scott Corbin drove Sarah's car up North Lamar, searching for an address he had copied from the yellow pages. He wore jeans, a short-sleeved sports shirt, a brown toothbrush mustache, and horn-rimmed glasses.

"I like the way this drives," he said.

From the passenger seat Sarah said, "It's a Honda Accord. *Auto Digest* rated it number one for two years running."

"Are you sure you want to do this?"

"No."

"No, you don't want to? You said—"

"No, I'm not sure. I haven't ridden in years."

"I can always take you back home."

The thought of being tied to that bed again was suffocating, which was why she had pleaded with him to take her along. Sarah watched his face and said, "When Marissa came by . . . ?"

"Yes?"

"You didn't even take Margot into the bedroom with you. Why not?"

Corbin glanced sideways at her, then back at the road. "Sarah, I wasn't going to hurt your cat."

"But you said—"

"Would you have called in sick Thursday if I hadn't threatened you in some way?"

"No."

"See? Same thing yesterday and again this morning."

"So you weren't serious about strangling her?"

"Look, I'm not particularly fond of cats, but I'd never hurt one. Any animal." His eyes misted as he remembered something. "I had a dog when I was a kid, name of Zack. I loved that dog better than anything. I see how much Margot means to you."

His words and misty eyes made a huge rent in her quilt of suspicions. Plus, in all their time together he had given no indication that he intended to harm her. Either this man was telling the truth about everything, or he was an incredibly good actor.

*Precisely as the prosecution had pointed out during his trial.*

After riding another block in silence Sarah said, "I look forward to going with you."

"You're sure?"

She hesitated. "I think so."

"You mean I don't have to hold Margot around the neck while we're in the store?"

She laughed aloud, and the sudden release of tension felt great. "That might be difficult with her asleep under the bed at home." She gave a short shake of her head. "No, Scott, I won't give you away."

"Do I have your word?"

She nodded. "You have my word."

He pulled to the side of the road and looked into Sarah's eyes. After several seconds elapsed without either saying a word, he said, "All right, I trust you. Whatever happens, I want you to remember that. I'm trusting you with my life."

Sarah's car resembled a gypsy wagon when they left University Cyclery. Two ten-speed bikes were strapped to the bumpers, and boxes of riding gear and sports apparel were piled in the backseat. He even stopped on the way home to replace the cords he had cut from her venetian blinds.

Corbin had paid for it all with cash. He wouldn't explain where his money came from other than to say he had been well paid for a job he'd recently held.

When they joined up later in Sarah's covered parking space, Corbin gave a low wolf whistle. Both were outfitted in summer-weight black spandex riding suits with chartreuse trim and matching helmets. Their eyes were covered by shatterproof dark goggles.

"Nice bod," he said.

She was too embarrassed to reply.

Corbin led the way down the driveway with Sarah right behind. She hoped he hadn't noticed her legs in those short shorts. She had hated her calves ever since she started gymnastics in high school. Loved gymnastics . . . hated muscular legs on a woman. At least, on her. Her mother had had beautiful slim legs until the day she died.

When they reached the entrance to the office

building Corbin sat astride his bike and said, "Tell me about the layout."

Sarah stood beside her bike. She had removed her goggles. He had not. This being the first Saturday of Austin's annual Bike Week, they blended readily into nearby groups of similarly attired riders.

"We occupy most of the fifth floor," she began. "Double doors at the entry with ISI in big bronze letters." She gave a detailed description of all offices inside. He was particularly interested in where files were kept.

"Everything is stored on hard drive these days, then backed up on floppy disks."

"Where are the dinosaur files? What I need would be from six years ago."

Sarah started to answer, but stopped. She saw Marvin Jamison get out of his car nearby and begin walking toward them. "Quick, turn around," she said. She immediately faced in the opposite direction and put on her goggles.

Jamison passed right by, entered the building, and stepped into the elevator.

Sarah's brow knotted into a frown. "What could he be doing here on a Saturday? I've never known Marvin to work overtime for any reason. And why didn't he park in the garage?"

"He sure hasn't aged well," Corbin said.

"What do you mean?"

"He must have put on thirty pounds since I last saw him, and he's growing bags under his eyes. He's going to seed."

Sarah looked around nervously, recognizing a

green motorcycle just inside the parking garage. "That's Cosmo's motorcycle," she said.

"Where?"

She pointed. "Chained to that column." She felt her pulse speed up. "There's something funny going on up there. Jamison and Rivers hardly speak to each other; now they've both come in on a Saturday?" She climbed on the seat of her bicycle. "Let's don't stay any longer, Scott. Somebody might see us."

"They won't recognize me."

"They will me, and I'm supposed to be at home, sick. We can come back tomorrow. Please."

Marvin Jamison looked up abruptly when somebody tried the front door to the offices. He quickly closed out the file on Marissa Young's computer, willing it to revert to screensaver mode before anybody might come inside. He scrambled to gather up the pages he had printed and stuffed them inside his shirt. Seconds later he was at his own desk in the main room. His breathing was rapid, but he felt safe now. Nobody would ever know he had accessed Marissa's files, let alone changed a thing or two.

Jamison's middle-aged rear was hardly in his seat when a back office door opened and what appeared to be a Venice Beach dropout flip-flopped toward him.

Cosmo Rivers stopped short, equally surprised to see Jamison.

"Hey Studmarv, what's the loverman doing in the mines on a nonworkday?"

Each man quickly fabricated a legitimate reason for being there; then they left the offices. Not exactly together, but at the same time. Perhaps five minutes later Anthony Shapiro eased out the front office door, adjusted his thick glasses on his nose, and took the elevator to the lobby. He wore a Polo sports shirt, expensive slacks, and carried an ostrich-hide attaché case. Shapiro had heard unexpected voices outside his private office, sounding like Cosmo and another man, and had remained very quiet. Being senior vice president, he could come and go as he pleased, any hour, any day. He had his own reasons, however, for not wanting anybody to see him in the office today. Or to even suspect that he'd been there.

Sarah stood wide-eyed and fascinated at the entrance to a club that evening, watching attractive young women wearing six-inch heels, micro-miniskirts, black bow ties around their necks, and nothing more. The women paraded nonchalantly about the crowded room as if their bare breasts weren't jiggling and bouncing with every high-heeled step. Their attention was directed instead at the trays of beer and mixed drinks they delivered. Sarah's eyes kept going back to their breasts whenever she thought nobody was watching. The women were much classier than she would have imagined. Some of them were quite beautiful.

Grateful to be fully covered in a black cotton turtleneck and slacks, Sarah received her share of speculative glances from men both young and old. Was it despite being fully covered, or because of it?

She was privately reassured that her own concealed anatomy measured up rather nicely, especially with her being probably ten years older than most of the women in sight.

Corbin aimed her through a smoke-filled sea of raucous men, toward a back booth. He had reluctantly agreed to bring her along, but now he was enjoying her reaction.

The man who waited in the booth widened his eyes as they approached, and said, "Holy shit, man, it really is you." He came to his feet.

The man looked like a handsome priest. In his late thirties, he was about five-nine, with a slight build, an olive complexion, jet-black curly hair, and a prominent nose. His eyes were large and a vivid blue. He appeared to be Italian.

His name was Peter Buda. Once in the booth Peter furrowed his brow and said, "I wasn't sure what was coming down over the phone. How in the world—"

"All I can tell you is," Scott Corbin said, "they executed the wrong man."

The two men spoke in low voices while Sarah sat tight-lipped and silent, like a frightened bird, sipping chardonnay and stealing glances at the waitresses nearby. Baseball, boxing, and hockey games blared from multiple giant screens, competing with exposed skin for masculine attention while Corbin and Peter arrived at some private arrangement.

Sarah learned that Scott had met Peter while both awaited trial in the Travis County Correctional Facility over in Del Valle. They had discovered a common bond, and struck up a friendship. Both had been born and raised in Tennessee, though Peter was of Armenian descent. At the time they met, each wished he had never ventured into the state of Texas. Peter had been arrested for breaking and entering. He swore to Scott that he was innocent—that particular time.

Above the cacophony in the sports bar Sarah couldn't hear details of whatever they were planning, other than Scott saying something about, ". . . no time, Peter . . . has to be this weekend."

Sarah suddenly wished she hadn't come along. Everything about the meeting seemed wrong to her. She didn't fit in at all.

Robert Garding parked his pickup truck behind the county morgue, turned off the headlights, and went inside. He had hardly made it home from Houston when Jack Barnaby called and asked him to meet him there. He hadn't even had time for dinner.

Barnaby had said he wanted to pick Garding's brain about an old case, which came as a surprise. They had worked together for years, but differed greatly in style. Garding had always been smoother in checking leads, investing the time to become friendly with witnesses, and unobtrusively gathering details, whereas Barnaby tended to forge ahead bluntly, often based on gut reactions.

They shook hands and exchanged greetings at the building's entrance. Detective Barnaby said, "Sorry to call you out on a Saturday night, Bob, but I want you to see something."

As they walked toward the refrigeration units

deep inside the morgue, an anorexic-looking attendant asked Garding, "How come you're still working, Detective? I figured your investigating would run more toward largemouth bass these days."

"Because you need a license to carry, Dennis. The crazies loose today, I don't leave home without it." Garding patted a modest bulge over his right hip and grinned his crooked grin. The bulge was a .38-caliber snub-nosed Smith & Wesson housed in a pancake holster inside his trousers.

Several minutes later the attendant rolled a metal tray back inside and shut the cooler's door. The desecrated remains of a sightless young woman named Stephanie disappeared into stale refrigerated air and eternal darkness.

Robert Garding voiced a grunt of exasperation. "Another Chameleon," he said.

"We've had copycats before, Bob. This guy is a fucking reincarnation."

"Is this the only victim?"

"Two, so far."

"Same MO on both?"

"Identical."

"Who's working with you?"

"Jim Moyers."

"A good man, detail-oriented."

"We subpoenaed both women's bank and phone records, cell phone and regular. Jim is comparing them as we speak."

They began walking back toward the front of the building. Garding asked, "Were the victims similar?"

"Attractive brunettes, early thirties, medium height. Both lived alone. One a graduate student at UT, the other a nurse. He played classical music real loud both times, probably to cover up their screams."

"Damn." Sarah Hill's descriptions of the men she had seen echoed in Garding's mind. He thought of his interview with Dr. Darvid King, and how the doctor had squirmed at the mention of Scott Corbin's name.

When they reached the front entrance Garding said, "Let's go someplace and get a cup of coffee, Jack. I need to tell you something."

They went to a nearby Denny's restaurant and sat in a nonsmoking booth. Garding decided to protect Sarah's identity until he had a chance to speak with her again. He also wanted another crack at Dr. King.

Robert Garding ordered the pot roast dinner, and Jack Barnaby ate a slice of pie and drank a cup of coffee while they talked. Garding began by telling Barnaby about reviewing Corbin's prison records in Huntsville.

"Why would you do that, Bob?"

"A client asked me to look into his execution. I'd rather not say who just yet, but I will tell you what I found." He related the information about Dr. King receiving Corbin's remains.

Barnaby didn't press for the client's name. He respected client confidentiality. "Was this doctor a relative?"

"No, he works for a genetic research lab in Houston. I spoke with the lab's director before I met with Dr. King. I believe King is hiding something."

"What?"

"I'm not sure, but he sure got nervous when I inquired about Corbin." Garding told Barnaby about the study Dr. King had been conducting regarding testosterone and Y chromosomes. "He acted like he was scared, but he may have been protecting somebody else."

"Which was it?"

"He shut down before I could find out. I didn't want to blow the rapport I'd established, so I backed off. I'll interview him again."

"What could he be hiding?"

"I've been asking myself that. Maybe he was using an illegal substance in his studies. Maybe he paid the mortician under the table to let him take the body so he could run his experiments. Maybe he sold the man's kidneys or something. Hell, maybe he's into necrophilia . . . I don't know."

"Was Corbin the only prisoner this doctor received?"

"There were two others, but Corbin was the last one. They discontinued the study after him."

"Did he say why?"

"He said, but his reasons sounded kinda weak to me. Somebody at the University of Colorado upstaged him and published a similar study ahead of his. That, and he never liked working with corpses to begin with."

"He'll tell you if we haul him into the station for a few hours of interrogation."

Jack's reaction reminded Bob Garding of their differences. Barnaby was ready to forge ahead, whereas Garding preferred a more subtle approach.

"I guarantee he would clam up, Jack. Then you'd be reading him his rights, he'd call his lawyer, and we'd never find out what he's hiding."

Barnaby sipped his coffee, considering. He didn't see any connection with the recent murders anyway. Finally he asked, "What else did you learn?"

"You've read records of convicts who were executed, haven't you?"

"A couple."

"Do you remember any where an autopsy was done?"

"I don't think so. No, there'd be no reason for one. Everybody knows how they died."

"Well, they did an autopsy on Scott Corbin."

"Who did?"

"Dr. King."

"Was that part of his experiment?"

"Maybe. The lab director did say that King examined Corbin's brain. Looking for a tumor or something, to explain why he murdered people."

Barnaby glanced at his wristwatch. "I called because I knew you'd studied the Chameleon inside and out, Bob. Thought maybe you could shed some light on our copycat. Can you think of anything that might help us?"

"Nothing I'm sure you don't already know. One question does come to mind, though. There never was an identity issue with Corbin, so there was no reason to look very deeply into his birth records.

Consequently, I never did, nor did anybody else, to my knowledge."

"Yeah, so . . . what's the question?"

"What if he had a twin brother?"

"What made you think of that?"

Garding realized he had almost made a slip. He did not want Jack Barnaby to know about Sarah's seeing somebody who looked like Scott Corbin. Barnaby would be all over Sarah, and she certainly didn't need that. Garding thought quickly, and said, "You said their MOs were identical. An identical twin might explain how."

Barnaby signaled their waitress for the check, thinking that Bob Garding was getting rusty in his retirement. "The MOs are close, but not really identical. The copycat jerks off into the victims' bellies after he opens them up."

"That's repulsive." Garding paused for a second, frowning. "Did you get his DNA?"

"We should have the results in a couple of weeks."

Garding left the tip and Barnaby paid at the checkout register. On the way out Barnaby asked, "You mind telling me why your client is so interested in the Chameleon?"

"Oh, you know how people are. It's somebody who followed the case closely and knew I was the arresting officer. They just wondered what happened after he was executed. If anybody ever figured out what made him do what he did."

"Can you at least say if it's a man or a woman?"

"Why?"

"Because if it's a man, you'd better be careful and you need to tell me who he is. He could be the copycat, Bob, trying to learn everything he can about the original."

"Take my word for it, Jack. My client is not your killer."

# Chapter Fourteen

Scott Corbin asked, "Where did you live when you were about . . . say, ten or twelve years old?"

Sarah pulled her legs beneath her on the sofa and sipped her wine. Both she and Corbin had changed into the velour jogging suits he had purchased that morning. Hers was pale pink, his a rich burgundy.

After leaving the sports bar earlier Corbin told Sarah that he and Peter Buda had really become friends when the man had come to his aid once in county lockup. Sarah had attempted to winnow more information about the man once they arrived home, so Corbin, characteristically, redirected the conversation to her. At least she had convinced him to spend the evening talking with her, instead of watching TV.

She answered his question about where she had lived, "We moved from the country to an apartment in Abilene after my father left."

"When was that?"

"I was in the fifth grade . . . right before my eleventh birthday."

"What happened, Sarah? Why did he leave?"

"He was a jerk. I mean . . . he really was. What can I say? He ran out on us."

"Too bad."

"Believe me, it was the best thing. My mother and I were far happier without him there." She studied her fingers for a moment. "It was hard, though. We didn't have much money. My mom took in laundry and cleaned rich people's houses. She took a secretarial course at night and finally got a better job."

"Did you work?"

"In high school. I did gift-wrapping at JC Penney for Christmas. Then I sold lingerie summers and after school." She smiled. "I'll never forget the bathrobe I bought with money I earned that first Christmas. I don't think my mom ever wore it. It was heavy flannel and way too hot. Most unflattering."

What Sarah remembered most about her childhood was the yelling at home. She told Corbin how her parents had argued—violent disagreements she'd overheard for years, mostly about her father's drinking and inability to hold a job. It always involved money. Then one day he just up and left, and they had never heard from him again.

With Corbin's prompting, Sarah said she took a regular job after she finished high school, and she and her mother found a two-bedroom apartment in a better section of town. She had lived there until her mother's death five years later, then moved to Austin and enrolled in a technical school to learn about computers and computer programming.

"What about boyfriends? Were you popular?"

She laughed. "Are you kidding? I was gangly and

awkward all through junior high and high school. I wanted to be a cheerleader more than anything, but never made it. I thought I wouldn't ever . . . you know . . . develop. My mother had a voluptuous body. I was built like a parking meter till I was almost twenty."

"You didn't go to college?"

"I couldn't . . . my mom was sick for a long time before she died. But I read everything I could get my hands on. I still love to read."

Corbin nodded. He had discovered hundreds of books in a hall closet, from romance novels to biographies to history—cataloged alphabetically by category and author. Assorted best-sellers lined two shelves in her living room.

"What about later? You never married?"

She unfolded her legs and sat upright. The muscles of her legs throbbed from the vigorous pedaling earlier. "No."

"Ever come close?"

She hesitated. "Why do you want to know?" She suddenly remembered reading, during Corbin's trial, "Serial killers are acute observers of human nature . . . they often study their victims' distinguishing traits in order to manipulate them into their web."

She also recalled a book she had read by Ann Rule, about her innocent working relationship with serial killer Theodore Bundy before anybody knew the horrible things he had done. The book was entitled *The Stranger Beside Me.*

Sarah gazed uncomfortably at the man beside her.

She'd be hard-pressed to imagine this man killing those women. But did she know for sure? Was she being lured into some sticky web? If so, why was the game important to him? Why not just kill her and get it over with? She quickly finished her glass of wine.

Corbin tried again. "You must have had some serious relationships. Were you ever engaged?"

"Once."

Prying personal information from Sarah was like scooping cold honey with a plastic spoon. But she finally told him about Edward McCann, the young man she had fallen head over heels for when she worked as a seamstress for a dressmaker in Abilene. She had been nineteen; Eddie was twenty. Sarah concluded by saying that Eddie hadn't been ready to settle down, so he joined the navy. She had dated a number of men since, but hadn't met anybody she cared seriously about since Eddie.

Uncomfortable with the subject, Sarah went to the kitchen and refilled her wineglass. "You haven't told me anything about yourself," she said, stacking her dishes in the dishwasher. If she was ever to know what to believe, she had to know more about this man. So far he had told her only what served his purpose.

Corbin shared bits and pieces of life growing up in the mountains of east Tennessee—the northeast corner of the state wedged between North Carolina and Virginia. He said the standard of living was so low among his schoolmates, he grew up believing his family was rich. By what yardstick? His father took them out for dinner once a month.

Corbin's mother had been an erudite, kind, considerate, and nurturing woman who had made Scott feel like the most special kid who'd ever been delivered into this world. She instilled a curiosity in her son for literature and music and far-off places long before she was diagnosed with Alzheimer's disease, only weeks after her fiftieth birthday.

"*True* Alzheimer's," Corbin said. "*Pre*-senile dementia—not the senile dementia of old age and clogged arteries that people mistakenly call Alzheimer's disease today." He lowered his eyes for a moment. "She died when I was twenty-five, thank God."

Sarah returned to the sofa and sat. "Why would you say that?"

"If you ever watch someone you adore literally disintegrate before your eyes, and there's nothing you or anybody else can do, you understand how death can be called the kindest cure. Also, if she had lived to see me go to prison, it would have destroyed everything that sweet woman ever believed in."

Sarah averted her eyes from the tears welling up in his. After a beat she asked, "What about your father? Is he alive?"

"I had an older sister, too, but the chimney fell on her in a freak storm when I was seven. I hardly remember her."

"How terrible for you and your family."

"That sort of thing happens back in the mountains. It's one reason most families have six or eight kids. They help with the chores."

After several false starts Corbin told her about his father.

"Growing up, I thought my dad was the strongest man alive. Not so much physically, though he'd been a pretty good athlete in his day. Mentally tough, you know? Morally. He could listen to anybody's problem, then offer a wise opinion about what they should do. People came to him for advice like he was a priest or something . . . he was a bookkeeper for a lumber company. Anybody who ever met the man respected him for his integrity. I must have heard a thousand times growing up, 'If Hank Corbin tells you something, you can put it in your hat.'

"He always taught me that a man's word is his bond. 'The good Lord gives you the body you're born with,' he'd say, 'and breathes life into you for a set number of years. What you do between the day you're born and the day you die determines how you'll be remembered. In the end the best a man can leave behind is educated, God-loving children and a good name.' "

A pang of guilt swept through Sarah for doubting this man. Yet he had still offered no proof. Was he for real? Or was she simply being sucked in again?

Was she even capable of telling the difference between sincerity and a flagrant con?

"That's quite a commendable philosophy," she finally said, still uncertain.

Corbin nodded and smiled proudly. "He was quite a guy."

"You said *was*. What happened?"

Corbin let out a slow, irregular breath. "He got killed right before I moved to Dallas."

"How?"

"Car crash. Went off Dead Man's Curve on the road to Bristol, straight into a red maple tree."

"How horrible." Sarah felt guilty that she had asked. Plus, she knew exactly how it felt to lose a father. In her case, however, her mother had been glad to see her father go. In time, so had she.

Corbin added, almost in a whisper, "I honestly believe my mother's illness destroyed my father, too."

Suave and sophisticated in black tie, Anthony Shapiro accompanied his striking dance partner back to their bar stools at the Forest Creek Country Club. Blond, lissome, tennis-tanned, and fashionable, Lillian was slightly tipsy. She leaned against Shapiro and whispered something in his ear, then laughed naughtily. None of the other couples paid any notice. At somebody's request the bartender turned up the TV's volume. A male newscaster reported two recent grisly murders, calling them Chameleon copycat killings. With few details available on the recent killings the reporter discussed two similar murders that remained unsolved from four years earlier. He gave details about the previous victims.

Lillian asked in a whiskey voice, "Whatever possessed you to hire that weirdo? What was his name, Corbin?"

"He told us he had just moved down from Dallas. Had good references. He was so convincing, nobody bothered to check." Shapiro slowly shook his head. "I'll rue that day forever . . . our stock went from sixty-four to seventeen when Wall Street learned where the Chameleon worked." He leaned closer and whispered, "What say we go to a hotel?"

"Why not your place?"

"I've told you, my ex has people watching my place."

"Smart girl. She wants those millions you have hidden away."

He winked. "She'll never find them." He produced a small, neatly wrapped box from his jacket pocket. "But you might, if you play your cards right."

"What's this?"

"A little something for my favorite girl."

Inside the box was a pair of diamond earrings. "Oh, Tony, they're beautiful." Lillian quickly replaced her rhinestone studs with the real things. Her dress rode up on a well-toned thigh when she crossed her long legs. "How can I ever thank you?"

"I think you know the answer to that question." He rested a hand on her leg and squeezed. "Are you ready to try a little stimulus tonight?"

"You mean . . . sniff something?"

He nodded.

"I don't want to drive home wired."

"It wears off fast."

"You're sure?"

"Absolutely. Believe me, you'll love it."

Lillian sipped her drink, considering. After a moment she asked, "When are you going to bring your other money home, Tony?"

"Why are you so concerned about my money? Is that the only reason you're attracted to me?"

"Of course not . . . how could you even think such a thing?" She looked hurt. "I just want you to be happy, and you're always talking about how much you lost in your divorce. I know you want a bigger house again, a nicer car. I'm only thinking of you."

When Shapiro didn't respond right away, she added, "I understand how important money is to you. I worry that maybe it isn't safe where it is. Other countries don't have the protection we do here. Laws and courts and the constitutional guarantees. What if somebody stole what you worked so hard to hide away? What would you do then?"

He shook his head. "You needn't worry about that . . . I checked it out thoroughly. I even went down there and met the head man at the trust company." He lowered his voice to a whisper. "They'd be really stupid to steal a client's money. Their entire business would collapse, and they're big. Really big."

Lil looked into his eyes. "If we can't go to Acapulco, why don't we fly down to the Bahamas, or wherever you took those stock certificates, and check on things? Maybe go visit your banker. There's nothing like a personal visit to let them know that you're keeping a close watch on things."

"If we did, would you be willing to try a little something to spice things up a bit?"

"Do I need spicing up?"

"Of course not. I didn't mean that. It's just . . . wait till you try it once and you'll see. It'll blow you away."

She touched one of her new earrings. "All right, Tony. But you'd better be telling me the truth."

He grinned lasciviously. "Drink up and let's go."

Shapiro placed a crisp new fifty on the bar and they left, laughing, arm in arm.

# Chapter Fifteen

Corbin had half a cantaloupe and a nectarine sliced and on the table when Sarah came into the kitchen the next morning. He was juicing three oranges for her, using, as she had pointed out the morning before, a juicer that bore the *Good Housekeeping* seal of approval. The machine was also a best buy in *Consumer Reports*. Corbin said he had already finished his breakfast. He put Sarah's wheat toast in the toaster and told her about trying to gather information from the Internet on some people.

"They make it look so easy on TV," he said, "but without their social security numbers, it isn't." He rotated his head in a circle and rubbed the back of his neck.

Their conversation was interrupted by the phone. Robert Garding spoke through the answering machine's speaker.

"Sarah, this is Bob Garding. I know you aren't feeling well, but I need to talk to you. Please pick up."

"Is that who I think it is?" asked Corbin warily.

"Yes."

A look of incredulity blanketed his face. "You called a Homicide detective? Robert Garding?"

Sarah felt her pulse quicken. "He's retired now . . . a private investigator. I phoned him when I first saw you." She added, "I was frightened, Scott."

Garding continued to speak to her machine. "Sarah? I know you're home. I can drive up there if you prefer, but I really need to talk to you."

"Answer it," Corbin said.

"You're sure?"

"You said you wouldn't give me away." He fixed her gaze with his. "I believe you, Sarah."

She nervously answered the phone, then listened while Garding told her about his visit to Huntsville. He did not share what he'd learned about Dr. Darvid King. No point upsetting Sarah with such gory details when he wasn't sure himself what had really gone on.

Sarah asked, "Have you drawn any conclusions, Mr. Garding?"

"Not yet, but I'm gonna keep looking." He paused. "I suppose you saw the report on TV."

"What report?"

"The two murders."

Sarah's heart leaped into her throat. "No, I didn't."

"It was on the news last night. Two young women killed this past week. I went over to the morgue last night and saw one of them. Whoever's responsible copied the Chameleon almost to a tee."

Sarah felt something heavy sink to the bottom of her stomach. She watched Corbin watch her. Her voice shook when she said, "That's terrible."

Garding replied, "You don't sound too good,

Sarah. Your office told me on Friday that you were out sick. Are you feeling that bad?"

She had to clear her throat. "A little weak, still. I guess I need to stay in bed today." The phone's receiver suddenly felt slippery in her hand.

"Well, I'll let you go. You take care of yourself. If you're not better by tomorrow, maybe you should see a doctor."

"Thank you. I may."

When she hung up, Corbin asked, "Everything all right?"

She nodded. "Fine." A thousand questions filled her mind. Not saying something to the private investigator might have been the dumbest thing she had ever done. But if Corbin was lying, he would have killed her the instant she opened her mouth. If he was telling the truth, she'd be responsible for an innocent man's going back to his certain death.

"Why'd he call?"

"What? Oh, to see how I was feeling."

"What made him think you were sick?"

"He called the office on Friday."

"Why would he do that?"

"I don't know . . . I suppose to see how I was doing. I was pretty upset the last time I spoke with him." Corbin's questions were making her even more uncomfortable.

"What did he tell you that was so terrible?"

"What do you mean?"

"You said something was terrible. Over the phone."

"Oh . . . uh, he was telling me about a case he'd heard about. Somebody got killed."

"Who?"

"I don't know. Why are you grilling me, Scott?"

"Sorry. I guess hearing Robert Garding's voice upset me more than I realized. He is not exactly my favorite person, you know."

She nodded.

After a few moments Sarah asked, "Where were you when I woke up this morning?"

"In the garage."

"How long had you been up?"

"A couple of hours."

"Doing what?"

"I meditated for forty-five minutes."

"Do you do that every morning?"

"It's the only thing that kept me sane in prison." He touched her hair, already brushed and in a hair band. "You looked so peaceful, I didn't want to wake you. I've already upset your life pretty badly."

Sarah recoiled from his touch. Confused now, she reflected on falling asleep the night before. She had objected to being belted in at first, but after another glass of wine, had finally conceded. In truth it had felt good to be close against another warm body. Breathing in concert with his rhythms. It had been so long.

So long since she'd been held by a man.

She forced her mind back to the present and asked, "What were you doing in the garage?"

"I left a makeup case in the car last night."

"Makeup for what?"

"My disguises."

Sarah stiffened, but didn't speak.

Corbin reacted to the shock that filled her face. He quickly added, "I told you I have to move around freely . . . I can't afford to be recognized." When she still didn't speak he said, "Sarah, I thought I could do what I need to by myself. I can't. I need help. I really need your help."

She looked askance at him, increasingly skeptical. "What kind of help?"

"I need to learn everything I can about people who worked at EBS when Rhonda was killed. Somebody didn't want me talking with her, and I'm convinced it had to do with selling the company to ISI because of how much money was involved."

Sarah listened, wondering what he would ask her to do now. Garding's words echoed in her mind—*Whoever's responsible copied the Chameleon almost to a tee.*

Corbin was saying, "In prison I became convinced that Franklyn Russett killed Rhonda. With his interest in porno tapes and hard-core sex magazines, I figured him to be the Chameleon. He was the right age, a quiet, meek guy like so many serial killers. But he couldn't have been."

"Why not?"

"Because two killings identical to the original six occurred here four years ago."

*And two more this week,* she thought. "The police said those were copycat killings."

"They had to call them that because they already

had me in prison. They wouldn't dare admit they had made a mistake."

She considered what he'd said. He was right about one thing: If Frank Russett was killed over four years ago, it couldn't have been Russett. *And it couldn't have been Scott Corbin.*

Corbin went on, "That's why I need information about the others. It had to be one of them."

"What kind of information?"

"Anything having to do with love, sex, drugs, money, or revenge . . . the reasons people usually commit murder. I want to know about their personal finances, bank accounts, credit cards, clues to hidden assets. Kinky habits, subscriptions to porno publications, membership in offbeat sex cults, extramarital affairs. Somebody was stealing big from EBS and they may still be doing it at ISI. People don't generally change once they find an easy way to make money, and they don't alter their sex habits. Maybe both things were involved, but somebody either had a lot to gain by Rhonda's death, or even more to lose if she stayed alive."

Sarah asked herself if Corbin had changed. Was he guilty? Was he involved in these recent killings? Or had he been innocent all along? She saw the desperation in his face. "What do you propose doing?"

"I want to get into your offices and go through old records. Phone bills, materials invoices, check stubs, contract-labor hours, hidden stock transfers or sales. Things that were going on before Rhonda was killed. But I also need personal information that wouldn't be kept at the office." He hesitated. "I asked Peter Buda to help me get inside their homes."

Sarah couldn't believe what she'd heard. "You did what?"

"He's a pro, Sarah. We can slip in and out and they'll never know we were there."

"You're planning to break into people's homes? The people I work with? My friends?"

"It's my only chance to find what I need. People into things like S & M or bondage or animal-sacrifice rituals keep letters and pictures and paraphernalia hidden somewhere. Peter knows how to find those secret hiding places."

Sarah was too upset to speak. She needed a glass of wine badly. Without another word she poured a glass of chardonnay and carried it to the bathroom. Once there, however, instead of drinking the wine she studied her reflection in the mirror, unable to suppress the anger welling up within her. Why had she allowed this man to totally disrupt her orderly life and put her at such risk?

Sarah set the wine down and marched outside. "Let me tell you something, Scott Corbin," she began, "or whoever the hell you are. I don't like it one bit that you're planning to break into anybody's home, especially people I've known for years and work with every day. What's more, I felt totally out of place and degraded in that sleazy bar last night with the naked women and your jailbird friend." Sarah's voice had risen steadily until she was shouting when she said, "I cannot believe I let you force me to lie to my friends at the office, and now to Mr. Garding. I had a very comfortable life before you came along and I was perfectly content. I'm tired of the anguish of not knowing what to believe, whether you're lying or telling the truth, and it is driving me out of my mind. You're ruining my life, Scott Corbin, and I want you out of my sight and out of my home this instant. No matter what you say, I never will be comfortable with you around. So go. Get out!"

Corbin lost it, too. "How are you comfortable, Sarah? Sitting home alone every night with your two-week-in-advance TV schedule? Afraid to go out? Reading romance novels instead of experiencing life, and sucking up wine till you're numb every night so you won't feel how miserable you really are? You think I can't see what kind of lousy existence you've carved out for yourself? Everything you have or do is because somebody else says it's okay. Your car, your magazines, the books on your shelves. Your orange-juice squeezer, for chrissake. You volunteer at the animal shelter twice a month, go to the ballet once or twice a year, occasionally collect for whales or seals or whatever somebody tells you is the latest cause, but what are you passionate about? What burns you up inside and makes you give a damn? Anything? Nothing? Are you just gonna stand on the sidelines and watch life go by?" He paused for breath, but his face had flushed a deep red and the veins on his forehead looked as though they might burst. "You were born with a brilliant mind and you're afraid to make a decision on your own. Not work stuff, that's easy . . . I'm talking about the hard choices. You're terrified of life because you got hurt once . . . maybe more than once, I don't know. Grow up, woman. Get involved. This isn't a dress rehearsal; it's the only shot you get. Either live or check out. To live, you have to take a chance now and again . . . maybe even trust somebody. It's your choice, so make it. Make a decision, Sarah!"

Sarah screamed at him, "You son of a bitch." She ran from the room in tears and slammed her bedroom door behind her.

Emerging from the bedroom over an hour later, Sarah was drained but strangely relieved—about what, she wasn't sure. She took a shower and applied makeup around her swollen eyes.

Corbin was waiting when she came out of the bathroom. "I'm sorry," he said, "I was out of line. I apologize for involving you in my situation . . . it was wrong."

She exhaled slowly. "I was out of line, too. It's been . . . I've been . . . I don't know, overwhelmed, I guess."

"We both need a break." He checked his wristwatch. "We have some time before I need to meet Peter. Grab a bathing suit and some towels and let's get out of here." He looked at her curiously. "You do own a bathing suit, don't you?"

Robert Garding stood in his barn surrounded by bleating sheep. He poured their pellets onto the ground, watching them push and shove. A few minutes later he headed back for the house. Having seen that girl's body the night before, then hearing the fear in Sarah's voice today, he couldn't wait until Monday to call Dr. Darvid King.

"I'll be here all afternoon," the doctor told him through the phone.

"Terrific," Garding said. "I'll pass right near your neighborhood on another matter anyway, so why don't I just drop by? I noticed that backboard and goal set up at the end of your driveway. Maybe we can shoot some hoops while we talk."

Dr. Darvid King was far more accurate at shooting goals than Garding. He was also nearly twenty years younger and in better shape, not to mention that Garding had just driven four hours straight to get there. After half an hour the investigator said he needed a rest, so they sat on the back stoop and drank cold soft drinks.

"You're a hell of a basketball player, Darv."

"Thank you, Mr. Garding."

"Call me Bob, please."

"You got it, Bob."

"You know, that fellow we were talking about . . . Scott Corbin . . . the one you picked up from the Huntsville prison?"

King's entire body changed and his voice tightened. "Yes?"

"Did you ever see any pictures of the women he killed?"

"No, sir . . . er, Bob."

"Well, you ought to, Darv. In fact, I think I may have some in the trunk of my car. Let me see if I can find them."

Minutes later perspiration streamed down Dr. Darvid King's face as Garding presented crime-scene photos of the Chameleon's victims.

"It is awfully hot today," Garding said, watching King mop his face. "Would you rather go inside?"

"No. Uh . . . my wife is watching a movie in the den. It's okay. I always perspire when I've been running around."

"Yeah, me too. I'll tell you something, Doc . . . if you think these are bad, you should see the woman I looked at last night. In the morgue up in Austin."

The doctor went rigid. His eyes darted everywhere except at Garding's face. He was also trying not to look at the photos. "What woman?"

"Somebody mutilated her exactly the way Scott Corbin used to mutilate his victims." Garding paused for an instant. "How old is your wife . . . Debbie? Is that her name?"

"Yes. Debbie's thirty-three."

"That's exactly how old the woman last night was. The one in the morgue." Garding lowered his voice. "Darv, he had ripped out both of her eyeballs. Slit her open from one end to the other and then masturbated till he came inside her belly."

"Who did?"

"The man who killed her. It sure looks like the Chameleon to me . . . but I guess it can't be. Everybody knows that Scott Corbin is dead. Right, Doc?"

"Of course."

Garding collected the photographs and began returning them to a manila envelope. "Man, this guy screwed up this time. We're gonna know for sure who killed this woman. Steph, they called her, or Steffie. There was another one a few days ago, too . . . Betty Lynne . . . a pretty little thing, about Debbie's size."

"How will you know?"

"The killer left his sperm inside both victims. We'll have his DNA by the end of the week."

Dr. King stood abruptly. He glanced around the backyard, then said, "I should probably be getting inside, Mr. Garding. I have a lot of work I should be doing."

Garding also stood. But his friendly smile had faded and the warmth went out of his voice when he said, "Before you do, Doc, why don't you tell me how you really came to claim Scott Corbin's body? And exactly what you did with it?"

# Chapter Sixteen

After buying a bathing suit for each of them, Scott and Sarah drove the fifty-five miles to Burnet, then on to Inks Lake State Park. They agreed not to discuss anything stressful for the remainder of the day.

Corbin wore no mustache today; rather, a baseball cap and wraparound sunglasses. They parked at a private campsite and swam in the Devil's Waterhole, a lush, cool cove where high granite cliffs jutted like a climbing wall out of pure springwater. Summer sounds and summer smells enveloped them.

Sarah hugged her knees close and sat watching groups of children playing in shallow water while Corbin swam to the docks and back for exercise. Over a mile. He really did have a wonderful physique. She refused to let herself think about Robert Garding's phone call. The recent murders.

An orange plastic ball got away from a little Hispanic girl nearby—probably three years old—in a sudden puff of wind. Sarah watched the ball skitter away on the water's surface while the child screamed in dismay. She sat up when the mother became angry and began reprimanding the child. She realized that the mother had probably spent her last dollar for the toy that was disappearing.

Sarah swam out and retrieved the plastic ball, then presented it to the excited little girl. The delight in the child's huge brown eyes and simple smile warmed Sarah's heart. It felt wonderful to play a role in such an immediate transformation.

When she eventually had a little girl of her own, Sarah hoped her child would smile exactly like this one. She also hoped that she could be half as fine a parent as her own mother had been. She blinked back her tears and looked out toward Corbin, returning toward her now. She forced her mind back to the present and waved to the little Mexican child. It was better not to think of past things.

Sarah swam out to meet Corbin, and they slowly came back to shore together. They toweled themselves dry, spread a blanket in the shade, and sat drinking iced tea from a thermos and enjoying the day.

Corbin surprised Sarah by producing an all-too-familiar spiral notebook from somewhere deep in a satchel.

"Where did you find that?" she demanded. Nobody had ever read a single poem she'd written—some of them dating back to high school. She tried desperately to retrieve her book.

Laughing, he playfully kept it out of her reach, then insisted that she sit quietly while he read composition after composition aloud. He read with respect and feeling.

When he finally closed the book he said, "They're beautiful, Sarah. You should write more."

She was embarrassed beyond words, but flattered at the same time. He really had seemed to like them.

"Your poem about the chains is my favorite," he said. "A man thinks a lot about freedom when he loses it. That's probably the worst thing about prison. The guards open the doors and the guards close the doors. They tell you when to eat, what to wear, what time to get up, when to turn right or go left, what you're not allowed to read or watch. You eat the same boring food day after day, year after year." He sat silent for a moment, then said, "The most incredible gift man has is his mind. No matter what anybody does to us, we can always think our own thoughts . . . make our private choices . . . even if only inside ourselves. If we stop doing that, we might as well be dead."

Later they walked past the crowded Catfish Barge restaurant before heading back toward their own secluded cove for a picnic and final swim.

As they walked Corbin unexpectedly said, "May I hold your hand?"

Sarah was taken aback. "Well, I . . . I suppose it would be all right. If you really want to."

"I'd like it very much."

They walked hand in hand for a ways without speaking. Sarah was surprised that she liked it too. His hand was large and strong. He adjusted position until their fingers intertwined. In that instant she was back in the Paramount Theater in Abilene, in the eighth grade, when Jimmy Treadway had first held her hand. She had forgotten just how sensitive the webs between her fingers could be.

Corbin disrupted her recollection. "The one thing I missed, those years on Death Row, was never feeling the touch of another human being."

Sarah hesitated. "Not even . . . other men? I've heard stories. . . ."

He shook his head. "That's how my arm got broken . . . in county jail when they first arrested me. Two big black guys tried to rape me. They didn't succeed, thanks to Peter. He rescued me." He smiled. "Peter is a lot stronger than he appears. He's an expert in martial arts."

No wonder Corbin felt so close to Peter. Sarah had wondered about the strange way Scott carried that arm. It had obviously never mended properly.

He continued, "That's one problem you don't have on Death Row . . . about the *only* one. You're in a six-foot-seven-inch by ten-foot cell, all alone, twenty-three out of every twenty-four hours for the rest of your life. The slit of a window you have is so high you have to stand on your bunk to see daylight. Picture yourself doing that every day of your life with no hope for change. That one hour a day when they do let you outside, you're all by yourself in a fourteen-by-twenty-eight-foot cement exercise yard with chain link on four sides and across the top. Guards watch every move you make. Believe me, I've stepped those measurements off a million times. I felt like I was in a dog run. I used to dream about walks like this . . . holding somebody's hand. Your skin is so soft, so warm." He looked down at their conjoined fingers as if to confirm that what he felt was real. "Or riding a motorcycle through the mountains of east Tennessee."

"A motorcycle?" Sarah was shocked.

He gave a short laugh. "In the little town I grew up in, one kid had a motorcycle—an old Indian Arrow, 1949 model . . . Indian red. I thought that bike was the finest thing I ever did see. Of course, we couldn't afford anything like that. When I moved to Dallas I bought a used Harley for my transportation. It's hard to describe the freedom you feel riding a motorcycle . . . nothing like it in the world."

"After all those years alone in a cell, I would think you'd want to be around as many people as possible."

"No . . . just somebody special. I crave the freedom I feel from riding a bike, but I want somebody with me to share what I feel . . . the things I see and hear. I don't know if that makes sense . . . wanting to be away from people but not alone." He turned to face her. "Have you ever ridden a motorcycle?"

"No."

"Would you like to?"

"Aren't they awfully dangerous?"

He grinned. "Not as dangerous as having a serial killer in your bed."

After a beat, she laughed. "Wouldn't I need to buy a special helmet or something?"

Dr. Darvid King feigned shock and disbelief, but it was no use. Robert Garding knew the doctor was guilty of something—now it was time to press. Having invested several hours in this man already, he wasn't about to let him off the hook now.

"Do you think I drove all the way down here on a Sunday afternoon for my health, Darv? We *know* what you did."

"What are you talking about? I didn't do anything wrong. I told you, I claimed his body. I performed a couple of experiments, then cremated him. That's all."

"Suit yourself, Doc, but you know what? I'm gonna level with you because I like you and I respect you. You spent a lot of years becoming a doctor, and I hate to see you get into trouble. I had a long talk last night with the Homicide detectives working these new murders, and that's why I'm here. You can either talk to me or go inside there and tell Debbie that you and I are gonna take a ride up to Austin tonight. Believe me, a nice young professional man like yourself is not gonna appreciate the kind of interrogation those guys do. Have you ever heard of Det. Jack Barnaby?"

"No."

"Well, you're lucky. He's known in Austin as the Pit Bull."

The sun was setting half an hour later when King's shoulders finally slumped and his hands dropped to his side. His body language told Barnaby that he had him. Now was the time to sit back and listen.

"I was doing a study on habitual criminals," King began, "and I asked for volunteers at the Huntsville prison."

"The testosterone and chromosome study."

"And serotonin, yes. Scott Corbin volunteered. Like some of the others, he was on Death Row. I interviewed him several times over a period of months, and drew serum testosterone and checked serotonin levels every two weeks. I did skin-punch biopsies to evaluate his chromosomes."

The private investigator let the doctor talk without interruption. Meanwhile he was alert for inconsistencies and half truths, to see if Dr. King would try to outsmart him as so many suspects did. Would he attempt to talk his way out of his situation?

"When I first met Scott Corbin, I assumed he was guilty. After talking with him on numerous occasions, he convinced me that he had never killed anybody. I was certain he'd been set up. Before Corbin, I had collected two bodies from the prison. One man had died of cancer, and the other they executed. They were running late the evening they executed that man, and I arrived in time to see the whole thing. Watching that execution was the worst thing I ever had to do. I've always been opposed to capital punishment, anyway, even before I actually witnessed one. It was awful.

"Scott Corbin told me that despite being innocent, he didn't want to live under the conditions on Death Row. He relinquished his appeals and asked to be executed." The doctor paused to take a deep breath. "That was the day . . . yes, that same day, he asked if I would claim his body after he was dead. Said he didn't want to be buried in the prison cemetery, and he didn't have anybody who'd claim him. He wanted to be cremated."

Up to the part about Corbin's asking King to claim his body, the doctor had seemed relaxed and open and his story had flowed easily. Following the pause and the deep breath, however, he had changed. Garding let it slide.

"So I did as he asked. I claimed his body, took him to the lab, and cremated him."

"Why would you do all that for a stranger?"

"I liked the man, Mr. Garding, and I believed he was innocent. It seemed like an innocuous request. And he *was* part of my study."

"What about the autopsy?"

"Yes, I did an autopsy. I examined his brain to be certain there were no tumors or other abnormalities."

The doctor had shaken his head from side to side during that answer, telling Garding that he had not performed the autopsy.

"Why would you do an autopsy, Doctor, if you already knew exactly how he died?"

"Well, for one thing, it was standard procedure in my study."

"Of habitual criminals."

"Yes."

"But you didn't believe that Corbin was a criminal, did you?"

"No, but . . . uh . . . as part of my study, I felt obligated to do the autopsy to rule out neoplasms, encephalitis, vascular abnormalities. So I did."

"I see. Please go on."

"There isn't anything more to tell. Mr. Corbin was cremated, we ended the study, and that's all there is." Dr. King tried to force a smile.

"I don't think so."

"What do you mean?"

"Well, Darv, I couldn't help noticing that we were getting along just fine till you mentioned the day that Corbin asked you to claim his body. Then we did okay again up to the part about the autopsy. Why would those two subjects make you uncomfortable?"

"I'm not uncomfortable, Mr. Garding."

"Bob."

King didn't respond other than to stare blankly at Garding. He was perspiring even more heavily now.

"You know what, Darv? I know for a fact that autopsies were not standard procedure in your study. Okay? Why would you lie to me? Here I am trying to keep you out of trouble and you're not telling me the whole story."

"What makes you think I'm lying?"

Garding suddenly raised his voice. "Cut the crap, Doctor. Before I became a private investigator I was a Homicide detective for twenty years. You do not want to get into a battle of wits with me. And if you think I'm bad, wait till the Pit Bull gets hold of you."

Dr. King seemed to shrink inside his skin. His eyes reddened. After several moments he nodded his head and whispered, "All right." He exhaled noisily. "Corbin wasn't dead."

Garding struggled to keep his face impassive. He said sympathetically, "Why don't you tell me all about it, Darv?"

# Chapter Seventeen

"Sure you won't go with me, Marvin?"

"I'd sooner write a thousand-dollar check to the theater guild. Just please don't bore me to death with another fund-raiser."

Marvin Jamison sipped his Johnnie Red on the rocks without missing the next pitch on TV. Three balls, two strikes; two men out and a runner on second.

"All right then," his wife said. She walked into the den where Marvin sat. Blond, lissome, and tennis-tanned, Lillian Jamison tightened the clasp of a diamond earring on one ear. "I'll see you later."

Backing her Mercedes out of the driveway, Lil dialed Anthony Shapiro's home number. "Just leaving, Tony. I'll meet you at the club in about fifteen minutes, okay?"

Inside, before his wife's car was out of the driveway, Jamison was on the phone, too.

"Amanda? Marvin. I found a neat one-bedroom you're gonna love. It has a whirlpool tub, an exercise room downstairs, and a deck overlooking the river."

Amanda Stowe said, "Really? It's on the river?"

"Well, not exactly *on* the river, but you can see the water from the deck. I'll take you to look at it after work tomorrow."

"It sounds wonderful, Marv."

"Say, what are you doing this evening? I was thinking we might take a drive somewhere. Maybe go to that little place I was telling you about that has VCRs in the rooms."

"When did you want to go?"

"Tell you what . . . I need to stop off someplace first. Why don't you meet me in the McDonald's lot on Martin Luther King Boulevard in about twenty minutes. I'll pick us up a movie to watch."

From the seat beside Peter Buda, Scott Corbin watched Marvin Jamison drive away in his silver Lexus. Peter had parked his car in the shadows of three sycamore trees shortly after dark, up the street from the address listed on the Internet. His recent-model white Toyota Camry looked at home in the neighborhood.

They were inside minutes later, thanks to Peter's expertise with locks. Scott wore khaki slacks and a navy cotton pullover. Buda had on a lightweight sport coat and tie—he said it made him appear less suspicious to prying eyes. Both wore latex gloves.

"Where do we start?" asked Corbin.

"First, don't hyperventilate. Your chest is heaving like you've run a hundred-yard dash."

"Sorry, I'm a little nervous. I've never done this before."

"You'll be all right. Start in the master bedroom.

Check all drawers, bedside tables, shelves, and boxes in the closets. Keep your gloves on and put everything back exactly the way you find it. I'll do the living room and kitchen."

Corbin rifled through lingerie, sweaters, socks, undershorts, and T-shirts in dresser drawers. He found condoms, a flashlight, night cream, antacid tablets, and paperback books in the bedside tables. Alongside shoes on the floor of their closets were boxes of old receipts and photographs. A dusty album of wedding photos occupied a top shelf, beneath a stack of hatboxes.

Scott jumped, startled by a loud clunking noise from down the hall. Convinced they had come home, he raced down the hallway, his heart pounding in his chest.

Peter Buda was walking nonchalantly from the living room toward the den.

"What was that noise?"

"The ice maker," Peter replied, "just dumped a batch of cubes into its plastic bin. Find anything?"

Corbin's throat was almost too dry to answer. "Not yet."

He returned to the master-bedroom closets and went through pockets in Marvin's clothing. He found nothing incriminating.

Peter Buda came in just as Scott was leaving the bedroom.

"Wait," Peter said. "Look." He pointed toward the smaller closet where Marvin's suits and jackets hung.

"What?"

"The pockets."

Scott saw it. A mirrored sliding door was open and two of the pants pockets were turned inside out. And he thought he had been so careful. He quickly stuffed the linings back inside.

Peter asked, "Were the doors open or closed when you began?"

"Closed."

"You sure?"

"I'm sure." Corbin closed the doors.

They went into the den. With Buda's help Corbin entered Jamison's personal computer. He found futures-market quotes, bank balances, and mortgage payments, plus a futures-trading account, video poker, and assorted computer games. After several attempts Peter was able to enter a coded and unlabeled account. They discovered additions of approximately five thousand dollars each month for the past three years, but there was no indication of the source of the funds, or where they might have been deposited. It was a running tally of some sort.

A blinding flash swept across Scott's face—a spotlight searching through the window near him.

"Oh, shit," he said loudly. "Peter! It's the police." Corbin thought he would have a coronary.

"Act normal," ordered Buda. "It's a private patrol." He directed Scott toward the sofa and had him switch on the TV. Peter casually waved toward the light outside as he ambled past the window with a drink glass in one hand. He joined Scott on the sofa and began flipping channels with the remote.

The neighborhood security patrol extinguished its spotlight and drove on.

Corbin's face and the armpits of his pullover were damp with perspiration. "Let's get out of here."

"Sure you don't want to have a drink or something? You look as though you could use one." Buda leaned back and crossed his legs. "Hey, look, the ball game's on. We can catch a couple of innings before we go."

Corbin stood, shaking his head. "You're nuts, Peter. Did you know that? I'm scared out of my wits that somebody's gonna come in and catch us, and you want to watch the stupid ball game. I'm leaving, buddy, with or without you."

Dr. Darvid King had been reluctant to talk at home, so Robert Garding drove them in his pickup to a nearby Sonic drive-in. Garding sipped from a Styrofoam cup of coffee while King related what had taken place.

"Like I told you, I agreed to receive Corbin's remains. When the time came I went to the prison and waited in a private room behind the execution chamber. I did not want to watch him die. The Huntsville Funeral Home normally picks bodies up from that room and takes them to their place to prepare them for burial. You know, they embalm them. Anyway, the guards brought Corbin in and left him with me. He was covered by a white sheet. One of the guards helped me roll the gurney out to the lab's Suburban I had brought—the same one I'd used to collect the first two inmates—and we loaded him in the back. The gate guard looked under the sheet and checked my paperwork on the way out; then I drove on back toward the lab.

"I must have driven forty or fifty miles when I heard a strange noise from the back of the Suburban, like a groan. I figured it was the usual postmortem escape of gases from the stomach, from being jiggled around, so I ignored it. I had the radio on, so I turned up the volume and kept driving. I arrived at the lab around eight-thirty P.M. We had one of those ambulance-type gurneys where the wheels fold up and unfold automatically, so I could unload him by myself. When I began to back the gurney out of the Suburban, the sheet slipped off his face." Dr. King inhaled deeply. "I swear, I almost fainted. Corbin's eyes were open and he was looking right at me."

Garding could hardly believe what he was hearing. He knew better than to interrupt the flow. He had always said, *An interview is a very fluid thing—it can shut off at any moment*. He said, "What'd you do, Darv?"

"Well, I could see that he was in shock. His face was ashen gray, and his skin, cold and clammy. His pulse was rapid and weak, thready. I wheeled him inside. He tried to say something, but I couldn't make it out. I couldn't just let him die . . . he was struggling so hard to stay alive. So I hooked up an IV of lactated Ringer's solution that I'd used in another experiment. His blood pressure started coming up almost immediately, and his pulse slowed down. About twenty minutes later he said my name. He was weak, but he was alive, Bob. It seemed like a miracle. He had somehow survived the lethal injection."

"What happened next?"

"I didn't know what to do, but I knew if I called the prison, they'd take him back and finish the job. Remember, I was one hundred percent convinced that he was innocent and I had been against his being executed in the first place. So I kept giving him IV fluids until he could sit up and talk. He wanted to leave right away, but he was too weak. He didn't even have anything to wear—he was still in his prison whites.

"There's a sleeping room in my part of the lab, for when one of us has to stay overnight for any reason. It has a bathroom with a shower. Nobody had ever used it since I'd been there, except once when Dr. Stratford wasn't feeling well and took a nap one afternoon. So I told Corbin he could stay there for a few days."

Garding ordered another cup of coffee. King still didn't want anything.

"The next day I fired up the crematorium and told people in the lab I had cremated his remains."

"What about the autopsy?"

"I figured if people could read a man's autopsy report, they'd never question whether he was dead. I fabricated a report."

"What happened next?"

"I slipped food in from home, and bought him some clothes. He started growing a beard. I read about how you can buy a fake driver's license and social security card. I suggested that he disappear across the border into Mexico, but he refused. All he talked about was going back to Austin to find out who had set him up. He still swore he hadn't killed anybody, but said he was certain that he knew who did."

Garding took his new cup of coffee from the curb hop and gave her a generous tip. He frowned. "Who did he say had committed the murders?"

"A man named Frank Russett, where Corbin used to work. He said Russett fit all the criteria of a serial killer, but he was also concerned about Cosmo Rivers and Marvin Jamison. Like a fool, I believed him. He probably made up the whole story."

"When did he leave Houston?"

"I'm embarrassed to tell you."

"No point in stopping now, Doc."

"I arranged to hire him as a lab assistant. He needed money and I needed help. He was plenty smart, and he caught on fast."

"Did Dr. Stratford know about him?"

"No. I bought him that fake ID and social security card, so he worked under a false name. Nobody recognized him."

"Till when?"

"Last week."

"Are you saying he lived in your lab for nearly six months?"

"No, he rented a room in town, but he showed up for work every day."

"Why would he do that?"

"I guess for the money. I had a grant that paid pretty well. He did help me complete the other study I was working on. I finished it one day; he left the next."

"Did he tell you where he was going?"

"No, he just didn't show up that morning. I tried to locate him, but he had moved out of the rooming house. I even drove up to Austin to see if I could find him. I was afraid he might do something foolish if he found Frank Russett. I thought I might stop him."

"That was your family emergency?"

"Yes."

"Did you see him in Austin?"

"No. He had disappeared. Next thing I know, you're at my home telling me he's killed two more women." Dr. King appeared genuinely contrite. "I can't tell you how terrible that makes me feel, Bob. I believed every word Corbin told me. I helped him stay alive, gave him a place to live and a place to work. He totally conned me. Now I'm responsible for those women's deaths."

When Corbin and Peter Buda returned, Sarah filled a large glass with chardonnay, excused herself, and went to soak in a bathtub filled with hot water. She didn't want to hear about breaking into Marvin Jamison's home.

Peter had left by the time she returned to the living room. Corbin sat at her computer, attempting to find information via the Internet on Cosmo Rivers. Sarah switched on the TV.

An exceptionally attractive woman newscaster with short dark hair and glasses was talking about two recent deaths in Austin.

"Our sources say that these latest murders so closely resemble earlier ones committed by Scott

Corbin, the man originally tagged 'the Chameleon,' that police are calling them Chameleon-clone killings. Homicide detectives at the Austin Police Department refuse to confirm or deny this information."

"Why now?" asked Sarah in a whisper. Just as she was beginning to believe Corbin, she was reminded again that women had begun to die.

Corbin closed out the computer program. Without expression he said, "Somebody knows I'm alive."

"What makes you think that?"

"If I'm caught, nobody is going to believe I didn't kill these women too. Either the real Chameleon or some other psycho knows I'm alive and out of prison. He's been in hiding; now he's free to kill as he pleases, knowing that I'll be blamed." Corbin angrily switched off the TV.

Sarah sat staring at her hands. She picked at something on a fingernail. A tear ran down one cheek and dripped from her chin into her lap. Graphic images from Corbin's trial intermingled with the newscaster's words in her mind. Scott's tender voice echoed in her ears, reading poetry softly beside the lake. She recalled a little Mexican girl's tearful smile, and the tingly sensation when Scott had held her hand as they walked beneath big shade trees. The gentle summer sounds.

Corbin turned to face her, then dried her cheek with one finger. Almost whispering he said, "Would you rather I leave, Sarah? I can go right now . . . tonight."

She considered his offer. Searched his face, the sincere pale brown eyes. He had just proposed what she had prayed for from the moment he had forced his way into her car. That he would go away and leave her unharmed. But now . . .

After several moments Sarah replied huskily, "No . . . stay. But hold me, please."

It was nearly midnight when Robert Garding finished questioning Dr. King. The man's story remained consistent, regardless of Garding's maneuvers.

Garding was pulling his truck into the driveway of the doctor's home when King said, "I guess you'll have me arrested now."

"You aided and abetted a convicted murderer, Darv. Helped him escape from prison and harbored a fugitive. That makes you an accessory to the recent murders he's committed."

Dr. King wiped a tear from his cheek with the back of one hand. "I can't believe I was so stupid."

Garding accompanied the physician inside and phoned the Houston police. While waiting for them to arrive he had Austin police headquarters patch him through to Det. Jack Barnaby at home.

Barnaby answered on the second ring.

"Jack, this is Bob Garding. Are you sitting down?"

In the dark later, not bound by a belt, Sarah lay on the far side of the bed and thought long and hard about what Scott Corbin had said to her. Words spoken in anger sometimes cut through the chaff. Was she living life on the sidelines? Afraid to get involved? He had asked what she cared about. Where her passion lay. If she were to die tomorrow, she asked herself, what would she want tonight?

She cared about her work. More than that, she *enjoyed* her work, and she was good at it. Her precious cat. Her reputation. Commanding respect and maintaining her dignity. She cared that she could pay her rent and wear decent clothes and drive a dependable car. She cared that she would own her own home someday.

Passion? As far as she could tell too much passion interfered with sound judgment, and clouded judgment could be dangerous. What did she want? What every woman wanted—a home, children, to be part of a family. She wanted to love a man and have him love her—if good men actually existed. She yearned for somebody to care about her. To give a damn whether she lived or died, if she was happy or sad. She wanted somebody to find her attractive. Desirable, even.

Her eyes stung. What was wrong with her? Was she unfit for love?

Sarah tentatively rolled over and tucked herself into the curve of Corbin's back. He was already asleep when she asked, "Scott . . . don't you find me attractive?"

His breathing changed; then he began to stir. "What?"

She repeated her question.

He coughed once, then cleared his throat. "Of course I do. You're very attractive."

"I just . . . I mean . . . you've never made any move toward me. You know . . . physically."

He turned to face her and kissed her forehead gently. "Sarah, I'm in no position to begin a relationship. If I were, you'd be the first woman I would ask."

She smiled in the darkness and exhaled a soft sigh. Maybe she wasn't so bad after all.

Corbin pulled her tightly against him and they fell asleep in each other's arms.

# Chapter Eighteen

Sarah phoned Marissa Young the next morning and requested a few more days off work. "A personal matter," she said.

"It's probably a good idea," Marissa said, always the understanding one, "after your recent illness and now all this frightening news on TV. It must bring back terrible memories for you. Would you like to use the retreat at the lake? I'll check my computer to see if it's available."

"No, thank you. I'll probably just stay at home for a few days."

"Keep me posted in case we need to reach you, dear. If you change your mind . . . let's see, I'm just checking . . . nobody has it reserved until a week from Wednesday . . . the Blackwells go in then. There's a place on the company Web site to enter your name and the dates you want to use it, then call 555-LAKE for directions. The front door has one of those push-button locks. The combination is BNK-one-three-five."

Robert Garding remembered one thing he did not miss as his pickup crawled along in Austin's Monday-morning traffic. It was obscene. He finally arrived at ISI's offices and was told by a pretty receptionist that Sarah wouldn't be in for a few days. The operations manager happened by and informed him that she had spoken with Sarah earlier that morning.

"She's had that summer flu virus that's going around," Marissa said, "and needed a few more days to recuperate. Is there anything I can help with?"

"No, I'm a friend from Fredericksburg. I thought I'd stop by and say hello. I'm in town for the day on business."

Amanda spoke up, "If you want to leave your name and number, I'll let her know you were here."

"Thanks, but I'll try her at home later. I have the number."

Det. Jack Barnaby said, "Exactly what did she say, Harry?" Barnaby and Det. Jim Moyers had located Det. Harry Wilkes in the men's room.

"Nothing that made any sense . . . typical prank call." Heavyset, pockmarked, and already jaded in his late twenties, Wilkes dried his hands on brown paper towels as he exited the men's room. The three of them walked toward his office cubicle on the second floor of police headquarters. "She thinks she sees a dead man, but one day he's a tall, handsome construction worker, and next time he's a short Mexican villain." Wilkes discarded the paper towels and began punching keys on his keyboard as soon as he reached his desk. "Here it is . . . first call, she says he was crossing the street. You should hear this broad . . . 'He entered the crosswalk at the northwest corner of Congress and Sixth, walking east on Sixth.'

"She was driving south on Congress. I'm surprised she didn't give his walking speed and what he'd had for breakfast. Said he was 'thirty-four years old, six feet tall, medium build with broad shoulders and a narrow waist. Approximately a hundred and seventy-five pounds, perhaps a little less now.' Those were her words. 'Black hair, combed straight back, with a widow's peak. Brown eyes so pale they're almost yellow, and always moving, like they're constantly watching for something or somebody. Strong cheekbones and chin. A straight nose with a high bridge and sculpted tip. He had a neatly trimmed short brown mustache today, but didn't used to. He has this strange habit of rolling his head around over his shoulders sometimes, as though he's held his head in one position too long and his neck is stiff. He wore . . . ' "

Moyers recorded every detail into his laptop, then asked a number of questions that Wilkes couldn't answer.

Barnaby said, "Why the hell didn't you tell me about this call? We've got a Chameleon copycat out there."

"Sorry, Jack, I didn't know."

"Have you been living on another planet?"

"I went to visit my brother in Atlanta the end of last week. All we did was fish and drink beer. Never even turned on a TV."

When they finished Moyers asked his coinvestigator what he thought.

"Yesterday I would've said it was impossible," Barnaby said, "but if what Bob Garding told me is true, we need to talk to Sarah Hill ASAP." He shook his head. "I can't believe he'd have the gall to come back into our city. How many times do we have to kill this son of a bitch? When we catch him this time, Jim, I may drive a wooden stake through his fuckin' heart."

Sarah seemed more nervous than usual when she invited Robert Garding inside her apartment and offered him a cup of instant coffee.

Garding made small talk while Sarah prepared the beverage and joined him on the sofa. He asked how she was feeling, about her work, animals at the shelter, and her interest in ballet. When she seemed to relax he asked about those two occasions when she thought she had seen Scott Corbin.

Sarah felt herself stiffen, but tried to hide it. "I know now that I was mistaken."

"How do you know?"

"Well . . . you faxed me his death certificate. And that return-of-death-warrant form from the prison."

"Are those the only reasons?"

Sarah wondered why Garding had a strange look on his face. "I also went back to that intersection and saw the man I had thought was him. It wasn't."

"You're sure it was the same man you'd seen before, Sarah?"

She hated lying to Robert Garding. He was more than a private investigator; he had become her friend. She said, "I'm sure."

"How was he different?"

"Huh? Well . . . he was just different, you know?" She shook her head. "His hair, his eyes. He was shorter than Mr. Corbin."

"Sorry, I couldn't hear that last part. You had your hand over your mouth."

Sarah lowered her hand. "The man I saw was shorter than Scott Corbin. A lot shorter."

"I see." Garding looked around the living room again. His gaze locked on something.

Following his gaze Sarah turned to see a man's sock in the hallway outside the bathroom. Her pulse skyrocketed.

Scott Corbin saw it at the same time from where he hid in the bedroom. He eased the door shut, anxious and perspiring heavily.

Garding smiled knowingly. "Have a new boyfriend, Sarah?"

She jumped to her feet and retrieved the sock. Reminding herself to appear nonchalant, she casually draped it over the back of a dining chair. "Why, yes, I do."

"What's his name?"

Her mind raced. "Peter. Peter Buda."

Garding seemed to relax. "Good for you. Do you have a picture of this young man?"

"Uh, no . . . we've just started going out." She immediately realized how that must look—just beginning to go out and this man had already slept over and left a sock. Her face flushed hot. She returned to the sofa and forced a smile, then sipped her tea.

Garding finished his coffee and returned the cup

to its dainty saucer. "Sarah, there's a strong possibility that the man you saw *was* Scott Corbin."

Sarah almost dropped her cup. She stammered, "Wh-what?"

"We don't know for sure yet, but we're checking. Corbin may have escaped from prison."

"But . . . uh . . . that can't be. I saw his death certificate, Mr. Garding. You saw it, too."

"I'm sorry to upset you, but you need to know."

"What makes you think he's alive?"

"For one thing, only the Chameleon would have committed those two murders they've been showing all over TV."

Sarah didn't speak. She held a napkin to her mouth.

"The other thing I can't tell you yet, but I have a reliable source. A doctor."

"A doctor? He saw a doctor?"

"I don't want you to worry. The police have the same information, and they'll comb the state till they find him. We will find him, Sarah."

Sarah thought her heart would jump right out of her chest. She clasped her hands tightly together in her lap, unable to speak.

"It's good you're not at work," Garding said. "There's a chance he may go to your office. I'd suggest you stay home for a few days till the police catch him."

"But what . . . I mean, why would he go there?"

"We have a tip that he might." Garding paused, then added, "He's not after you, Sarah. You'll be safe at home." He stood. "I'd better be getting on down the road. There are some people I need to talk to."

"Mr. Garding . . ."

"Yes?"

"Before you go . . . have you ever considered that maybe Scott Corbin didn't kill Rhonda?"

He angled his head slightly, frowning. "Why would you ask that?"

"I don't know, I . . . seeing that man on the street started me thinking. And I watched a program on TV a while back about those innocent men on Death Row up in Illinois. What if somebody else killed those women and planted the evidence in Scott's apartment and car?"

"You didn't doubt his guilt when you testified at his trial."

"I know, but . . . well, the entire year that I worked with him, he seemed so nice. I've been having second thoughts, and I really don't believe he could have killed anybody. What if somebody from work set him up?"

Garding was jolted. Dr. King had raised the same question. "What would make you wonder about that after all this time?"

"I guess the TV show. Students at Northwestern proved that a number of men on Death Row were innocent. And Corbin claimed during the entire trial that somebody had set him up. Don't you remember? He felt certain it was somebody from Electronic Business Systems."

"Do you have somebody in mind?"

"No, but you could find out."

"Why should I?"

"I don't want to go through life wondering if I testified against the wrong man." She hesitated, then said, "I'll gladly pay you if you'll just ask a few questions."

"Questions of who?"

"People we worked with." She named them. "The more I think about it, the more I'm convinced that I was wrong before. Scott Corbin couldn't have killed those women. Any of them."

Garding smirked. "Don't kid yourself, Sarah. Sounds like he sucked you in almost as bad as he did his victims. The man is a master con artist. And a vicious killer."

Garding reviewed what Sarah had said as he drove away. Of course she was upset—he had expected that. But she had seemed on edge even before he'd told her that Corbin might be alive. He asked himself what had made her change her story about seeing Corbin on the street—she had been so firmly convinced before. And what was this bit about suddenly doubting Corbin's guilt? Speculating that somebody at work had set him up? It seemed awfully coincidental that Dr. King had voiced the same concern.

Garding decided to do exactly what Sarah had asked. He would speak with those people where Sarah worked. Then he'd come back and talk to her again.

Scott Corbin hurried from the bedroom and embraced Sarah. "Thank you," he said.

Sarah clung to him, still shaking inside. "I was so scared, Scott. I kept worrying that you might sneeze or something and he'd hear you. I was petrified."

"You did fine."

"I hated having to lie to him. He's always been so . . . so kind to me."

"That's the man who arrested me, Sarah. He put me on Death Row."

"I know, but . . . he's not a bad person. Really. I'm sure he believed he was doing the right thing."

"Yeah, well, he was wrong. And he sure wasn't kind to me." Corbin turned away and walked into the kitchen.

Sarah hesitated. "Were you sick? Did you go see a doctor?"

"No."

"Then what was he talking about? He said some doctor told him you were alive."

"I don't know."

Sarah watched Corbin open the refrigerator, then shut it, without looking at her. He opened the refrigerator's door again.

"What did he mean about a doctor, Scott?"

"I can't tell you."

She felt her face flush. "Can't tell me? After what I just went through, you can't tell me? You mean you *won't* tell me."

A knock on the kitchen door interrupted their conversation.

"Oh, my God," Sarah said, "he's back."

Corbin ducked behind a cabinet. "Don't let him in."

Sarah hurried to the door, wiping sweaty palms on her skirt. She almost laughed with relief when she saw who it was.

Peter Buda came inside, smiling broadly. "Hope I'm not interrupting anything," he said.

Sarah felt so weak that her knees almost buckled. She barely said hello to Peter, then excused herself and went to her bedroom.

Robert Garding approached the reception desk at ISI.

"Hi again," Amanda said. "Were you able to speak with Sarah?"

"Yes, I did."

"Is she feeling any better?"

"Some, but she'll probably be out for a few more days. I was wondering, is Frank Russett in?"

"Who?"

"Frank Russett."

"There's nobody here by that name."

"You're sure? He used to work here. Or he worked at Electronic Business Systems before ISI bought them out."

"Sorry, I've never even heard the name."

"What about Cosmo Rivers or Marvin Jamison?"

"They're both busy this morning." She smiled warmly. "May I ask what you want to see them about?"

"I'm not only Sarah's friend, miss, I'm a private investigator. I need to talk to the people who were here when Scott Corbin worked for EBS."

Amanda leaned forward, offering a glimpse of

Grand Canyon–caliber cleavage, then settled back in her chair and smiled again. "Mr. Shapiro had a cancellation this morning. Let me see if he's available."

Minutes later Garding asked, "How close was Sarah Hill to Scott Corbin, Mr. Shapiro?"

Shapiro shifted in his seat. He seemed agitated for some reason, and spoke quite rapidly. "Corbin was only with us for a year. They worked together, but Sarah doesn't get close to people. She hasn't formed what I would call warm-and-fuzzy relationships with anybody in the office. Don't get me wrong, Mr. Garding; she's an excellent worker—organized and efficient. Everything on her desk is in its special place, like the files in her computer. Her purse is organized, her hair is always perfect, and her clothing . . . never flashy or the latest fashion, but neat. Conservative and practical. If anything, she dresses down so as not to attract attention. Probably to avoid conflict . . . being hassled, you know."

"You mean like sexual harassment? Has that ever been a problem?"

"With Sarah?" Shapiro smiled faintly and shook his head. "No, nothing like that. What I mean is, Sarah has organized her life exactly the way she wants it, and doesn't allow anyone to intrude. Not really a control freak . . . more like playing it safe, I'd say." Shapiro twirled a pencil in his fingers as he spoke, then put it down and picked it up again. Garding wondered if he was on something.

"What can you tell me about Scott Corbin?"

"Nothing you don't already know if you watch

television. He killed six women before they put him in prison." Shapiro narrowed his eyes. "Say, weren't you the detective who caught him six years ago?"

"Yes, sir, I was. What I'd like to know now is about his personal life. Hobbies, friends, where he hung out. Disagreements he might have had with other employees."

"May I ask why you're concerned with Corbin after all this time?"

"I have a client who's interested, Mr. Shapiro. They don't always tell me why." He asked again about Corbin's personal life.

Shapiro said, "I really didn't know the man, thank God." He put the pencil down and folded his arms across his chest.

Garding could see that Shapiro was shutting down, but he had only one or two more questions, so he persisted. "What do you know about Corbin's relationship with Frank Russett?"

"They worked in the same office. That's about it. I assume you know that Russett was killed."

"Yes, sir. How did Corbin get along with either Marvin Jamison or Cosmo Rivers?"

"I wouldn't know anything about that. Would you like to ask them yourself?"

"I would."

Shapiro quickly pressed a button on his intercom and instructed Amanda to set up appointments for Mr. Garding to speak with Jamison and Rivers. "Oh, yes, and Tad Roman," he added. He turned to Garding. "Mr. Roman worked with Corbin as well."

As Garding stood to leave, Shapiro added, "I must warn you . . . Rivers is strange."

Peter Buda was sitting across the dining room table from Scott when Sarah emerged from her bedroom. They went silent when somebody rang her front doorbell. Peter crept over and peeked outside through the blinds.

"There's two of them," Peter whispered. "They look like cops."

# Chapter Nineteen

Corbin whispered, "Peter and I will hide in the bedroom while you get rid of them." He took Sarah's hands, looking deeply into her eyes. "Whatever happens, I trust you. And you did great before. You'll be just fine." The doorbell rang again.

Detectives Barnaby and Moyers showed their identification and came inside. Barnaby said, "You reported seeing somebody who looked like Scott Corbin last week, Miss Hill. Would you mind telling us about that?"

"I'm sorry, gentlemen, I made a mistake."

"What kind of mistake?"

"I had had a nightmare about the Chameleon a few nights before, and his image must have remained in my mind." She strained to conceal her anxiety while Barnaby inquired about her second sighting.

Detective Moyers set his laptop on the coffee table. He read aloud her reports, verbatim, then looked up questioningly.

Sarah said, more forcefully than she'd intended, "I hadn't been sleeping very well at the time and it's hard to remember what I said, but I went back to where I saw him, a couple of days later, and saw the man I had thought was him, and it wasn't. I'm really sorry if I caused you any trouble."

Barnaby nodded, frowning slightly. "You must have seen the reports of those two copycat murders on TV."

"Yes."

"What was your reaction?"

"What would anybody's reaction be, Detective? I was horrified."

"You didn't think maybe the man you saw might be responsible?"

"Of course not. The man I saw was not the Chameleon." Sarah kept waiting for them to drop the bomb that Corbin was alive and had escaped. They did not.

Barnaby studied her face. "You worked with Scott Corbin at one time, right?"

"Yes, sir."

"How long did you work together?"

"A year."

"So you knew him pretty well."

"Yes."

"How far away was he when you thought you saw him?"

"Which time?"

"Both times."

"I don't know . . . perhaps twelve or fourteen feet the first time. More the second . . . maybe fifty feet or so. I'm not good at estimating distances."

"And the last occasion, when you decided it wasn't him?"

"Oh . . . well, he was much closer then." She shook her head. "Almost right in front of me."

Jim Moyers asked, "Do you think the third man you saw was the same as the first one or the second one?"

"I don't understand what you're asking."

"Let me rephrase. Your first report described an average American workingman with a short brown mustache. Your second described a Mexican man with a long handlebar mustache. What did the man look like when you decided you had made a mistake?"

"Oh. Well . . . both."

"Excuse me?"

"He resembled both men." She shook her head again. "The first time I called, the man was actually darker than I had thought. I realized that later. And I hadn't been able to see his mustache well . . . the sun was in my eyes because of where he was standing. There was a glare on my windshield." She was more than a little annoyed with this cat-and-mouse scenario, and her stomach was churning wildly. She wished they would leave.

Neither detective spoke.

Sarah added, "How am I supposed to remember? I was frightened at the time. I thought I had seen a dead man, don't you understand? When I calmed down, and then I saw him again, I realized I had made a mistake. Haven't you ever made a mistake, Officers?"

Barnaby asked, "Which one did he resemble, ma'am? The Mexican or the other one?"

She folded her arms across her chest and exhaled. "He looked like a Mexican farmworker."

"I see." Barnaby looked at Moyers. "Anything else, Jim?"

Moyers shook his head and closed his laptop.

"All right, Miss Hill," Barnaby said. "We appreciate your report. If you should see either of those men again, or anybody else who resembles Scott Corbin, would you give us a call?" He handed her his card.

"Of course." She stood at the door as they left. "I'm sorry if I caused you any trouble." She closed the door behind them, her knees weak.

Walking back to their car Jack Barnaby said, "She's lying."

"Sure appears that way," replied Moyers.

"She hemmed and hawed, stalling. She was searching for answers."

"Nothing like the woman who gave those descriptions to Harry Wilkes."

"And wouldn't an average woman be curious as to why we'd tell her to call if she saw anybody resembling Corbin? Especially after the recent murders?"

"I sure would think so."

"She's either scared for herself or protecting somebody else."

"But who? And why?"

"I don't know, but I want another go at her after we talk to the warden. Sarah Hill is holding something back."

* * *

Corbin and Peter Buda came from the bedroom. Scott said, "That was a very brave thing to do. Thank you."

"For harboring a fugitive who won't even tell me how he can possibly be alive? I must've lost my mind."

Corbin asked Buda to wait in the car.

"All right, Sarah," Scott said when Peter had left, "I'll tell you, but not now. It's going to take a while, and I don't want Peter to hear."

"When?"

"After I return. Peter and I need to investigate something first."

"Like what, another one of my friends' homes?"

Corbin looked at her without replying.

"Whose is it this time?"

"I have to go now. I'll be back as soon as I can."

Warden John Paine, of the TDCJ's prison in Huntsville, returned Jack Barnaby's call at police headquarters.

"I just got off the phone with Detective Armbruster in Houston," Warden Paine said. "After spending most of last night interrogating Dr. King, he confirmed pretty much what Bob Garding told you. If the doctor is telling the truth, we've got a serious problem."

"So you do think it's possible?"

"I've talked to two different physicians whom I respect. Both say it could happen if the drugs were either tampered with, improperly mixed, or defective when they came from the manufacturer. Specifically, the potassium chloride."

"Is there any way to find out if that's what happened?"

"Not this long after the execution. We're interviewing guards now, trying to determine who gave the injections."

"Don't you keep the name in a file?"

"That's one piece of information we never record or give out. If we did, nobody would accept the job . . . be too dangerous."

"Are you saying nobody knows? Not even you?"

"It's a long-standing policy. We know which guards were on duty that night, but according to what Dr. King told Armbruster, none of them noticed anything unusual. Nobody did."

"Damn." After a long pause, Barnaby said, "I spoke with a woman today who reported seeing Corbin in Austin last week. Right before our first murder."

"How many have there been?"

"Two, so far."

"Both Corbin's MO?"

"Practically identical."

"He'll kill again. They always do."

"They? Have others escaped?"

"Not from our Death Row. Six got away in Virginia a few years back and slaughtered a bunch of people. After a five-year dry spell, Corbin will, too."

"If we don't catch him quick."

A long sigh came through the phone. "Keep me posted, Detective. We're not going to release any information about the doctor or *how* Corbin escaped until we're forced to. However, I've asked the governor to put out a statewide alert on Scott Corbin. He's one monster we cannot afford to fool around with."

Robert Garding took his seat across the desk from Clarence Rivers. Rivers wore a Hawaiian luau shirt, ragged jeans cut off at midthigh, and rubber flip-flop sandals. Stringy hair hung loose over his shoulders, and his eyes were covered by tiny dark glasses.

"So you're a real PI," Rivers said. "Do you carry a piece?"

"I do."

"Can I see it?"

"No."

"I wasn't gonna shoot you or anything."

"Good. I'd like to ask you a few questions, Mr. Rivers."

"Cosmo, because I'm cosmic. You call me Cosmo and I'll call you Mr. PI. Deal?"

Garding cleared his throat. "I understand you worked at Electronic Business Systems at the same time Scott Corbin did. Is that right?"

"Hey, you're good. Only a few thousand of my closest friends have that information."

"Am I correct, Cosmo?"

"Right on, bro . . . the slasher dude. Somebody must've royally pissed him off. Or that Rhonda chick wouldn't give him no pussy. That'd piss a man off, right?"

"Did you have any dealings with Corbin other than work-related activities?"

"You mean, like, did we party together? Naah. He was too square. Or made out like he was till the sun went down. Then, wooo-ooo-ooo-ooo." Rivers made a horrible face to accompany his ghoulish sound, slashing the air with one finger as though it were a fencing foil. He mimicked somebody's throat being cut and fell forward, facedown on his desk. "Arggh."

Obtaining a baseline reading on Rivers was going to be virtually impossible. The man bounced off walls. Possibly to camouflage his true self? Garding tried to see beyond his antics. "What can you tell me about Corbin's personal habits?"

"You mean like how he wiped his ass, or whether he flossed after each meal?"

"I mean like where he hung out, who his friends were, what he did for entertainment."

"Duh, Mr. PI . . . killing his friends *was* his entertainment."

"You never joined him for a beer anywhere? Saw him with anybody?"

"Nope."

"Did you ever have a disagreement with Mr. Corbin?"

"If I did, I'd be dead, right? Come on, Mr. PI, you can do better than that."

Rivers was purposely diverting attention from himself back to Garding. Arrogantly so.

Garding asked, "Did you ever hear of any disagreements he might have had, either with people in the office or elsewhere?"

"Just Rotting Rhonda."

"What type of disagreement did they have?"

"He killed her."

"Why do you suppose he did that?"

Cosmo shook his head. "Same reason guys always have. No pussy on demand."

"Did you know Rhonda Talbot?"

"Met her once when ISI swarmed in to kick our tires."

"Do you have personal knowledge of any disagreement between Corbin and her?"

He shrugged. "Ain't it always the same?"

"Is that a no?"

"Damn, you're perceptive. You ever think about going into investigative work?"

"What do you know about Marvin Jamison?"

"Studmarv? A full-time alcoholic lecher and part-time reject from Gamblers Anonymous . . . or vice versa, depending on the hour of the day. All in all, my kind of guy, but I wouldn't take a shower with him."

"Why not?"

"What if I dropped my soap?"

"Are you suggesting that he's homosexual?"

"He wouldn't waste time checking for gender; he'd just aim and fire."

"I see." Garding thought for a moment. "Did Jamison know Rhonda Talbot?"

"Did she ovulate?"

"Is that a yes, Cosmo?"

Cosmo leaned forward, almost serious for a moment. "Marv was all over her the day they came for a test-drive. Sniffing like a bloodhound, pointing like a bird dog."

"Who is *they*?"

"ISI. Their top execs came to check out EBS. It was disgusting the way Shapiro licked their asses."

"Were you opposed to the buyout?"

Cosmo shrugged. "Would it matter?"

"Do you know if Jamison ever saw Rhonda again?"

"You can bet he tried."

"Does that mean you don't know for sure?"

"Hey . . . junior G-man. Score another direct hit."

Cosmo leaned back in his chair again, responding as if the interview were an entertaining diversion.

Garding asked, "What was Jamison's relationship with Scott Corbin?"

"The only intimate relationship I remember is the day they had hall sex."

Garding sat forward. "They had what?"

"One day as they passed each other in the hall, Corbin asked Marv something and Marv said, "Fuck you, Corbin." Cosmo laughed demonically. *"Hall sex."*

"What had Corbin asked?"

"Beats me. Ask the Studmarv."

"You're referring to Mr. Jamison?"

"I knew you'd grow up to be a real detective someday. You've just won a Spymaster ring with its very own secret compartment."

Garding changed position in his seat. "What can you tell me about Mr. Shapiro?"

"Demanding, self-centered, plays well with others, but unwilling to share. I'd give him a C in deportment."

"Meaning what?"

"He's greedy, Mr. PI, though his ex did lessen his need for that tendency."

"What does that mean?"

"She vacuumed before she left. Cleaned him out."

"Who, in your opinion, gained most from the sale of EBS to ISI?"

"Shapiro got the big bucks."

"Anybody else?"

"All the slaves had stock options. That's how Shapiro avoided paying a living wage."

"So you personally benefited from the sale?"

"Not like Shifty Shap."

"You're referring to Mr. Shapiro?"

"Hey, now you get your very own badge, too. How are you at neurolinguistics, or reading subtle alterations in communication cues?" Rivers mimed stabbing himself in the chest with a knife.

"What do you know about Tad Roman?"

"A mama's boy with greasy hair. Unweaned."

"Other than work duties, did you ever see Roman or Shapiro with Scott Corbin or Rhonda Talbot?"

Rivers nodded his head forcefully up and down. "Nope."

"Marvin Jamison?"

He nodded again. "Nope."

Garding inhaled deeply and stood. This man was bizarre.

Cosmo exaggerated a pained expression. "You didn't ask about Scrupulous Sarah. She spent more time with Corbin than anybody."

"All right. What do you know about her?"

"You ask me, the Virgin Queen soaked her panties for the serial man."

"Sarah Hill? And Scott Corbin?"

"Hey . . . they rubbed elbows in there for a long time. Maybe other things. She never got that dreamy look in her eyes for me. Could be that's why she testified . . . a woman scorned, and all."

Garding considered Cosmo's speculations. He turned to leave. "Thanks for your time, Mr. Rivers."

"Awww, don't go . . . I haven't had this much fun since solitary confinement at reform school. And call me Cosmo."

"No, Peter, put it back."

"Come on, Scott. It's been sittin' here just waiting for me."

Scott Corbin stood next to Peter Buda at the open door of a wall safe in Anthony Shapiro's condominium. It had required less than fifteen minutes for Peter to locate the hidden safe, then dial in its combination using the latest electronic gadgetry. They discovered nearly a hundred thousand dollars inside, in neatly stacked fifty- and hundred-dollar bills. Scott also found the business card of a trust officer at Scotia Bank in Hamilton, Bermuda. He copied the name and phone number from the card, then carefully replaced it.

"He won't notice a paltry ten or twenty thousand," Peter insisted. "This goes against everything I've ever even imagined."

"That is not why we're here. I can't afford to tip him off."

Peter reluctantly closed the safe and accompanied Corbin into the den.

Shapiro's personal computer was protected by a security code neither could break, denying them access to his personal files. Scott rifled through desk drawers, hurriedly scanning credit-card receipts, phone and electric bills, and dues statements from a country club. His breath caught when a car pulled into the driveway outside. "Shhh," he said to Peter. He quietly closed the desk drawers.

They crouched in a corner and listened. Corbin eased a window blind aside, searching for a means of escape. The windows were rollouts that a grown man could never fit through. They were trapped.

Perspiration dripping down his face, Scott couldn't decide whether to hide in a bedroom closet or try to reach a rear door before somebody came inside.

Buda touched Corbin's arm and motioned with his head. Scott followed as Peter walked quickly toward the door to the garage. Along the way Scott accidentally brushed against a bookshelf, toppling several volumes onto the floor. He managed to break the books' fall with his hands and one foot, then scrambled to return them the way he guessed they had been. Footsteps approached along the sidewalk outside, then up the stairs to the front entrance.

"If he comes in the front," Peter whispered, "we run out the garage door, then split up. Otherwise we go out the side, where we came in."

Scott nodded. His throat was dry and his pulse

raced. His hands felt wet and sticky inside the latex gloves. "What about the car?"

"Come back for it later or leave it and find another one. It isn't registered to me."

Scott strained to hear above his pounding pulse. Somebody was at the front door now. Hinges squeaked as the screen door opened. Scott wrapped one hand around the doorknob leading to the garage, praying that the control to raise the outside door would be in plain sight.

# CHAPTER TWENTY

Something thudded near the front door; then the screen slammed shut. Footsteps retreated down the stairs and disappeared along the sidewalk. Moments later a car backed out of the driveway and pulled away.

Corbin's chest felt tight. His breath was still coming hard. "Let's get out of here."

"Relax, friend; it was only a delivery. Whoever it was has gone now."

"That was too close. We've seen everything we need to, Peter. He's skimming cash like crazy, probably shipping it to Bermuda."

Peter was still salivating over the cash when Corbin tripped on a corner of a Persian rug and stumbled against the front door. Though Peter had bypassed the security system on the side door to gain access, with no intention of using the front door, he had ignored that alarm. The deafening siren that suddenly wailed above their heads nearly shattered their eardrums.

Corbin shouted, "Run, dammit, run."

"Don't run . . . walk. And stuff your gloves in a

pocket once we're out the door. We haven't seen or heard a thing."

Garding introduced himself, then commented on photographs on Marvin Jamison's desk. The photos depicted an attractive blond woman in various situations. Lillian Jamison.

"Very pretty lady," Garding said. "Do you play tennis, too?"

"Not anymore."

"I bet you were pretty good though, huh?"

"Not bad. I was a B player."

"Do you have children?"

"No. No . . . Lil never wanted children. Says she isn't the maternal type." Marvin appeared relaxed, open, friendly.

After several minutes Garding said, "Can I ask what sort of relationship you had with Scott Corbin, Mr. Jamison? When he worked at EBS?"

"Are you serious?"

"Yes, I am."

Jamison almost laughed. "I never liked the man."

"Why is that, sir?"

"Why do you want to know?"

"I have a client who's doing a psychological profile on him."

"Who is this client?"

"I'm not at liberty to say."

"Then maybe I'm not at liberty to tell you what I know."

"Perhaps I made a mistake. . . . Mr. Shapiro said he

didn't think you'd mind. He was quite open with me."

Jamison mulled that over. Finally he said, "Well, there was always something strange about Corbin, as far as I was concerned. I proved to be right, too."

"Was he friendly to you? At first?"

"Tried to be."

"What happened?"

Marvin's responses had changed. His eyes had narrowed. He was frowning more. He leaned forward on his desk in an aggressive posture. "Hell, he was a psycho, Mr. Garding. He killed six women."

"I understand. What I meant was, how did he change toward you?"

"I don't see what that has to do with anything."

"I'm just curious. I believe Mr. Shapiro said you were the operations manager back then. Right?"

"That's right."

"Did Corbin's work seem satisfactory?"

Jamison sat back in his chair. "Not in my opinion."

"In what way?"

"He was okay the first couple of months or so, while he was still training. After that, he spent nearly as much time trying to see what everybody else was doing as he did tending to his own duties."

"Did you discuss this with him?"

Jamison tapped a letter opener on his desk. He exhaled sharply. "Yeah, I told him he'd better shape up."

"What was his reaction?"

"Oh, he straightened out for a short while." Jamison shook his head. "I thought he was just a busybody. Little did I know, he was trying to get personal information about all of us. Probably planning to kill us, too."

"What type of personal information?"

"Oh, I don't know . . . things he had no business knowing."

"Such as?"

"One time when I came back from lunch he was going through my desk drawers."

"What was his reason?"

"He said he had an upset stomach. Claimed he was searching for my bottle of Tums, but I knew better."

"How?"

"They were right there on top where they always are. He knew exactly where they were." Jamison opened his top drawer and presented an economy-size plastic container of antacid tablets. He replaced them beside a pack of chlorophyll breath mints.

"What was Scott Corbin's relationship with Rhonda Talbot?"

"How would I know? I never met the woman." The tone of Marvin's voice rose. He leaned back in his chair and interlaced his hands across his abdomen. When Garding didn't speak, Jamison declared firmly, "I don't know what he did or who he saw after work. His personal life was none of my business."

Amanda Stowe rushed into Marvin's office, looking at a magazine and talking excitedly. "Marv, I found the dreamiest . . . Oh, excuse me, I didn't mean to interrupt." Her face flushed bright pink. She quickly closed the magazine, then spun around and left.

Garding merely smiled at Jamison.

"What? You run out of questions?"

"No." Garding cleared his throat. "I was wondering . . . were you present when the executives from ISI did an on-site visit to EBS?"

Jamison frowned. "Well, I don't remember . . . maybe that was . . ." He looked up toward the ceiling and nodded. "Yeah, I think I did come by while they were here, but only for a few minutes. I must have had appointments outside the office that day."

Garding watched Jamison "itch" the tip of his nose as he answered, his hand partially covering his mouth. *Keeping the lie inside?*

"Do you recall meeting Rhonda Talbot that day?"

"No, I told you . . . I never met the woman."

"She didn't accompany the other executives?"

"If she did, I didn't see her."

Jamison had shaken his head while verbally responding. Was he confirming or denying what he said? Cosmo had related earlier that Jamison had been all over Rhonda that day.

"But like I said," Jamison added, "I only came by for a short time. I really don't remember who was here." He frowned. "What does that have to do with Scott Corbin? You're supposed to be asking about him, not me."

"I was wondering if, perhaps, that's how Corbin met Miss Talbot."

"Oh. Sure, that could be. That's probably when it was."

Garding asked about Cosmo Rivers.

"He ought to be on medication."

Garding asked a few more questions, then left. He reflected on the interviews, certain that Jamison had lied about meeting Rhonda Talbot. How well he had known her was anybody's guess. Anthony Shapiro had seemed antsy about something. He was either nervous that Garding was asking questions, or exceptionally uptight. He reminded Garding of people on amphetamines or cocaine. Who knew what Cosmo Rivers was about? Garding could easily picture Cosmo going over the edge and killing somebody. Shadowy figures unquestionably skulked about dank dungeons in that man's brain.

Tad Roman's house was small and neat, in a quiet family neighborhood a few blocks off Ben White Boulevard. Peter parked the white Camry around the corner; then he and Scott walked to Roman's front door and rang the bell. Both wore sport coats, sunglasses, and ties. Scott carried two encyclopedias. They had watched Roman's wife drive away minutes earlier, from up the street.

As they had hoped, nobody answered the bell. It required less than a minute to gain access and disappear inside.

Corbin took the bedroom while Buda went through the kitchen, living room, and front closets. Scott scanned countless boxes of baby pictures. Their child was named Merrilee, and she appeared to be about eighteen months old in the most recent photos.

Other photographs showed the baby with both sets of grandparents. Tad resembled his own mother.

"Find anything?" asked Peter.

Scott closed the door to a closet. "Just baby stuff and lots of photographs."

"Yeah, me, too." Peter nodded. "Of course, it's usually the baby-faced ones with families who cruise the streets at night looking for somebody to kill."

"Hard to believe."

"You said one of the victims was a hooker, right?"

"She worked for an escort service."

"Same thing. If he couldn't stay out late without his wife getting suspicious, he'd set up a date with a hooker. He could slice up the woman, get his rocks off, and be home for the ten-o'clock news."

"You have an evil mind, Peter."

"I've met guys like him."

They talked while they searched the den. Roman's computer easily divulged their household budget, checking- and savings-account information, and a score of computer games.

Scott was closing out a computer program when somebody opened the kitchen door directly behind him. Before he could turn around a woman screamed.

Corbin panicked. He jumped up, pulled his jacket over his face, and ran past the shrieking woman and out the door. Gasping for breath when he heard footsteps gaining on him, he tried to run even faster.

"Slow down," Peter Buda shouted. "We're half a block away and out of sight. Walk the rest of the way to the car."

Scott slowed to a fast walk. Buda came up beside him and they continued to the car, got in, and drove away.

"Never run," Peter said when he had caught his breath. "It makes you look as though you've done something wrong."

"We did, Peter; we broke into somebody's house."

"Nobody knows that except you, until you run."

"Roman's wife knew."

"That wasn't the same woman who drove away with the baby in her car. This woman was Hispanic. She was their housekeeper."

"I never looked."

"How could you with your coat over your head? I was about to tell her that the Romans had won a set of encyclopedias for their baby and that we were delivering the first two volumes. But no, you buried your head and tore out the door."

"Sorry."

"She would have bought it, too. Mrs. Roman would be eagerly waiting for next month's installment."

Sarah parked in her assigned space behind her apartment, assuming that Peter had already brought Scott home. Inside, however, she discovered that Scott hadn't arrived. She was unloading groceries in the kitchen when her front doorbell rang.

A most uncomfortable feeling settled over her when she saw the white car outside with the black rubber posts on the bumper—it was those two police detectives again, and Scott was due home any second. She opened the door, but did not invite them in.

Detective Barnaby said, "Excuse me, ma'am, but we forgot to ask something when we were here earlier."

"Yes?"

"Do you mind if we come inside?"

"I've just returned from grocery shopping, gentlemen, and I'm expecting a friend for dinner. I need to get things prepared and take a shower before he arrives."

"This will only take a minute. It's extremely important."

Sarah couldn't afford to appear uncooperative, which might make them suspicious. Her heart already racing, she asked, "What did you want to ask?"

"This man you reported seeing . . . that is, those two men—did either of them see you?"

"I don't think so."

Barnaby frowned. "That's good."

"Why do you say that?"

"Well, ma'am, we don't mean to frighten you, but it appears that the Chameleon isn't dead after all. The warden of the Huntsville prison confirms that Scott Corbin is not only alive; he has escaped."

Before Sarah could speak Detective Moyers asked, "Haven't you been watching the news?"

"I was out most of the day. I haven't had a chance to turn my TV on."

Moyers said, "There's a statewide alert out for him."

Sarah tried to imagine how she would react if she didn't already know that Scott was alive. She could hardly be any more upset than she was, albeit for different reasons.

She said, "Why didn't you tell me that when you were here earlier?"

Barnaby said, "We were waiting for confirmation from the warden."

"Do they know where he went?"

"There's a good chance he's still in Austin."

"What makes you think that?"

"In addition to the two murders last week? You saw him."

"But I told you, I made a mistake."

Barnaby said, "That seems awfully coincidental, Miss Hill. Maybe you did see him one of those times."

"No, I'm sure it was somebody else. Besides, he's probably in Mexico or somewhere by now. Surely he wouldn't be foolish enough to hang around Austin."

Barnaby was growing impatient. "Would you rather come down to headquarters with us, Miss Hill?"

"What for?"

"To help you remember. Your description of what you saw was very exact when you called the station. Both times. Now you don't seem to want to talk about it. Why not?"

"I've told you everything I know, Detective."

"Well, it isn't enough, okay? And why are you so fidgety all of a sudden?"

Sarah's adrenaline flooded her system. Peter

Buda's car was coming down the street, and she had no doubt that Scott would be in the passenger seat. The white Camry slowed and its turn signal began to blink as it approached the rear of the detectives' car. Peter and Scott were turning into her parking lot.

# Chapter Twenty-one

Peter Buda laughed as he swung into the parking lot. "Man, when that maid screamed—"

"Stop!" Corbin said, grasping Peter's arm. "Turn around, quick. Get out of here."

"What?" The car stopped with a lurch.

"Cops."

"Oh, my God."

Peter began to back out of the lot.

Sarah managed to say, "I'm sorry, Detective Barnaby . . . what did you ask me?"

"I said, why are you so fidgety?" Barnaby glanced around toward a white Toyota Camry backing from the parking lot into the street.

Sarah's anxiety erupted as anger. She almost shouted, "What would you expect, Detective? You come here telling me that a man I testified against is out of prison and right here in Austin instead of being dead like I thought he was." She tried to stop herself, searching for control. She forced her voice to calm somewhat as she asked, "Do you know Det. Robert Garding?"

"Of course. Why?"

"Because he's a friend of mine, that's why, and I have already talked with him several times."

"Why him?"

Watching Buda drive away she said, "Because nobody at police headquarters would help me when I called last week. Your Detective Wilkes didn't believe a word I said. Mr. Garding took the time to look into things. He helped me realize that I'd made a mistake. In fact, he made a special trip here this morning to inform me of the escape, and I told him exactly what I've told you. I made an honest mistake. I did not see Scott Corbin."

"You talked to Bob Garding today?"

"Yes, I did."

Barnaby considered what she had said. That would explain why she hadn't reacted more strongly to the news of Corbin's escape.

"If there's anything more," Sarah said, "I suggest you ask Mr. Garding. Now, if you don't mind, I'm expecting a guest."

Barnaby studied her earnest face for a few seconds, then said, "All right, Miss Hill. We wanted to let you know about the escape. If Corbin is in Austin, we'll catch him. Meanwhile, if you see or hear anything suspicious, let us know right away."

"Oh, I will, Detective." Sarah shook her head. "You can count on that."

Peter Buda forced his foot to sit lightly on his car's accelerator, cruising slowly away from Sarah's apartment.

"Damn," Corbin said. "Now what?"

"I couldn't see. Who was it?"

"Those same two detectives who were here this morning. They were at the front door, talking to Sarah."

Buda drove silently for a moment, then said, "You need another place to stay, friend."

Corbin didn't respond.

Peter added, "They know something."

"They came out because she reported seeing me last week. She already told them she'd made a mistake."

"So why did they come back?"

"I don't know."

"I'm telling you, Scott . . . staying with Sarah is too dangerous."

"Maybe." Corbin stared out the window for several seconds, then said, "Drive around for a while, then take me back there. I need to find out what they wanted."

Sarah was flipping channels on her TV when Scott and Peter came in. The local news hadn't begun. She turned the set off and they discussed their close call. Then she told them exactly what the detectives had asked, and what they'd said.

Corbin said they had heard on the radio about the statewide alert.

When Peter left, Sarah asked, "Where did you go today?"

"It's better that you don't know."

"I'm tired of not knowing things, Scott. You're always talking about trust . . . how do you expect me to trust you when you hold out on me?"

Corbin opened a can of Dr Pepper from the refrigerator. He took a drink of the soda, then detailed where he and Peter had gone and exactly what they had found. He wound up by saying, "Marvin Jamison probably killed Rhonda, Sarah."

Sarah was shocked. She had worked alongside Jamison for years. He had his faults. But murder?

"If it wasn't Frank Russett, then everything points to Jamison. He was stealing heavily . . . overpaying for components and outside contract labor. Still is, judging by what we found on his PC. Also, to watch his reaction, I had purposely let it slip to Marvin that I was having dinner with Rhonda that night." Corbin shook his head sadly. "God, I wish I'd never done that. It was really stupid." After a moment he said, "If Shapiro suspected Marvin, he didn't do anything because of the buyout . . . Shapiro obviously wanted the money. And that's a whole other story. He's probably hiding a ton of money in Bermuda."

Sarah considered what Scott had told her, then said, "I figured it was Cosmo."

Corbin nodded his head and cocked one eyebrow. "Cosmo is capable of anything."

"How will you ever know?"

"One of them killed Rhonda—most likely Jamison—but I don't believe that either one is the Chameleon. Whoever's killing these women now must be tied to Rhonda's murder. The killer knows I'm alive, and has to assume that I know about him. He'll come after me if he figures out where I am."

Corbin sipped his soda. "I have to force him to make a move before anybody else tracks me down."

Sarah fed Margot later, then joined Corbin on the sofa. "You promised you'd tell me how you escaped, Scott."

He reached for the TV's remote, but she covered his hand with her own. "Please," she said, "who helped you escape?"

"That is one thing I cannot tell you."

She pressed for an answer.

"I agreed to tell you how, but not *who* helped me. I gave my word."

Sarah nodded. "All right."

He sipped his soft drink, then began. "While I was on Death Row I was approached by a doctor who worked in a genetic-engineering firm in Houston. He was conducting a study on criminal behavior. He told me that habitual criminals sometimes have an extra chromosome in their genes, and others have super-high testosterone levels or not enough serotonin. I joined his study mostly to get out of my cell for an extra hour or so every couple of weeks. Over the next few months we shared some confidences. He was concerned with the number of innocent people convicted of capital crimes in our country. Especially how many get executed. He's a member of Amnesty International, and adamantly opposed the death penalty."

"Is this the same doctor that Mr. Garding called a reliable source?"

"I don't know who Garding was talking about. This man would never disclose what happened."

"Please go on."

"Maybe because I had normal testosterone and serotonin and no extra chromosomes, or maybe just because he believed what I said, the doctor told me about how physicians or medical laboratories sometimes claim the bodies of executed prisoners."

"Such as when they've donated their organs?"

"No, organ banks won't accept organs from condemned prisoners. They're afraid of the effects of drug abuse and AIDS and other infections. Plus, I guess the lethal injection messes up the organs somehow."

"Sorry, I didn't mean to interrupt."

"He gave me an example of how it worked. The prison at Huntsville executed a prisoner named Joseph Jernigan by lethal injection in 1993. Jernigan had donated his body to medical science. As soon as he was pronounced dead, doctors froze his body and took it away. They sliced him into millimeter cross sections with a laser, then took detailed photographs of each section for anatomical studies. They even have a Web site about it on the Internet: Mcc.Murdoch.edu something. Frankly, I've never wanted to look at it.

"Anyway, before the state executes you, you fill out a form saying who's to get your remains. If nobody claims your body, it gets buried in the Captain Joe Byrd Cemetery near the prison."

Corbin turned to face Sarah more squarely. "This doctor said the last time he'd claimed a body from the prison, the executioner offered him the option of monitoring the lethal injection himself, which he had not done. But he could, and the offer still stood. First off, he could load the syringes. Being an M.D., he could also pronounce the offender dead and then take the body to his laboratory.

"After we talked several times, this doctor said he had figured out a way that might keep me alive." Corbin paused to take another sip of his soda.

"They have three syringes and a device that automatically pushes the plungers, in the injection room . . . a small area behind a one-way mirror, next to where the inmate is strapped down. Witnesses can watch the inmate through glass windows in two observation rooms, but only the person monitoring the injections is privy to what goes on behind the mirror. The doctor said he could load the first two syringes with less-than-lethal doses of sodium thiopental and pancuronium bromide . . . the drugs that put you to sleep and stop your breathing. He would substitute sodium chloride solution in the third syringe for the potassium chloride solution they use to stop your heart. A few minutes after the injections began, I'd be unconscious, not breathing, and would appear dead to anybody watching. He said it would look exactly like a standard execution."

Sarah recalled Robert Garding's telling her how he had kept his eyes glued to the observation window that stormy night, watching the lethal injection flow into Corbin's veins. Little did Garding know, he had actually witnessed a resurrection.

Scott continued, "Since the EKG monitor sits behind the one-way mirror where the doctor would be, he'd say my heart had stopped and quickly disconnect the EKG leads. There'd be no reason for anybody to question his diagnosis. Security in the chamber gets pretty lax as soon as the inmate is pronounced dead, and since executions are always right after six P.M., people are in a hurry to go to dinner or back to work, so everybody leaves. The doctor would immediately wheel me into the prep room behind the chamber and resuscitate me. Nobody goes in there except the undertaker from town, and he wouldn't be around, since the doctor would be claiming my body himself. He explained how he would wake me up by using neostigmine, atropine, and oxygen to reverse the effects of what he had injected. He even let me read about the different drugs.

"Then, with copies of the death certificate and release-of-remains forms, he'd load my 'body' and drive me right out of the prison. Normally the Huntsville Funeral Home removes the corpse from the Death House as soon as witnesses are cleared, so gate guards are accustomed to a body leaving just minutes after the execution. All I'd have to do would be to hold my breath and look dead in case anybody looked under the sheet. He said a little white makeup would take care of that."

Corbin exhaled abruptly. "Later, when he showed me the official form authorizing him to claim my remains, I withdrew my appeals. I agreed to the execution."

Sarah sank back on the sofa, shaking her head. When she could speak, she said, "I can't believe you'd trust anybody that much."

"He believed what I told *him*."

"Yes, but—"

"He gave me his word, Sarah." Corbin paused. "Think about my situation . . . everybody else in the world wanted me dead. That doctor was the only person who believed I should live. All my options had been taken away. I had one decision left and it was the toughest I ever had to make. I knew it might be my final choice, but at least it was mine. So I made it."

After a moment Sarah said, "The doctor took a huge chance, too. What did he want in return?"

"Two things. First, he asked me to participate in his genetic-engineering studies for six months, for which I would be well paid. Second, I should never admit who helped me escape."

"You still won't tell me his name?"

"I can't. I will tell you that he's a member of Physicians for Human Rights. You might have seen him on CNN last month with a group of doctors out west, campaigning against capital punishment. He goes all over."

Sarah was astounded. "It's . . . I'm overwhelmed that you would even consider what he suggested."

"I was ready to die when he offered me a way out. Living in a cold, hard cell day in and day out isn't being alive. Alone. Bored out of my mind. Unable to do the things I had always planned to do. I'd prefer a pine-box parole any day."

Sarah watched the muscles work in his jaw. Saw the fiery intensity in his eyes. Whose life had he just described?

Suddenly the focus on her own life sharpened. Living alone. Bored. Waiting for what, chronic alcoholism? She visualized a thin metal box lined with cheap satin. Saw her mother's stiff body in that Abilene funeral home, a mannequin of the woman Sarah had known.

Sarah had been on the edge of a major decision since Inks Lake. Watching that little Mexican girl with the tear-streaked face. Holding Scott's hand.

Without another word she melted against Corbin and hugged him tightly to her. She knew in that instant that she was ready to believe this man without reservation. To take a huge chance—the biggest of her life. She wanted so desperately to trust again. Perhaps, someday, even to love.

She thought of the items he had said he needed from her office. Phone bills, materials invoices, check stubs, contract-labor hours, and anything that might point to hidden stock transfers or sales. Whatever was going on around the time Rhonda was killed.

She said, "The other day, you said you couldn't do what you need to by yourself. I want to help . . . but to find the things you want, I'll need to go back into the office. I can't do it from here."

Corbin looked uncertain. The muscles around his eyes tightened and his Adam's apple bobbed up and down. He didn't speak.

With a tear blazing an erratic path down one cheek, Sarah softly added, "Trust has to flow both ways, you know."

Corbin finally responded. "Thank you. I can't tell you how much it means, just knowing that you believe in me." After a moment of strained silence he smiled and asked, "Do you like country-and-western clubs?"

"I've never been to one."

"What about the blues clubs on Sixth Street?"

"Never been."

Disbelief filled his face. He stood and pulled her to her feet. "You live in Austin, Texas, and you've never . . . ? Sarah, what have you been doing with your life? Do you own a pair of western boots?"

"No."

"Damn, girl." He smiled broadly. "Don't just stand there; go put on some jeans and a blouse. I'm taking you dancing tonight. Then we'll go listen to some blues."

She protested, "You can't go out, Scott. The police are searching everywhere for you."

"They're looking for a convict on the run, not some lucky fellow out on the town with his beautiful girl. Sixth Street will be filled with couples who'll look just like us."

A heavy, dark cloud seemed to vanish from around Sarah, and she suddenly felt light and cheerful. She was going dancing. She hurried toward her closets, but turned back. "Have you ever seen the bats at dusk?"

"No."

"You live in Austin, Texas, and you've never . . ." She grinned. "I'll take you to see the bats, first . . . then we'll visit your clubs."

Instead of taking his wife out for dinner as planned, Jack Barnaby adjusted his sport coat on a hanger and sat at his desk. Jim Moyers stood across the aisle in front of his own office cubicle, arms folded and ankles crossed. PI Robert Garding leaned back in a swivel chair near Barnaby's desk and rubbed the back of his head. It had already been a long day for each when Barnaby had asked Robert Garding to join them.

Barnaby said, "You know Sarah Hill better than we do, Bob. What's she holding back? And why?"

"I'm not sure," Garding answered, "but it isn't like her to back down from what she believes. Of course, I've never known her to have a boyfriend before. Maybe he's put some doubts in her mind."

Moyers asked, "How was she when you spoke to her?"

"Well, she . . . she definitely seemed less sure of herself. She's questioning things she was absolutely convinced were true a short while back."

"Such as?"

"Such as whether Scott Corbin killed Rhonda Talbot."

"How could anybody doubt that?"

Garding shook his head. "She saw a TV show where several convicts on Death Row up in Illinois turned out to be innocent. She's worried that maybe she helped send an innocent man to prison."

Barnaby said, "Her testimony wasn't all that crucial, anyway. You had scads of evidence."

"Yeah, but she thinks it was. She's the type who'd worry about something like that. Giving the devil his due, she did lead me to a couple of interesting situations today."

"What situations?"

"I talked to some people who worked with Corbin . . . the same office where Sarah worked." Garding related his discussions with Shapiro, Rivers, and Jamison. He concluded by saying, "If I were still on the force, I'd investigate Cosmo Rivers a lot more thoroughly. That man is dangerous."

Moyers spoke up. "But you just said that Marvin Jamison lied to you about knowing Rhonda Talbot."

Garding nodded. "Probably. Then again, maybe Cosmo was the one who lied, to make it appear that Jamison was hiding something."

"Why would he do that?"

"Possibly shifting suspicion away from himself in case anybody ever starts digging around. He's smart enough to do that. Frankly, they all seemed nervous when I started asking about Rhonda's murder." He paused. "Corbin swore all along that somebody at EBS killed her and set him up for it."

Barnaby almost laughed. "You're not suggesting that Corbin was telling the truth, Bob?"

"No. Don't get me wrong; I'm convinced that he's the Chameleon. But something went on over there at EBS that somebody sure wants kept under wraps."

Jack Barnaby stretched his arms until one shoulder popped. "Well, my concern is putting Corbin's ass back on Death Row. He hasn't shown up anywhere else, and it's been mighty quiet around Austin these past few days. I don't know about you, but that makes me nervous as hell."

# Chapter Twenty-two

The sun set minutes before the Lone Star Riverboat cruised under the Congress Avenue bridge. Sarah and a man who looked nothing like Scott Corbin stood arm in arm on the riverboat's upper deck. Sarah thought Corbin looked exceptionally handsome in jeans, a western shirt, a Stetson hat, and boots. She even liked his bushy brown mustache and beard. More than a thousand spectators lined the east side of the bridge as first one, then three or four, then more than 1.5 million Mexican free-tailed bats exploded into the air from fifteen crevices under the bridge. A collective gasp could be heard—the display was so spectacular, it was breathtaking.

"They live here because they've been evicted from their natural habitat," Sarah told Corbin. One of Scott's arms slowly encircled her waist as they leaned against a railing. He appeared awestruck by the magnitude of the display.

She continued, "Most of the caves they used to live in are open to the public now, so they come here to have their pups. Each female has only one a year. This is one of the largest colonies of Mexican freetails in the world."

"Whoa," was all Scott could manage to say.

* * *

Later that night Sarah turned off the lights in the bathroom and, nervous as a teenager at her first prom, padded across the hall in her best silk nightgown. It had been a marvelous evening—first the bat display, then club-hopping and listening to the best live country-and-western music and Texas blues she had ever heard. They must've passed twenty-five music clubs in addition to the four they entered—all packed with enthusiastic people having a rollicking good time. She had even learned to line dance, and was pretty good at it. She could hardly wait to buy her first pair of cowboy boots. Maybe one of those calico skirts.

She eased in beside Corbin, expecting him to take her in his arms immediately. Instead he lay perfectly still on his back. She could hear him breathing.

"You smell nice," he finally said. "I like that about you . . . you're always so clean and fresh."

"Thank you. I had a really good time tonight."

"So did I. Those bats were awesome."

He extended one arm and she slid over beside him, resting her head on his shoulder.

He nuzzled her hair, breathing in her scent, then traced small circles on her bare arm with one finger. His lips brushed the skin of her neck as he asked, "May I kiss you?"

"Would you like to?"

"Very much."

"Uh . . . do you have some sort of . . . you know? In case we . . . ?"

"Yes."

She turned her face and they kissed, slowly at first, tentatively. Corbin drew back and looked at her in the dim light. "You have absolutely beautiful eyes," he said. "An incredible mouth."

She had already begun to tingle all over.

"I'd like to kiss you again," he said.

This time the kiss was deeper, stronger, and searching. His fingers traced delicate lines across the thin material covering her breasts. A strong hand caressed her buttocks.

God, he knew how to kiss.

Muscles she had watched ripple the day he swam at Inks Lake were taut now and knotted, at once hard and smooth beneath her fingers. She loved that he felt so solid in her arms. So strong.

His mouth seemed to be everywhere at once, so gentle on her ear she could hardly detect it, so aggressive on her lips that it almost hurt. Her mind flooded with unexpected sensations till she had to force herself to breathe.

"I love how you taste," he said in a throaty growl. Minutes later he stripped her gown over her head in a single fluid motion and tossed it aside. He cupped both full breasts in his hands, and his tongue flicked across her chest while his eyes opened wide to drink her in. Her nipples were hard now, projecting, begging to be taken. He kissed all around both breasts, teasing, tantalizing, his breath hot and his tongue wet, drawing small circles on her skin.

An unfamiliar sound escaped Sarah's throat when Scott pulled one throbbing nipple inside his mouth, his teeth nipping, his tongue flicking. She groaned aloud, more a low, throaty moan than a cry.

She curved her body into his and felt his hardness against her belly, pulsing, pushing, hot and firm. Her thighs were damp; she was flooded with uncontrollable desire. Never had she wanted a man so badly. Her hands searched his body, exploring, feeling, stroking, and anticipating.

He teased her with his tongue, tantalized her thighs with silky strokes of his fingers, never quite entering her directly. She arched her back and pushed up toward him, consumed with a ravenous hunger.

"Tell me what you like," he whispered.

"This," she responded huskily. "You . . . everything you do."

"Do you like to be kissed?"

"Oh, yes, I love the way you kiss me."

To her amazement Corbin quickly slid down the length of her, caressing and kissing her burning skin, her belly, the wetness of her thighs, and then her most intimate parts. She thought she would surely go out of her mind as he made love to her with his lips and his magical tongue, devouring her. Never one to lose control, Sarah flew past the point of no return with no chance of turning back. Exhilarated by his touch and overwhelmed with need, she opened herself to this man as she had never done before. She twisted his hair in her fingers as her first tremors began, wild now, unable to stop her shaking thighs or thrusting pelvis.

Before she knew what was happening Corbin was

on top of her, his mouth covering hers with his own demanding kisses. He deftly slipped on a condom and entered her slowly and fully. The sensation of having him inside her was overpowering, and she clung to his hard back, her knees in the air, legs and arms pulling him faster in a frenzy of excitement and uncontrollable passion. His body lunged against hers, harder, deeper, and faster until she cried out his name, clasping and squeezing him tightly inside.

Suddenly frightened by the intensity of her feelings, Sarah thought for an instant to stop, but retreat was impossible. Corbin continued to move rapidly atop her, building her pleasure again to a point beyond reason or conscious thought. His sinewy muscles were hard and straining, his teeth clenched, his eyes squeezed shut. Blue veins distended under the flushed skin of his neck as he thrust deep inside her again and again. Her mindless body fully joined his until a tidal wave of ecstasy crashed over and swept her up, churning, thrashing, drowning out whatever reality she had ever known. She cried aloud once more, and Corbin fell against her seconds later, their skin slippery and their chests heaving together as they gasped for breath.

Sarah was too astounded to speak. They clung tightly to each other in the dark while their hearts and breathing slowed.

Sarah felt thoroughly ravaged—but at peace.

Corbin finally spoke. "Whoa."

Several moments passed without either saying another word. Finally he rolled to one side and pulled her close. "That was wonderful."

She looked into his pale brown eyes. "It was beautiful."

"*You're* beautiful."

She knew better. She had never thought of herself as beautiful. Smart, maybe. Capable. Not beautiful. "Thank you," she managed. She nuzzled her head against his chest.

After a lengthy silence Sarah said, "I've been thinking about what you said . . . about living in that cell. Just existing."

Corbin made a sound more a *hmmm* than a reply.

"I've been living in a cell, too. There are so many things I wanted to do as a girl that I've never done. Never actually tried." She paused. "I guess I've been afraid, and I'm not even sure of what." She toyed with the hairs on his chest, comforted by the beat of his heart.

They talked quietly for several minutes before Sarah said, "If you hadn't come along, I wonder how long it would've been before I took an overdose of sleeping pills . . . or left the gas on in the stove one night. I wouldn't even have had the courage to slit my wrists." She broke down then, and began sobbing.

Corbin held her close, her cheek against his chest. He kissed the top of her head and stroked her back consolingly.

When she regained her composure Sarah asked, "Are you getting ready to leave me?"

"Why do you ask that?"

"I feel so good when I'm with you, but I can't

relax. I have this constant feeling that you're about to go away."

"I haven't lied to you, Sarah . . . you know I could be arrested any minute."

*Or worse,* she thought. She refused to dwell on that possibility.

He interrupted her thoughts. "How come you never married?"

"Oh, I . . . you know . . . never met the right man, I suppose."

"That's hard to believe. You're a bright, capable woman. Very pretty."

"I've never thought so. Pretty, I mean."

"Well, you are. You even look good when you first wake up." He chuckled softly. "My ex was a natural blonde. She didn't have a face in the morning without spending an hour at her makeup mirror."

Sarah hesitated, then said, "I was engaged once."

"When?"

"Just out of high school. I may've told you that I sewed dresses for a woman in Abilene. Her nephew kept coming by the shop and we went out a couple of times, you know, to get a milk shake or something. Then we started dating. I . . . really liked him."

"Go on."

"We eventually got engaged. He didn't buy me a ring, but we talked about getting married. We both wanted to. One morning he came by the shop and told me he had joined the navy. He was leaving that same day."

Corbin recalled her telling him about a young man who had joined the navy. Not wanting to interrupt the moment, however, he said, "He hadn't told you before?"

"Not a word."

"What happened?"

"Oh, he wrote me a couple of letters, but I never saw him again. He was in town on leave a few months later, but he didn't come to see me."

"How terrible."

Sarah shifted position in Corbin's arms. After a lengthy silence, she said, "I was pregnant, Scott, and he knew it before he left. Eddie knew about it . . . that was his name. He knew about it because we had discussed what to do and he said we would get married. Then he left."

"What a bastard." Corbin pulled her tighter against him. He held her silently for several moments. "What happened with the baby?"

"I wasn't quite three months pregnant, so I hadn't started to show or anything. I still dream about what she would've looked like. She'd be in the seventh grade now." Sarah brushed a tear from her cheek. "I had a miscarriage, Scott. I always wondered if my disappointment caused it somehow." After a beat she said, "Every day of my life I imagine the little dresses I would buy her. How I'd fix her hair."

"Maybe it was a boy."

"No, she was a girl. I could tell."

Corbin lay silent for a moment, then said, "Why did your father really leave, Sarah?"

"I'd rather not talk about that."

"Tell me. I sincerely want to know."

Finally she told him. About how she used to lie in

her bed at night listening to her mother and father fight. She could hear her mother screaming that he was no good—always comparing him to her own father. Sarah's father never measured up. She said she remembered hearing names like *sex maniac* and *sot*. Her mother telling her father to take his sick desires elsewhere.

"He eventually did take them elsewhere," Sarah said. "But not very far." She exhaled abruptly. "I always had a special relationship with my dad. You know, he'd buy me little gifts . . . a cheap necklace, a book of poems, Cracker Jacks, things like that. One night after he and my mother had a terrible fight, he came into my room and held me real tight. He was crying. I had my arms around him and was rubbing his back. After a while he began to caress me, too . . . my head, my back, my shoulders. It felt good. But he started touching places where I knew nobody should touch, and I got frightened."

Sarah had to stop to collect herself. Continuing, she said, "I asked him to stop, but he wouldn't. He said it would be our little secret . . . that I would be his woman. I was shaking all over and I know I cried. I was pleading with him to stop."

She wiped her cheeks. "He stopped then, and told me he was very, very sorry. Then he got up and left without saying another word. I could hear him crying as he went out my bedroom door.

"When I woke up the next morning, Daddy was gone. He never came back."

"Never?"

"No. We never saw or heard from him again after that night."

Corbin lay silent for a long while before asking, "What do you believe made him leave?"

The question surprised her. Wasn't the answer obvious? "He molested me, Scott. He was afraid I'd tell."

"Would you have?"

"I've never told anybody before."

"Nobody?"

"No. Not even my mother."

"Why not?"

"He was my daddy. I loved him."

Scott remained silent for several more moments, then asked, very softly, "Why did you believe he left back then? When you were, what . . . ten, eleven?"

"Almost eleven." She had to clear her throat. "I thought I wasn't pretty enough to please him. I wasn't nearly as pretty as my mother, and I didn't know how to do whatever he had wanted me to do."

Corbin let out a slow sigh. "Why do you think Eddie left you?"

"He was scared to death of his parents. He was only twenty."

"Not now, Sarah . . . then. What did you believe at the time?"

She lay perfectly still for several seconds. "That I wasn't good enough. That I hadn't pleased him . . . you know, in bed."

Corbin turned her face up to his. Tears streamed silently down her face. He kissed her, tasting her salty tears. "May I tell you something?"

"What?" Doubt filled her voice. Insecurity.

"Two things. First, the men in your life left because there was something broken inside *them* . . . not because of anything you did or didn't do."

Sarah didn't speak for a moment; then she asked, "What's the other thing?"

"You are fantastic in bed."

"What!"

"I mean it. You're warm, you're sensitive, you respond to every little touch. You have a natural sense of rhythm. You're . . . Best of all, Sarah, you make me feel like I'm the greatest lover since Rudolph Valentino."

She laughed and sobbed all at the same time. "You *are* the greatest."

"No, I'm not, but you respond like I am, and I love it. I enjoy knowing that I please you."

"Oh, but you do. You please me so very much. I love you, Scott. I love you more than I've ever loved anybody."

He hugged her tightly to him and she buried her head against his chest, waiting. Waiting. Praying for him to tell her, too.

Corbin did not say what she needed so desperately to hear. After far too much time had elapsed, he said, "Thank you, Sarah." He sat up in bed and smiled. "Anybody gettin' hungry around here? I could use a bite to eat."

After a light snack they took an erotic shower together, then returned to bed and made long, slow, delicious love.

Lying in Corbin's arms afterward, Sarah asked if she might tell him something else. Something personal.

"Of course. What is it?"

"My mother committed suicide."

"I'm so sorry."

"I've never told anybody that, except a therapist I went to for a short time after she was buried. She slit her wrists, Scott . . . in a drunken stupor."

"You poor thing."

"I found her in the bathtub at our apartment in Abilene."

Sarah said that the therapist she had consulted explained that her mother likely suffered from bipolar disorder—manic-depressive illness. Sarah had become convinced of it as soon as she read up on the symptoms at the library. Her mother should have been on medication, and should never have ingested alcohol of any kind.

"What a terrible experience," Corbin said. He pulled her even closer, as one might comfort a child. "The influence parents have on children is so tremendous it's downright scary."

"How do you mean?"

"So many of our adult decisions are nothing more than reactions to what we saw as children . . . when our minds were thirsty little sponges soaking up every new experience.

"Like birds fledging their young, if our parents are wise and loving and considerate, we have a shot at flying successfully on our own someday. But if a parent's picture of reality is blurred, often by some distorted perception passed down from their own mother or father, we'll almost certainly shadow that same off-center view."

Sarah recalled her mother quoting things that she had learned from her own mother. She didn't speak.

"If we could only see our parents as imperfect, as they really were, we might not pass on that same egregious behavior." Corbin paused for a moment. "Most children believe their parents are perfect because they have nothing to compare to. But parents take advantage of a child's trust—like lying about Santa Claus and the Tooth Fairy—then they expect children to grow up trusting others. In prison I used to ask myself, Why isn't it enough for a parent just to be human? To admit that imperfect is all right? That it's normal?"

When Sarah didn't say anything he went on. "All that talk about victims on TV lately . . . hell, we're all victims—of our past. Our hope should be that each of us is the *final* victim in his own long line of damaged souls. Like Harry Truman and the buck . . . the aberration stops here."

Corbin lowered his voice and said, "Learn something from your mom, Sarah. Whether it was her upbringing or a chemical imbalance, something condemned her to live as a tortured soul. Don't let that happen to you. You really do have that choice."

Sarah pondered what he had said, and her mind called up a dozen incidents from her youth. Some memories were pleasant, a few comical, others too painful to bear. But she had arrived at one firm decision as Corbin spoke: She would never allow herself to depend on alcohol again. She felt certain her mother would still be alive if it hadn't been for that.

Sarah fell asleep in Corbin's arms a short while later, spent, her breathing deep and regular.

Corbin stared unblinking at shifting patterns of light that filtered through windblown bushes outside. Then he quietly untangled his arms from Sarah's and slipped out of bed.

An old man dressed in baggy clothes stood motionless but eager, hunched over amid rustling bushes outside a Spicewood Springs apartment. A storm front was moving in from the south, and the air felt more humid than when he had watched the woman go inside with her young man. He touched himself as the excitement of anticipation grew, and felt a familiar stirring between his legs. He listened to the young woman inside arguing in a heavy Southern accent with her increasingly frustrated young man. Minutes later the boyfriend stomped out in a huff.

The old man stepped from the shadows the instant the young man's car roared away. He walked to the front door and rang the bell.

The woman's emotionally charged voice asked who it was. Music with a heavy beat resounded from behind the door. One red-rimmed green eye appeared at the peephole.

"I'm so sorry . . . to disturb you," the man said, gasping between word groupings, "but my car . . . broke down and . . . my emphysema . . . is so bad . . .

I can't walk. If I can . . . phone my wife she'll . . . have somebody . . . pick me up."

He stepped back into the light, permitting a better view.

The woman watched for a moment, then blew her nose and cleared her throat. She unlocked and unchained the door.

"Sure, why not? My grandfather has emphysema. If you'll—"

The man jammed a handgun in her abdomen and forced his way inside. He quickly changed her stereo's dial from hard rock to a classical FM station, and increased the volume.

"What are you doing?" the woman demanded. "My fiancé gave me that stereo three days ago. Don't you touch it."

He smiled behind his mask, scanning the woman with his eyes. She was about thirty years old, brunette, five-foot-three. A lavender leotard clung to every curve and hollow of her firm and shapely body. Her breasts were full, their cleavage deep, and her tummy flat. Prominent nipples strained against the tight lavender material. Her arms were toned, with a hint of muscle below each shoulder, and her nails were manicured and bloodred. Her calves and thighs appeared tight, like a dancer's, and her buttocks were well shaped.

The man extended a gloved hand to touch one of her breasts.

"Stop that!" She slapped his gloved hand away. "Who are you?"

He smiled again, watching fire shoot from her

eyes. He grabbed the woman's wrist and spun her around, twisting the arm behind her back until she cried out. Quickly moving closer, he brushed his penis against a firm buttock. His erection stiffened even more.

"Damn you," the woman shouted. She struggled to get away.

In one rapid motion the man pocketed the pistol and reached around her, clutching one breast roughly in his free hand. He stepped still closer and began humping her buttock like a sex-crazed dog.

"You pervert!" she shrieked. She struggled violently against his greater strength.

He laughed aloud. "Oh, yes," he said. "Twist it around. Push against me. Ooh, yes, like that."

Minutes later the man slammed his pistol against the woman's head to stop her struggles. He cut off her leotard and panties and dragged her, nude, into the dining room. He propped her upright in a dining room chair and bound her arms and legs with duct tape. Separating her thighs with his knee, he was probing inside her with a gloved finger when she regained her senses.

She screamed out and made a desperate attempt to bite, but he moved away just in time.

Taking a ten-inch knife from inside his jacket he traced delicate lines on the woman's chest—drawing blood across the fullness of one breast, around its areola, then into the valley between and up onto the other breast.

The young woman screamed out in agony, hysterical now.

"Yes," he said, immersing his soul in her pain. "Tell me exactly what you feel."

He stopped short when her eyes suddenly opened wide and glared wildly at him, unfocused, her teeth grinding together now. Her screaming stopped abruptly, and she began to froth at the mouth. An unearthly sound came from somewhere deep in her throat. One torn edge of her lower lip was wedged between her teeth, though she didn't seem to notice, and bright red blood pulsed down her chin as she chewed the ragged piece in two.

The man calmly put down the long knife, then pulled another—a shorter blade, stout, and rounded on the end.

The woman gnashed her teeth, bloody saliva foaming from her mouth while he scooped out her vivid green eyes—one at a time.

An hour later stringy extraocular muscles dangled as limp as rubber bands from the woman's eye sockets. Blood that had trickled erratically down both cheeks now slowly congealed. Her intestines spilled out onto beige nylon carpet. Near where she was fastened to her dining room chair, an artfully sliced kidney rested alongside her broken heart.

Soft moans escalated into full orgasmic cries as Ruggero Leoncavallo's 1892 opera of passion and murder, *I pagliacci,* resounded throughout the apartment.

The man jerked in convulsive spasms, spurting his seed into the dead woman's chest and abdomen. When his spasms subsided he sank to his knees, weak now, breathing hard. He frowned momentarily, as if unable to comprehend why his erection seemed to melt in his hand.

Having been allowed release after all that time, the urges were growing stronger, crying out for more—and more frequent—satisfaction.

He rose to his feet and smiled. Why worry? Hadn't he spent his life making people believe whatever served him? Convincing any and all that he was warm and affectionate, and felt things the same as they did?

He had often wondered what motivated others. What hidden pleasures could justify an existence so mundane? Compared to his, their lives were supremely boring, yet they went on. Not only that, they cried out to live when they saw their death approach, no matter how badly he made them suffer. He had to admit such behavior amused him, though he'd never fully understand why they even cared.

He did know one thing for certain: It wouldn't be long before he would kill again. That act alone made everything he had ever been forced to endure worthwhile.

# Chapter Twenty-Three

Scott Corbin laughed softly while Sarah fought to catch her breath after their early-morning lovemaking. Bright sunshine streamed through partially open blinds at a nearby window. Corbin got out of bed minutes later.

Sarah dozed, but stirred when Corbin returned with a steaming cup of tea in a china cup and saucer.

"Oh, God, that was incredible," she said. She propped herself upright on two pillows, brushing her hair back with her fingers.

"No, *you're* incredible." He sat beside her and they kissed again.

"Do you really think so?"

"I know so."

After several minutes of planning their day, Scott said, "The whole world knows I'm alive and out of prison now. I need some new disguises, and I need to force the killer's hand quickly. If it is somebody at ISI, I've got to make him believe I know who he is."

"What do you want me to do?"

"First I need those old phone records from EBS. I'm certain Shapiro tracked everybody's calls through the PBX system, so ISI should have them stored somewhere. I need to know if anybody spoke with Rhonda before that night. Specifically Jamison, Shapiro, or Cosmo Rivers. Maybe one of them already knew Rhonda outside the office . . . if so, he may have called her several times. Any one of them could've also called the escort service where the other woman worked . . . the one he killed before Rhonda. Make sure you check Tad Roman's extension for that number. The next thing I need will be . . ."

Sarah called her office and told Amanda that she was feeling much better, so she would be in. Then she left for work.

Scott Corbin stood at the bathroom mirror in shorts and a T-shirt a short time later, shaving, when the doorbell rang. He tiptoed to the front window and peeked outside. A UPS truck was parked at the curb, the driver ringing the bell. Scott ignored it and went back to his shaving.

Minutes later the front bell rang again. This time Sarah's landlord was at the door. Scott chose to ignore her too. He was walking back toward the bathroom when he heard a key slide into the front door's lock. He raced into the bedroom, wiping his face on a towel, and pulled the door shut behind him. He hurriedly grabbed up a shirt and a pair of trousers.

"Hello? Hello-ohh. Anybody home?"

Corbin cracked open the bedroom door to watch. A squat little woman with strands of unkempt gray hair and a mustard-stained housecoat came inside.

Letty Whitstone, whom Sarah had pointed out a few days before.

Mrs. Whitstone placed the UPS package on the dining table, then went through Sarah's kitchen, blatantly inspecting cupboards and pantry. She flipped through the magazines on the coffee table, careful to replace each one exactly as it had been, then came down the hall. In the bathroom she inspected Corbin's razor and can of shaving cream on the sink, then pushed aside a pair of discarded undershorts with the toe of one pink slipper.

Corbin eased the door shut and flattened himself against the wall. The woman had started for the bedroom. He jerked one leg away when Margot sidled up against him, rubbing herself on his bare ankles. He almost jumped out of his skin when the phone rang.

"Hello, this is 555-9793 . . ." It was Sarah's voice on the answering machine. Whoever had called, hung up.

Mrs. Whitstone called out, "Margot. Margot?"

Corbin eased the door open a crack and guided the cat through.

"There you are," Mrs. Whitstone said, picking up the cat. "My pretty baby. You want a fresh can of tuna? Hmmm? Come on, sweetie; Letty's gonna get you something to eat."

Corbin wiped perspiration from his face as the woman slowly walked back up the hall with the little cat. Minutes later she left.

* * *

Homicide detectives and crime-scene techs went through the motions in the Spicewood Springs apartment, though they already knew what they would not find. There would be no fingerprints. No weapon. No eyeballs in the eye sockets. No distinctive fibers or teeth marks or skin beneath the fingernails of the corpse. They would and did find a few pubic hairs in the dead woman's gutted chest and abdomen, along with what appeared to be dried semen.

Technicians took specimens for DNA fingerprinting, but only for confirmatory evidence when they caught the killer. Everybody knew exactly who was responsible for this latest carnage.

The scene was virtually identical to the previous two, except this time, one kidney was neatly sliced and stacked on the dining room table alongside the dead woman's intact heart.

Detective Barnaby announced as he came back in from outside, "Nobody saw nothing, nobody heard nothing. The guy next door did think the music a little strange, since Brandi here preferred pop or jazz." Barnaby forced himself to sound cavalier, and switched on the overhead lights. No amount of light, however, could penetrate the gloom that clung to this woman's grotesque form. He wondered how even the finality of death could quell the pain that must have screamed out from her every ragged nerve.

Jim Moyers emerged from a crawl space at the rear of a hall storage closet. "Did he know anything about where she worked? Boyfriends, family?"

"He didn't, but her landlord did. He says Brandi was a Jazzercise instructor . . . supposed to get married in two weeks. He's looking up her parents' address and phone number now." Barnaby could not let himself imagine the sorrow such a call would bring to this girl's father.

"Did he know the fiancé's name?"

"No, but her mother will . . . as if we need the information. Do you have any doubts as to who killed this girl?"

Moyers shook his head. "No." He stripped off his surgical gloves and tossed them into a plastic bag, then began entering information into his laptop.

Barnaby said, almost to himself, "They had his ass on Death Row, and the son of a bitch still got away."

Robert Garding joined detectives Barnaby and Moyers at the murder scene later that morning.

Garding said, "It doesn't seem possible that a body so small could've contained this much blood."

"It's the same as all the others," Jack Barnaby said, trying to ignore the agonizing screams that seemed to emanate from every blood corpuscle spattered throughout the room. He could feel the young woman's desperate struggles, almost taste her fear.

"What time?" asked Garding.

Moyers answered, but had to clear his throat. "ME's investigator thinks between midnight and six A.M."

Garding shook his head wearily. "The bastard has been saving it up . . . now he's in a feeding frenzy like sharks in a pool full of body parts." He walked slowly through the apartment, then returned. "No question about it, Jack. The Chameleon did this."

"My worst fears have come true," Barnaby said. "Not only is Corbin alive, he's hiding somewhere in my city."

Garding looked around again and shook his head. "The hell of it is, he could be almost anywhere, doing damn near anything, and there's no telling what he looks like. He's not only a con artist, he's a master of disguise."

Barnaby stopped what he was doing and narrowed his eyes. "You may have just given me the best idea yet, Bob."

"How's that?"

"If you had come to town last week thinking that nobody knew you were alive, and suddenly your face was on every channel on TV, what would you try to do?"

The man who sidled into Shakespeare & Company Theatrical Supply wore western clothes and boots, a brown Stetson hat, and a full brown mustache. The shop sat at the edge of the University of Texas campus, on Guadalupe Street, a few short blocks from where Charles Whitman murdered more than a dozen people from atop the Texas Tower on August 1, 1966.

"May I help you, cowboy?" A lean but athletic-appearing man of about fifty stood behind a counter, wearing tight jeans and a red T-shirt. He smiled suggestively with obscene red lips, and batted eyelashes unnaturally dark and long.

Scott Corbin ignored the man's overtures and calmly replied, "I need several items. We're doing

*The Man Who Came to Dinner* next month, and a play every other month after, so I'm going to need a couple of suits, hats, and a lightweight raincoat. I also need to restock my makeup supplies . . . I see you carry Ben Nye, Kryolan, and Bob Kelly. Good. Oh, and a couple of those wigs and beards and some colored hair spray."

"I adore the theater. Who are you with?"

"We're a new group down in Boerne . . . The Stage Players."

Marissa Young stopped by Sarah's office on the way to lunch. "You're certain you won't join us, dear? We're going to pick something up from the deli and go eat by the lake."

"Thank you, Marissa, but I'm way behind on things. I brought something to eat here at my desk."

"Are you sure you're feeling all right? Nobody would have minded if you had taken a few extra days for yourself."

"I'm fine. Really. You go ahead with the others, and have a nice lunch."

Sarah waited anxiously after the women had gone, and until Anthony Shapiro left with Harrison Hodge. At last she was alone in the office suite. She hurried into Shapiro's private office.

"The fastest printer Hewlett-Packard makes," Sarah mumbled to herself minutes later, "and it feels like somebody lubricated the gears with molasses." She quickly read the travel itinerary being printed. Shapiro had flown to Miami, then on to Bermuda, then returned the following day. The quickie trip had taken place nearly six months before his divorce.

She stopped suddenly. Something had creaked outside Shapiro's door.

Sarah's heart sped up even more. As loudly as her pulse pounded in her head she probably wouldn't hear if Shapiro returned and shouted at her.

She closed out that file and quickly ran next door, to Mr. Hodge's office. Once there she keyed in a specified sequence of numbers, then typed: "I KNOW WHAT YOU'RE DOING! I WILL EXPOSE YOU!"

Sarah entered the necessary command. The words she had typed would scroll endlessly across every screen in the office in big, bold letters until deleted at each station. When traced, as it was certain to be, the originator of the message would show as Harrison Hodge—president of ISI.

The only person with ready access to Mr. Hodge's computer was his private secretary, Tracy Leigon—Fireplug Woman herself, with the little toy feet.

Sarah smiled, immensely pleased with her plan.

Thirty minutes later Sarah exited the women's rest room to see what all the fuss was about.

Marvin Jamison's eyes widened perceptibly when he read the message on his monitor's screen, unaware that Sarah was watching. He feigned a laugh of dismissal and quickly erased the message, but beads of perspiration dotted his upper lip.

Anthony Shapiro read his message, then scowled and shut his office door.

Since Tracy Leigon had not returned from lunch,

Sarah nonchalantly positioned herself beside Tracy's desk, watching a telephone extension light up. She carefully lifted the receiver as if making a call, and eavesdropped.

"Everybody knows," Shapiro was saying. "It's on all the computer screens." He read the message aloud.

"Was it him?" A woman's voice.

"Who else could it be?"

A silence followed. "What does he want?"

"I don't know, but we need to talk. Can you meet me around four-thirty today?"

"The usual place?"

"Perfect."

They hung up.

Unable to see Cosmo Rivers's reaction behind the closed door to the rubber room, Sarah fabricated a reason to go inside.

"Hey, there!" Cosmo said as she entered. "Seen any kamikaze child molesters today, Sarah?"

Marissa Young came in right behind Sarah. She apologized for interrupting their discussion.

Sarah left, but remained outside the door long enough to hear Marissa accuse Cosmo of generating the message.

Cosmo said he couldn't remember if it was him or not. Said he had been "astral-projecting through the ethers with subsequent deletion of all temporo-spatial recall." He said if the message "included photos of nubile young women having sex with African wildebeests," it very likely came from him.

Sarah had seen, when she had first entered his office, that Cosmo had already deleted his message.

In the middle of the afternoon Sarah pulled a third ancient phone bill from its folder in the storage room and replaced the rubber band.

"Yes!" she exclaimed under her breath.

She hoisted the dust-covered box back into position. The room was unbelievably musty, and she'd gone through more than twenty boxes before finding her treasures. She stifled a sneeze, then adjusted the stack. Every carton was back in the exact order she had found it. She stuffed the sheets of paper inside her skirt and hurried to the door.

She peeked into the interior hallway, scanning the offices nearby. Nobody in sight. A sudden commotion came from Rivers's office as Sarah stepped into the hall; then his door partially opened. Marissa Young stood with her back to Sarah, telling Cosmo that he should know better. In the entire year that Marissa had been there, Sarah had never heard the woman raise her voice. Marissa wasn't exactly yelling, but for her, it was pretty loud.

Cosmo angled his head and peered around Marissa toward Sarah, then at the storage-room door. His eyes narrowed warily, but he didn't acknowledge Sarah at all. He slowly got out of his chair and closed his office door.

Sarah hurried back to her desk and stowed the stolen invoices in her bag.

* * *

"The man we're after may look something like this," Det. Jim Moyers said. He presented a six-year-old photograph of Scott Corbin.

"Or not," Jack Barnaby added. "He's a master of disguise, which is why we're here."

They stood outside the entrance to a black-box theater at the University of Texas, speaking with Mr. Venard Christian, chairman of the drama department. Something medieval-looking was being rehearsed inside.

Christian was a dumpy little man with pasty-white skin, shoulder-length hair, and a Vandyke beard. He said he hadn't seen anybody resembling Corbin, but suggested they try theatrical makeup and supply shops. Said there were several in the neighborhood.

It was nearly six P.M. when Anthony Shapiro swung his leased Jaguar into the driveway of the lake house. He glanced at Lil's Mercedes and hurried inside.

ISI had purchased the prime property four years earlier as a corporate retreat. A four-bedroom beige stucco with Spanish-tile roof, the house and its plantings afforded privacy from shouting-distance neighbors and sat well back from the farm-to-market-2147 access road. This particular area was known as Bay Country, a Bay West subdivision of Horseshoe Bay. Texans took great pride in this luxury development on prized, constant-level Lake LBJ, valued even more because it was named for former president of the

United States and local good ol' boy Lyndon Baines Johnson.

Once inside, Shapiro checked two terraces before he found his elegantly coifed and bejeweled lady on the shaded patio off the dining area. Rather than appearing the cool, sophisticated woman he had recently danced with at the country club, Lil sat stiffly upright, tan arms interlocked over her chest, swinging one crossed leg with a vengeance. She was pissed, big-time.

Shapiro pushed his thick glasses up on his nose and opened the sliding glass door. He apologized for being late—the traffic between his house and Lake LBJ had been frightful.

Lil glared at him.

"I had to go home first," he explained. "My burglar alarm went off again."

Crow's-feet momentarily showed around her striking eyes. "He broke into your home again? The same day he sent the message?"

"Do you really believe it's the same person?"

"It has to be one of two." She frowned, then shook her head. "But burglary isn't Marv's style." She paused, watching Shapiro's face. "Did the bastard find anything?"

"Hey . . . I'm not stupid."

"Still, he knows too much, doesn't he?"

"Is *that* ever an understatement."

"What are you going to do?"

"Sit tight for now."

"He's dangerous." She uncrossed her long legs and stood. "Have you sold the stock yet?"

"Some of it."

"When will you get the money?"

"I told you, the divorce waves must settle first."

The lithe woman nodded slowly, then seemed to relax. After a beat she put her arms around Shapiro's neck and kissed him. He cupped a full breast in one hand and they began to pet. One elegantly manicured hand slowly eased down between them, searching for where his erection should've been.

Lillian pulled back, surprised. "What's the matter?"

Shapiro let out a sharp sigh and turned away from her. "I'm sorry," he said. "I guess that threat on my computer upset me more than I realized."

"Apparently. You've never had this problem before."

"I'm worried, Lil. Really worried. I've worked too hard for too long to let this bastard tear everything apart."

Lillian saw a look in Shapiro's eyes she had never witnessed before—something downright frightening. She asked, "What are you going to do?"

"Same thing I always do . . . whatever it takes to survive."

# Chapter Twenty-Four

Sarah was momentarily taken aback when she saw an unfamiliar man approach her kitchen door. Then Scott Corbin came inside, removed his wig and dark beard, and took her in his arms.

"I missed you today," he said.

"I missed you too."

She kissed him full on the lips, then said, "I have good news." She excitedly told him about her day at the office—finding Shapiro's flight itinerary to Bermuda and the invoices from the phone company. And about people's reactions to the screensaver message.

Corbin was delighted. Seconds later he turned up the TV's volume when a news flash came on. A woman reporter stood outside an apartment building where someone had been "viciously murdered by the Chameleon." The reporter gave Corbin's name, then showed a photograph taken when he had first been confined to prison.

Corbin switched off the TV. "He's really setting me up this time."

"We'll prove that you're innocent, Scott. Somehow."

Sarah hurried to retrieve the invoices she had found, and presented them to Corbin. She had gone two months farther back than he'd requested, just in case.

"Perfect," he said, scanning the pages. "These show every call placed through the PBX. Not only the number called, but the originating extension, length of each call, and time of day. I've prayed for five years that EBS kept these records."

Sarah took dinner from the freezer while Scott pored over the detailed invoices. He had said he loved Italian food, and her homemade lasagna was tasty—even better after being frozen, then warmed up again. She hoped he wouldn't mind that it contained no meat. With lots of garlic bread and Caesar salad, the lasagna would prove what a good cook she was.

Scott not only complimented Sarah on the delicious dinner, he asked for seconds.

Later, after carefully reviewing the telephone-company invoices, Corbin said, "I was right about who made the calls to the escort service—that was Frank Russett's extension. He made three calls in one month, all late at night."

"That ties him to the prostitute," Sarah said, "but not necessarily to Rhonda."

Scott inhaled deeply. "You know, maybe Russett didn't make those calls. If somebody knew that our PBX calls were logged, he might purposely have used Russett's phone."

"Who?"

"Marv Jamison knew I was going to see Rhonda

that night. And he didn't like it one bit when I raised a question about how much he was paying contract programmers."

"What happened?"

"He told me in no uncertain terms what I could do to myself. That was less than a week before Rhonda was killed."

Sarah sat silent for a moment. "I really thought Cosmo would turn out to be the Chameleon."

"He may be, but I always sensed that Cosmo disliked Jamison. If Rivers was the Chameleon, he'd more than likely have used Jamison's phone to call the escort service, to set Marvin up." Corbin paused for a moment. "I really need to get inside Cosmo's place. Can you imagine the rat's nest he must live in?" He set the invoices on the table. "Then again, Shapiro had the most to lose if the sale didn't go through. If he knew what I was telling Rhonda, he would definitely not have wanted her to pass it on."

"The only person you haven't mentioned is Tad Roman . . . and I agree. I can't imagine Tad doing anything bad to anybody."

Corbin nodded, then raised his brow. "What do they always say about serial killers? The ones you least suspect?"

Detective Moyers parked their unmarked car on Guadalupe Street at ten o'clock the following morning and accompanied Jack Barnaby inside Shakespeare & Company Theatrical Supply. As they had at several similar businesses, they asked if anybody had recently purchased a quantity of materials that might be used as disguises.

"Lots of people buy costumes and makeup," the lean clerk drawled. He threw Barnaby an appraising look.

Barnaby shot his cuffs and adjusted his necktie, quickly looking away.

Jim Moyers presented the photograph of Scott Corbin to the clerk.

"I don't know . . . maybe." The clerk pressed a painted fingernail to his lipstick-coated lips. "Is this an old picture?"

"About five years," Barnaby replied brusquely.

"So he could have worked out quite a bit since then. The man I'm thinking of had a much better body . . . I mean, from what I can see in this picture. And a mustache. He wasn't this heavy. And he held one arm funny, you know?" The clerk was silent for several moments. "No, I'm positive . . . I'm terrible with names, but I'd never forget such a handsome face. This is definitely the man I saw. He was in here yesterday, midmorning. From Boerne." The clerk looked at a wall clock. "Just about twenty-four hours ago."

Barnaby said, "Don't you watch TV? This picture is being shown at least fifteen times a day."

"How uncouth," the clerk responded. "Who watches TV with so many more interesting things to do? Personally, I'd rather go dancing or listen to some really good jazz." He batted his eyelashes.

Barnaby shook his head. "Can you give us a list of the things he bought?"

"Of course."

Moyers asked, "Did he use a credit card?"

"Paid cash. Surprising, really . . . almost nobody does anymore."

Sarah's message on the computer monitors had created a flurry of activity. Mr. Hodge and Mr. Shapiro spent most of the day questioning office workers, trying to determine who was the culprit. Other than Mr. Hodge's asking Sarah if she had seen or heard anything that might make her suspicious, they did not interview her. Tracy Leigon sat unmoving at her desk like a stone frog guarding its garden.

It was difficult for Sarah to ascertain levels of concern because everybody seemed to be on edge, including herself. But if somebody in her office was setting Scott up, she had to find out who, and she needed to do it fast. The police were looking everywhere for him.

On her way to the ladies' room she saw Cosmo Rivers going into Anthony Shapiro's office. Each man stared daggers at the other.

Amanda Stowe was shaking her finger at Marvin Jamison when Sarah cautiously approached the reception desk.

Amanda was saying, ". . . tired of you promising you're gonna do something and then you don't."

"What, suddenly you're my wife? You're the one who backed out on what you said you'd do."

"It's too scary."

"How would you know till you try it? I've got

enough to worry about without your insipid whining."

Both immediately went silent when Sarah walked past.

Sarah said, "Good morning, Amanda. Marvin."

"Good morning, Sarah," Amanda replied.

Jamison didn't respond.

Sarah was straightening up her kitchen that evening when she spotted a recorked bottle of chardonnay in the refrigerator. Her first thought was that a glass of wine might relieve some of her tension, but she stopped as she reached for the bottle, closing the refrigerator door instead. She went into the bedroom and studied her reflection in the mirror. A blush colored her cheeks that she hadn't seen in . . . actually she couldn't remember ever looking so refreshed.

She thought of what Scott had said on Sunday when he became so upset with her, before they went to the lake. She had thought about it a hundred times since, and he was absolutely right.

Then again, he was right about so many things. For instance, maybe she did rely too heavily on the opinions of others. She'd never questioned this, since others seemed to know more about cars and books and plays and microwaves and . . . even a device that squeezed juice from an orange. When it came to work she trusted her own judgment implicitly, but not in matters outside the office, where she'd had no specialized training.

Why not? Why couldn't she trust herself? She was an intelligent woman . . . everybody said so.

There, she was doing it again.

Being with Scott had made Sarah realize that her judgment *could* be trusted. Everybody said he was a bad man. A murderer. Who said it? The police, newscasters on TV, all the people at the office—everybody she had known and respected. She had even said so herself at one time. Swore it on a Bible.

Sarah had once believed, with all her heart, that Scott was a despicable creature. She knew today, however, in every crevice of that same heart, that she had been dead wrong before. Scott wasn't a bad man. He was a wonderful, loving, warm, and caring man. Perhaps the first she had ever known, aside from her father—before he had changed.

Dusk descended minutes before a figure in a black windbreaker, dark trousers, cap, and running shoes slipped into the space between the bushes and the outside wall of Sarah's apartment. He moved stealthily from one window to the next, attempting to see inside. The bottom edge of one set of blinds was higher on one side than the other, allowing a shaft of light to spill out. The man knelt in the dirt to see inside Sarah's bedroom.

Sarah was standing in front of her dressing table, studying her reflection in the mirror.

He watched as she slowly removed her blouse and skirt, then hung each item in a closet. He could feel his excitement building, the growing weight of blood engorging his penis, and his need escalated even more. He imagined the scent of her hair, its texture between his fingers. He could almost touch her milky thighs as she walked past the window. So near. So delicious. A hand slipped between his legs to touch his growing hardness, but he jumped, startled, when something clanged against a pipe near his feet. The knife he used to scoop out their eyes had slipped from his jacket pocket, striking a metal pipe alongside the building.

At the same instant Sarah stopped what she was doing and looked around the room, her eyes alert, and as green and moist as wet ivy. He had looked into those eyes so many times, dreaming of the moment he would take them for himself. Fantasizing about the day he could take all of her. He would mix his essence, finally and forevermore, with hers.

He had to suppress a sudden impulse to laugh, aware that Sarah hadn't the slightest inkling of his secret urges. He could always tell. Knowing that he had deceived her was almost as exciting as the look he'd see when she realized how completely she had been misled. He would enjoy the thrill of that moment nearly as much as watching her blood spurt and flow and drip.

Sarah seemed to relax. She removed her earrings and placed them in a decorative box on the dresser.

The man breathed again and retrieved his knife. He slipped away from the window and crept around the rear of the building. It was even darker in back, near the parking area. She wouldn't see or hear him enter through the kitchen door.

* * *

Sarah studied herself in the dressing table mirror again—a tear sliding down one rosy cheek. She suddenly saw her mother's face mask her own. That mystified look in those haunting eyes.

She knew she used wine as a crutch, as her mother had before her. Exactly the way Scott had said. She did anesthetize herself against hurt and loneliness and the pain of rejection.

Correction . . . she *had* used it.

On an impulse Sarah returned to the kitchen and poured her last bottle of wine down the drain with a flourish. She flung open the kitchen door, carried the empty bottle to the trash bin outside, and smashed it to smithereens. This feeling of uneasiness would pass, and it would just have to pass on its own. She already felt better. Being with Scott made her feel so good, she would never need alcohol again to dull her senses. She had no desire to dull anything. She wanted to feel everything from this moment on. Every touch. Every caress. Every blessed moment she would ever experience with this man.

The man in black flattened himself against the building when the door opened unexpectedly. His breathing quickened and he savored the sense of excitement as his heart raced and his face flushed hot. He loved the chase—stalking his prey while they went about their mundane existences with no inkling that he was there.

Somebody had run from the open door to a trash Dumpster across the paved drive. A shattering of glass followed; then he heard feet on the pavement again. He dared to peek and his throat went dry. It was Sarah, with the shamrock-green eyes. He could just make out her face in a shaft of light cascading from her door. He touched himself again, thrilled that she was so near. She was coming to him now. A few more steps and he would leap out and cover her mouth and pull her inside before she could make a sound. She was moving closer now. He could almost feel her radiant skin.

As Sarah hurried back toward her kitchen door, something darted out of the darkness, racing straight at her.

Sarah screamed.

# Chapter Twenty-Five

A hairy brown rat scampered directly in front of Sarah's feet and disappeared beneath a parked car. Her heart was in her throat as her trembling hands felt for the kitchen door.

She did not see the figure in black advancing toward her.

"What's going on here?"

Sarah fought to catch her breath, then turned and exclaimed, "Thank God it's you, Mrs. Whitstone. The biggest, ugliest rat I ever saw just ran right in front of me."

Letty Whitstone hurried along the drive from the front of the apartment complex, her hair a fright, a rifle in her hands. "Where'd he go?"

Sarah pointed.

"With what we pay exterminators, there's no excuse for this. I'm sorry, Sarah. It won't happen again if I have to sit out here with my twenty-two every night. You go on inside now. I'll take care of that stinking rat."

Sarah didn't sleep well all night. Scott had not come home till nearly 11 P.M., then was too preoccupied to be good company. He pored over materials-and-supply orders and additional invoices she'd brought from the office, then sat up flipping channels on TV until after 2 A.M.

She hadn't even had time to set her purse under her desk the next morning when Amanda Stowe came in to ask how she was feeling.

Seconds later the receptionist freaked.

"Oh, my God," Amanda cried. She clamped a hand over her mouth, eyes wide with alarm.

Horrified, Sarah stared unbelievingly at the image assembling itself on her computer screen. A graphic depiction of a decapitated woman appeared—blood spurting from her neck and gushing in erratic rivulets down her nude form, into a widening crimson pool. A disembodied head floated to one side, cackling in a witch's voice, "Keep your mouth shut. You could be next. Keep your mouth shut. You could be next."

Something slithery seemed to coil itself in Sarah's stomach. The face on the floating head bore a distinct resemblance to her own. Sarah didn't recall later that either she or Amanda had screamed out, but when she looked up, Anthony Shapiro and Marvin Jamison were at her office entrance. Both men bore unreadable expressions, looking back and forth from the monitor's screen to Sarah's face.

The Austin Police Department sent out a High-Tech Crime unit to evaluate the animated-head message. To Sarah's great relief she had not been the sole target of the warning—it appeared on every terminal in the network. Officer Brenda Brown, the lead investigator, felt that the face depicted was generic, not intended to resemble anyone in particular. In the end they were unable to determine its origin, other than that it originated within the office network.

Sarah confided to Marissa that she suspected Cosmo Rivers. When confronted Cosmo was wearing a graphically offensive T-shirt, black shorts, and red-and-white motorcycle-racing boots. He, like everyone else in the office, denied any knowledge of the head's creator.

The High-Tech Crime unit returned to police headquarters and filed its report. Officer Brown told her associate, "This sort of prank normally wouldn't bother me, but with the Chameleon on the loose, I'm gonna let Jim Moyers know about it. He said at the meeting yesterday to report anything unusual."

Minutes later Jack Barnaby said, "Wait a minute . . . you're telling me this floating head showed up where Sarah Hill works? The same place Scott Corbin used to work?"

Moyers said, "You got it."

Sarah answered Detective Barnaby's question again. "I don't know who might have done it."

"But you wavered slightly when I asked about Mr. Rivers. Why?"

Sarah sat at her desk with detectives Barnaby and Moyers seated across from her. "I just . . . he might find it amusing, that's all."

"Was anybody amused?"

"No, it was horrible. Ask Amanda or any of the others. Everybody saw it."

"We will." Barnaby nibbled something inside his lower lip for a moment, deep in thought, then stood abruptly. "All right, ma'am. Thank you."

Out of earshot of Sarah, Barnaby told Moyers, "Ask Sergeant Fuller to put an undercover unit on Sarah Hill immediately. Her house, the office, anyplace she goes."

"You think Corbin's coming after her?"

"We'd be foolish to discount the possibility. Tell Fuller to keep his officers out of sight . . . Sarah has to go about her business naturally or Corbin will smell a trap. Meanwhile I'll sweat Cosmo Rivers a bit, find out what he's made of. If Bob Garding thinks Rivers is dangerous, he probably is. Bob wasn't often wrong."

Two men wearing Southwestern Bell windbreakers, baseball caps, and carrying a box of tools approached a dilapidated duplex in a run-down neighborhood in south Austin. Scott Corbin also wore a dark wig and full beard. The locks on the door were more sophisticated than either had expected, so Peter Buda spent five fitful minutes gaining entrance to Cosmo Rivers's apartment. None of the kids playing in the street seemed to notice.

The apartment inside was filled with sophisticated computer equipment and sound systems. Ghoulish rock-group posters hung on flat-black walls, intermingled with photos of bearded outlaws on *bad* motorcycles and skeevy women with obscenely large, tattooed breasts.

"This guy is a mental case," Corbin said. He tentatively inspected a black leather whip resting behind a bedroom door. On an adjacent wall hung six shrunken heads, their small foreheads deeply furrowed and their lifelike eyes glaring menacingly into space.

"Get a load of these," Peter said, pointing to outfits of black leather and chains in a closet. "He's into some strange shit."

In the refrigerator Corbin saw four six-packs of Lone Star beer, the dried-out remains of a pizza, huge mushrooms, and molding mung bean sprouts. A living, growing flat of grass occupied the bottom shelf. Somebody had mowed one section with a pair of orange-handled scissors, which now rested atop an open can of beer.

Scott nearly jumped out of his skin when Buda's cell phone rang.

Peter calmly answered the phone, then switched it off. "Wrong number," he said.

A locked door in the rear of the apartment required several attempts before Peter opened it. Inside was a small office complete with a personal computer. They finally gained access to Cosmo's files.

In addition to several weird and perverted Web sites tagged as "favorites," Cosmo maintained personal and confidential records on nearly everybody at ISI—investment accounts, bank balances, credit-card statements. He also had ISI's supply orders, vendor accounts, and delivery schedules. Scott was beside himself with his good fortune.

One file indicated that Marvin Jamison had received more than $600,000 in ISI stock from the buyout of EBS, while Shapiro netted $20 million. Two people identified only as Frick and Frack had received $12 million between them.

"They must've been the original partners that Shapiro bought out," Corbin surmised.

Frank Russett got $350,000. Rivers received only $100,000, but had been a fairly new employee at the time of the buyout. Cosmo's current investment account totaled over $415,000. Sarah had received $125,000, though she had been with the company for several years. Judging from this information, women had consistently received less than their male counterparts.

A joint futures-trading account was registered to both Marvin Jamison and somebody named Benard. It appeared that Cosmo had been receiving regular monthly transfers of between three thousand and five thousand dollars from that account into his own investment account.

Corbin told Peter, "I'll give you odds that Cosmo is blackmailing Jamison. If Jamison killed Rhonda, Cosmo knows about it."

Peter said, "What if Jamison paid Rivers to kill Rhonda so he could collect his six hundred thou? Maybe he's still paying Rivers off."

"Look at this. As ISI's purchasing agent, Jamison has been overpaying like crazy for hardware components, then getting kickbacks from the suppliers. Big ones. It's all right here."

Without warning Peter clutched Corbin's arm. "Shhh," he said. "Listen."

The chugging sound of a motor rapidly approached, advancing until it was directly outside the window of the small office. Then it shut off.

"Shit."

"What do we do now?" Scott's pulse drummed loudly in his ears. He had recognized the low, rumbling, *po-tato-po-tato* sound instantly: a Harley-Davidson.

"Be quiet and listen," Peter said.

Somebody walked heavily up the gravel driveway, then onto the porch. A loud knock rattled the front door and a man's voice called out Cosmo's name. Seconds later Scott heard keys being inserted into two different locks, and somebody came inside.

"Hey, Rivers," the gruff voice shouted. "You in here?"

Scott quietly turned off the computer and followed Peter's lead. They stood beside the door to the hallway, their backs against the wall.

The man called out again. "Hey, asshole. Where are you?"

Scott could imagine the huge Hell's Angel who had come inside. Beads of perspiration on Peter's upper lip and forehead were nothing compared to the ones streaming down Scott's sides. He was roasting hot beneath his wig and beard. Even breathing had become an effort.

The refrigerator door opened. Something popped,

then hissed, like a beer being opened. After a few silent moments they heard a long sigh. Heavy footsteps approached the door where they stood.

Scott tensed all over. He could imagine the fight that would ensue. The biker in the hallway belched loudly, then turned and walked away. The unmistakable sound of a man urinating into a toilet followed, and went on for what seemed an eternity. The toilet never flushed.

Agonizing moments later the front door slammed. The man returned to his motorcycle, fired up, and rode away.

"Oh, no," Sarah said.

Sarah returned home from work and set her purse and keys on the kitchen counter. She went to check for packages outside her front door when she noticed a car easing into a shady spot up the street. Except for being dark blue instead of white, the car was identical to the one those Homicide detectives had driven, with black rubber posts on the front bumpers. Two men sat in the car attempting not to look her way.

Sarah quickly shut the door and raced to the phone. A woman at Peter Buda's favorite sports bar said he had left not ten minutes earlier. He and his buddy.

There was no answer on Peter's cellular.

Sarah expected Peter to pull into the driveway any second, with Scott in the seat beside him. She had to warn them. But how?

She grabbed a package of blueberry muffins from the freezer and hurriedly filled two cups with water.

She ignored the water she spilled on the counter and chipped a nail jabbing the start button on the microwave.

Minutes later Sarah pulled alongside the two police officers hunched down in their seats trying desperately to be inconspicuous. She rolled down her Accord's window, beeped her horn, and waved. "Hello, there . . . I brought you some coffee and hot muffins."

The undercover officers glanced nervously at each other, then rolled down the window nearest Sarah.

"Do you work with detectives Barnaby and Moyers?"

Peter's car turned the corner just then and headed straight for Sarah's apartment. Scott Corbin sat in the passenger seat, laughing at something.

Sarah's heart leaped into her throat when she saw Scott. No doubt feeling safe to finally be at home, he was removing his beard.

Sarah immediately passed the tray of goodies through her car window, *accidentally* leaning hard against her horn. She had forgotten just how loud it could be.

The closest detective spilled coffee on his shirt. At the same instant Peter saw what was happening and immediately took off.

"My God, that's the Chameleon," exclaimed the officer in the passenger seat. He held up a photograph of Scott Corbin. "I recognize his profile. It really is him." He grabbed the mike hanging on the dash.

Sarah's decorative tray and china teacups clattered

to the pavement as the unmarked police car raced off to give chase.

Buda's car was fast, but no match for the vehicle closing in from behind. While Corbin anxiously kept watch behind them, Peter accelerated like a maniac, then braked furiously to avoid a near collision. He skidded around corners and, with his horn blaring, raced through three consecutive stop signs. Approaching a narrow intersection blocked by heavy traffic, he jumped a curb and slid sideways through someone's front lawn before their wheels found pavement again. He careened onto MLK Boulevard seconds later and gunned the engine.

"We're coming up on the freeway," Corbin shouted.

"Too easy to track us there," Buda said. He veered around a group of bicyclists and raced under the freeway overpass.

Scott Corbin reached for Peter's cell phone and punched in a number.

Sarah hurriedly parked her car and ran inside her apartment. The red light was blinking on her answering machine. Her hands shook when she pressed the play button.

Scott Corbin's recorded voice came through the speaker, shouting above squealing tires and wailing sirens. "Thanks for the warning, Sarah . . . they would've had us for sure. No time to talk, but you've been great. Even if I make it this time, I'll keep going . . . I've already caused too much trouble. Get rid of all my clothes and disguises. The cops will search your place for sure. And erase this—"

Two fast explosions followed, like firecrackers; then the line went dead.

# CHAPTER TWENTY-SIX

Scott Corbin had been right. When Sarah returned from the Dumpster behind H-E-B Food Stores the police were at her door. Thank God Scott had warned her to throw away his things. On her own she had thought to wipe down any and all surfaces he might have touched, including the computer keyboard.

Detectives Barnaby and Moyers arrived minutes later with a warrant. Moyers directed policemen who swarmed over her apartment, searching everywhere.

Jack Barnaby came to where Sarah sat on her living room sofa. Her hands were wet with perspiration and her blouse felt soaked through. Margot watched anxiously from Sarah's lap.

"You are living very dangerously, young woman."

"How do you mean?"

"Forget whatever this man told you and listen to me. I have a wife and a daughter very much like you. Any one of you could be Scott Corbin's next victim. He's a killer who has already murdered three women since he hit town. Did you know you can go to jail for harboring a fugitive?"

Sarah swallowed hard. "What makes you think I've harbored anybody?"

"Don't play games with me, Sarah . . . we don't have time for it, and I sure as hell don't have the patience. Where did he go?"

"I don't know what you're talking about."

"Oh, I think you do. You lied about not seeing him on the street, then pretended you didn't know he was alive and out of prison. Why would you do that, Sarah?"

Her heart pounded unmercifully. She had never been so frightened, except the first day Scott arrived and she had thought he was going to kill her. Now she feared that *he* might not survive. She struggled to hide her anxiety.

Shaking her head, Sarah said, "I've told you everything I know, Mr. Barnaby. I took some muffins and coffee to your colleagues in the car across the street, when suddenly their tires screeched and their siren started screaming, and they took off after another car. They nearly ran me over."

"Who was the other man?"

"What other man?"

"The one driving. Corbin was the passenger."

"I don't know anything about that."

"You were there, Sarah. You saw what happened."

"I didn't see. I was delivering a tray of muffins and coffee."

Sarah knew that if she was to be believed, she had to convince herself that what she was saying was true. No matter how rough Barnaby got, how much she perspired, or how badly she trembled inside, she had to stick to her story.

Detective Moyers came back into the living room.

"Find anything?" asked Barnaby.

"Not yet. The techs are dusting for prints."

"He still running?"

Moyers nodded. "They went out toward the airport, then turned south. They're sticking to surface streets in residential neighborhoods."

"Damn," Barnaby said.

Corbin and Buda raced wildly toward the next intersection when a police motorcycle unexpectedly turned the corner, heading straight toward them. A long string of cars followed behind the motorcycle, their headlights on.

"Watch out," Scott shouted, but it was too late. The motorcycle ran up over the curb, dumping the patrolman into a stand of bushes.

Buda plowed straight ahead, nearly slamming into a hearse. Perspiration poured down his florid face as he veered sharply to his right, then cut back across the procession. They sped down the one-way street in the wrong direction, on the passenger sides of oncoming vehicles. At the next intersection Peter turned sharply back across the line of cars and down another one-way street against traffic. He slammed on his brakes unexpectedly, screeching to a halt, then backed up and shot down a narrow alleyway. The Camry's wheels spun gravel as Peter gunned the engine again, and the muscles in his jaw worked furiously.

It took nearly an hour for police to complete their search of Sarah's apartment and car. Jim Moyers returned and took Barnaby aside. They'd found no evidence that anybody other than Sarah had occupied the dwelling. Sarah had explained the absence of even her own fingerprints by saying that she always cleaned her apartment thoroughly every week, and had done so earlier that day. Moyers said that they had found footprints, however, left by athletic shoes in the soft dirt outside Sarah's windows—mostly her bedroom window.

Barnaby considered what Moyers said, then asked, "Still no Corbin?"

Moyers shook his head. "Not yet."

"Dammit! What happened?"

"They blasted right through some funeral procession, then disappeared down a back alley in southeast Austin. Probably abandoned their vehicle and are on foot. The neighborhood's been sealed off and our guys are going door-to-door now. K-nine units have been called in."

"Then let's go. I want to be there when we bring this bastard down."

Barnaby returned to Sarah. "You're gonna be real sorry you lied to me."

Sarah didn't answer. She hugged Margot closer to her chest.

"Are you aware that somebody has been watching you at night?"

She stiffened. "No, sir."

"His footprints are all over the dirt outside your bedroom window." Barnaby inhaled deeply, then slowly let his air out. "There's no doubt in my mind that it was the Chameleon."

Sarah brushed a tear from her cheek. She also harbored no doubt that Barnaby was correct—if somebody had indeed been out there, it was the Chameleon. But she couldn't admit what she knew—that the Chameleon had either been looking for Scott or had come to kill her and make it appear that Corbin had done it. If she even hinted that Scott had been there, regardless of his reasons, Barnaby would arrest her immediately. How could she help Scott from jail?

Barnaby continued, "We're the best friends you've got, Miss Hill. Right now we may be the only ones. This man is the worst kind of human predator, and he preys on women like yourself. Do you have anything to tell me before I go?"

"No, sir."

The detective's face flushed red. "Lock your doors and windows and don't open them for anybody. I'm ordering a twenty-four-hour guard on your home until we have this man in custody."

Sarah sat by her phone all evening, uncertain what to wish for. Should it ring? Should it not ring? Was he any place where he could call? Would it be safe to call?

More than anything she wanted Scott to come home, but that was impossible. Police would be all over the neighborhood. She wished he could get word to her that he was all right. Or tell her where to meet him. They could go away somewhere. Anywhere, so long as they'd be together.

She turned off the answering machine just in case,

but knew that he wouldn't call. Couldn't call. She wondered how long it required to tap a phone line. Minutes? A few hours at most.

Where would he go? Possibly to Peter's place, but Sarah had never asked where Peter lived. Where was he now? Down near Brownsville? On the way to Mexico? Or California or New York?

With the entire state looking for him—no, the entire country—and his image imprinted on every conscious mind, Scott would almost certainly be caught. His protective camouflage was buried deep in a trash container behind a supermarket across town. But he was as clever as anybody she had ever known. If, through some miracle, he did manage to escape, he would disappear. Go to another country, perhaps. That was what he had been telling her on the phone. She wished she could have saved those precious final words, but had been afraid to, and wisely so. Detective Moyers had checked the answering machine straightaway. Scott was saying good-bye. He had called to let her know that he cared, but it was over. He would never see her again. And he was right.

If he stayed he would be shot on sight.

Scott Corbin and Peter Buda were speeding down a residential alley just after dark when Peter spotted an open garage. Having gained a slight visual lead over their pursuers, Buda extinguished his headlights and Corbin frantically shoved aside a rusty lawn mower and dust-covered bicycle to make room. Scott lowered the overhead door the instant the car was inside. Brief moments later they held their breath, cringing, as a long line of police vehicles raced by.

They crouched near a front fender of the car, drenched with perspiration, listening intently for several minutes after the last siren disappeared into the night. The Camry's engine began to tick, cooling down.

"We can't stay here," Peter whispered.

"We sure as hell can't leave," Corbin replied. He thought for a moment, then asked, "Where'd you learn to drive like that?"

"Bristol, before they built the new track."

Through a crack between the side door and its frame, a slice of moonlight penetrated the pitch black of the garage. A dog barked somewhere down the alley.

"Their dogs will sniff us out," Peter said.

"You don't know if that's a police dog."

"You wanna stay and find out?"

Something scurried about on an overhead shelf. Corbin's perspiration stung his eyes and a stench of mildew assaulted his nose. He mopped his brow again. The night was roasting hot, the humidity unbearable.

"You go ahead, Peter," Scott said. "They're not after you."

"You're sure?"

"I'm sure."

"What'll you do?"

"I'll think of something."

They managed to shake hands in the darkness. Peter whispered, "Good luck, man."

"You, too, Peter. Thanks for everything."

Buda quickly slipped through the door and disappeared into the night.

Scott Corbin sat perfectly still, exploring his options. His thoughts raced nearly as fast as his pulse. Suddenly, hearing a different sound, he held his breath again, alert, wary. A man's voice was saying something in the distance. Another male voice responded.

Corbin tried to wipe the sweat out of his eyes, but it only made them burn even worse. He struggled to suppress the panic welling up within him. He heard a voice again, closer this time.

The men sounded Hispanic, fairly young, and were advancing slowly in Scott's direction. Something metallic squeaked, followed by a faint crunching on gravel as they approached. Scott could not identify footsteps, but he knew what he was hearing.

Seconds later Corbin stepped from a narrow pathway between two garages, into the moonlit alley. As casually as possible he pushed a bicycle toward the approaching men. His chest was bare and his undershirt stuffed inside his trousers, along with his wig and beard. Smudges of dirt crisscrossed his face and chest. The bicycle he had stolen from the garage had a flat front tire.

When close enough to speak Scott said, "Hey, *hombres . . . Qué pasa?*"

"Who is that?"

"I'm Robert. Who are you?"

The young Mexican men clearly did not recognize

him. They advanced cautiously, then told him their names. They asked what he was doing there.

Scott said he had been visiting a señorita up the way, and his bicycle got a flat tire when it came time to go home.

They stepped down from their own bikes to look. They inspected the tire, but said they had nothing with them to fix the flat.

"How far you live?" Scott asked.

The man named Carlos pointed up the alley. "Two more blocks." He angled his head slightly and asked, "What girl you came to see?"

A siren wailed in the distance. Scott frantically searched for a name. "Maria?"

The man named Juan half laughed. "Maria Rodriguez?" He threw an amused look at Carlos.

Carlos smiled knowingly. "*Sí,* we know Maria. Everybody knows Maria."

Scott returned their smiles and shook his head. He wiped his forehead, making a show of appraising both "his" bicycle and the two others. All had seen better days. "Somebody maybe wanna trade?"

Carlos looked at Scott's bicycle, then at his friend. "My bike is *más* better than yours."

Scott took several bills from his pocket, counting them carefully. The dog he'd heard barking earlier was joined by a second one, and both sounded closer than before. "Then I'll pay the difference. I live too far from here, you know?"

"How much?"

After several tense moments of negotiating, Scott rode away on Carlos's bicycle, having grossly overpaid. He donned his dark wig and beard as soon as he was out of sight of the two delighted young men, then pedaled quickly away from the barking dogs.

Sarah turned up the TV's volume when the eleven-o'clock news came on. A white-haired newscaster reported, "Earlier today Austin detectives made visual contact with a man believed to be Scott Corbin, the notorious serial killer tagged 'the Chameleon' by police six years ago."

An old picture of Corbin filled the screen.

The reporter continued, "Our information is sketchy at this point, but we will bring you live updates as new reports come in. What is known is that Scott Corbin was convicted of the savage murders of three Austin women nearly six years ago, and was charged with killing three others. Corbin is also thought to be responsible for three recent slayings in the Austin metropolitan area. A report that Corbin was executed by lethal injection on January twelfth of this year at the state prison in Huntsville, Texas, is now known to be false. A spokesperson at the prison says that an investigation is under way regarding the source of that report. It is not known at this time exactly when or how Corbin escaped from the prison facility. A manhunt is under way in Austin at this very moment. Police say they expect to have Corbin in custody within the hour."

# Chapter Twenty-seven

Det. Jack Barnaby had finished three enormous cups of Starbucks coffee by nine the next morning. He paced as he spoke from the front of the room on the second floor of police headquarters. Standing along-side five other Homicide detectives, Jim Moyers stopped testing his personal global positioning system device when Barnaby began to speak.

"... found the car abandoned in a garage on Wilburn Street at three A.M." Barnaby was saying. "No sign of either Corbin or the man who was driving. Both are on foot, so they can't have gone far. No stolen vehicles were reported in the area overnight. My biggest concern is that they might take a hostage... they may have already done so, and Corbin won't hesitate to kill. Officers in the neighborhood have been instructed to shoot Corbin on sight. I advise you to do the same if you encounter him."

Linda Torres asked, "What do we know about the other man?"

"Very little. They were driving at high speeds the entire time officers had him in sight. Detective Barlow described him as Caucasian, mid-thirties, black hair, olive complexion. We don't have a name. And they may have split up."

"Who was the car registered to?"

Barnaby blinked rapidly several times. "It was reported stolen two weeks ago in Dallas by a woman named Sandra Erwin, an insurance company executive."

Melissa McBain asked, "How's the motorcycle cop who dumped his bike during the chase?"

"Aside from bending a turn signal," Moyers said, "the only thing hurt was his pride."

When nobody asked anything more Barnaby said, "All right, guys, let's get out on the streets and find this bastard."

Sarah was bombarded for most of the morning by office coworkers who had heard about her close call with the Chameleon.

Anthony Shapiro asked, "What made the police think he was after you?"

"They found his footprints in the dirt outside my bedroom window."

Marvin Jamison asked, "How could they be sure whose footprints they were?"

"I don't know . . . that's just what they told me. Maybe they have plaster molds or something."

"And the man they're saying was Scott Corbin," Shapiro said, "you didn't see his face?"

"No. I was taking some muffins and coffee to the policemen across the street."

Marissa Young asked, "What were they doing out there, dear?"

"Watching my apartment in case the Chameleon showed up, I suppose . . . because of my report when I thought I saw him over on Congress."

Cosmo Rivers peered over Marissa's shoulder. "Face it, Sarah, you were Chameleon bait. Cast a maiden upon the waters—"

Tad Roman interrupted, saying, "That isn't very nice, Cosmo. Can't you see that Sarah is upset?"

Rivers mimicked Roman. "Can't you see that the innocent maiden is still alive, Tad? The big, bad Chameleon didn't take the bait. Yet."

"It's all very frightening," Amanda said, ignoring Rivers. "You must have been terrified, Sarah."

That afternoon Amanda's voice came through the speakerphone. "Long distance on line two, Sarah . . . a Mr. Bellingham. Are you feeling any better?"

"A little, thank you." Sarah glanced at the clock on her office wall—two forty-five P.M. She depressed the phone's lighted plastic button, wondering which bank employee had messed up their system this time. The software was virtually foolproof if people would only follow a few simple directions.

Out of habit she forced herself to smile before speaking into the mouthpiece. "This is Sarah Hill . . . how may I help you?"

"Sarah, just listen before you say anything . . . my name is Bellingham and I'm a client from somewhere out of town. Can you meet me tonight?"

Sarah almost swallowed her tongue to keep from shouting her glee. She managed to sound reasonably calm when she said, "Yes, I'll do that. Have you tried rebooting the computer?"

"I need some money."

"I see. How much would you estimate spending?"

"Coupla thousand . . . more if you can get it."

"All right."

"They'll be watching your car, so leave it wherever it is. Make sure you're not followed. Rent an inconspicuous car, but not from one of the big companies, and try not to use your credit card. I'll meet you at the Diamond Shamrock station at eight o'clock. Twenty-five-twenty Broadway. Okay?"

"What city was that again?"

"Sorry. San Antonio."

"That will be fine, Mr. Bellingham. I'll speak with you then."

"Great, see you tonight. And Sarah . . . thank you." Corbin hung up.

Exhilarated that he'd called, Sarah felt her mind whirl. She suddenly had a zillion things to do. She'd have to get to the bank before closing. Rent a car. Ask Mrs. Whitstone to take care of Margot. What about clothes? She had no idea where they might go or when she'd be coming back.

Marissa Young was at the reception desk minutes later, going over the week's appointments with Amanda Stowe. Both looked up when Sarah approached, carrying her purse and obviously in a hurry.

"My head is hurting too badly to concentrate on

work," Sarah said. "I think I'll go home and go to bed."

"Of course," Marissa said. "After all you've been through, I'm not surprised."

Amanda added, "Take a couple of aspirin and put a cold cloth on your forehead, Sarah. That always helps me."

"Thanks, I will." Sarah hurried out the door.

Rather than taking the elevator directly to the parking garage as usual, Sarah exited on the second level. She hurried past closed office doors toward the fire exit at the end of the hall, praying that she wouldn't see anybody she knew. Two women came out of a rest room, animatedly talking, and walked straight toward Sarah. She had seen them before, but didn't know their names. They smiled as they passed by, never slowing their conversation.

Sarah opened the door at the end of the corridor and hurried into the concrete-and-steel stairwell down to street level. Halfway down she stopped short, listening. Somebody was behind her, their footfalls hurrying down the metal stairs from above.

Sarah quickly reversed course and began walking up the stairs. A blond man carrying a brown attaché case raced past and down to street level, then flew through the door to the outside. Sarah turned around and followed him out the same door onto the sidewalk.

She donned her sunglasses, attempting to appear as inconspicuous as possible. She walked over to San Jacinto, stopping twice to look behind her in the reflections of storefront windows. She continued on to the Four Seasons Hotel, where a doorman hailed her a taxi. She had the driver take her to the Austin North Hilton, in Highland Mall. Once there she looked up auto-rental agencies, and reserved a car over the phone. Fairly certain by now that she hadn't been followed, she took another taxi to her bank, then on to Able Car-for-You on Manchaca Road. Her driver's license, a blank personal check confirming her residence address, and a three-hundred-dollar cash deposit put her into a 1999 Toyota Corolla.

It was growing dark outside when Robert Garding hurried into Sarah's apartment. "Find her yet?"

Jack Barnaby shook his head. "She left work in the middle of the afternoon. The receptionist said she got a long-distance call around three, then suddenly took sick. No idea where the call came from."

"We put out an APB," Jim Moyers said.

Garding said, "I assume her car is gone."

"No, but her cat is," Barnaby replied. "Her car's in the parking garage at her office. She called to have her landlady pick up her cat, but didn't say where she was going. Said she'd be back in a couple of days."

Robert Garding rubbed the back of his neck, deep in thought.

Moyers asked, "Can you think of any place else she might have gone, Bob? We don't know for sure that she intends to meet Corbin. Does she have relatives nearby? Close friends?"

Garding slowly shook his head. "She doesn't have

anybody. It's hard for me to believe she'd hook up with Corbin under any circumstances, but if she did, that's how the bastard got to her. What kind of life can she have? She'd be an easy mark."

"And Corbin could make her believe he's the Easter bunny," Barnaby added.

Garding paused, then said, "I'm sure the airport and bus terminals are covered."

Moyers nodded. "We already had people looking for Corbin, so as soon as we realized that Sarah had skipped, we circulated her picture, too."

"She can't get far with no vehicle," Barnaby said, "which means Corbin is still in town somewhere."

"Maybe he picked her up."

"Or had the other guy pick her up. We still don't know who he is, either."

Garding said, "What if she rented a car?"

"Harry Wilkes is checking with rental companies now, and Melissa McBain is working on a subpoena for Sarah's credit-card records. If she rented a vehicle, we'll have a description and license-plate number by morning."

Friday evening traffic was heavy in San Antonio when a maroon Toyota Corolla turned into the Diamond Shamrock service station at two minutes before eight P.M. Three cars and a pickup truck were getting gas at the pumps. Sarah pulled to an outside pump and got out of the car. She looked around nervously but did not see anybody resembling Scott Corbin. She ran her Visa card through the slot and began fueling.

"Clean your windshield, ma'am?"

Her heart almost stopped. She would never have recognized the bearded man in the grungy T-shirt, but his voice was unmistakable. "Yes," Sarah said. "Thank you."

As soon as the tank was full Corbin joined her inside the small car. "Did you use your credit card at the pump?"

"Yes . . . I'm sorry, Scott, I forgot."

"It's all right. Turn left when you pull out, heading south."

She did as he said. At the first intersection he said, "Turn left again and go around the block. We need to go back in the opposite direction."

She had gone less than a full block when he said, "Pull over."

Confused, she pulled to the side of the road and stopped. "What?" she asked.

"Come here." Corbin pulled her to him and they embraced. He kissed her long and deep. "God, I've missed you," he said.

"Oh, Scott, I missed you, too. I was so afraid for you." After a moment she said, "Where can we go?"

"Back to Austin."

"But you can't. Somebody will recognize you."

"I don't have a choice, Sarah. I need a couple of days to let things settle down; then I have to force the Chameleon to come after me. It's the only way I'll ever be free."

A thousand questions filled Sarah's mind, but the most important ones had already been answered.

Scott was alive. He was all right, and she was there with him.

Robert Garding drove by Sarah's apartment once again. He pulled his pickup into the parking lot and circled through the back, his eyes searching each vehicle beneath the covered parking. Sarah's space remained vacant. No lights burned inside her apartment. He cruised through the complex at idle speed, nodding toward two plainclothes officers caught in his headlights at the edge of a fence. If they recognized him they gave no indication.

An ominous feeling permeated his gut. He sincerely hoped that Sarah was all right. Poor girl was like a scared squirrel on a highway, not knowing which way to run. She didn't understand the ways of the world. She reminded him a little of Mary Beth when they had first met in college—putting up a front that she always knew what she was doing no matter what, then locking her doors behind her. Sometimes sobbing into the night.

Garding sucked in a long breath. He needed a cigarette. He suddenly realized just how worried he must be—he hadn't smoked in five years. Hadn't thought about a cigarette for nearly three. Hell, he didn't even like the way they smelled anymore.

Marvin Jamison's excitement escalated as he pumped furiously into the pale figure writhing beneath him. He peaked at the exact moment she began to shudder, and felt her nails digging into his bare back. He collapsed onto her, breathing hard. Only when Amanda's fists continued pounding on his shoulders did he remember. He quickly raised himself on both elbows and removed the plastic bag covering her head.

Amanda coughed, gasping for air, and the dusky blue color of her lips slowly returned to pink.

"That was fantastic," Marvin said. "Didn't I tell you?"

"I nearly passed out."

"Yeah, but that was the biggest come yet. Probably the best you ever had, right?"

"I feel like I'm gonna throw up, Marv. My head is spinning."

"Sit up. I'll fix you another drink."

Jamison padded over to the motel room's dresser and refilled both glasses with vodka and tonic water. On the way back to the bed he switched on the TV.

An attractive middle-aged brunette woman with a white apostrophe in her hair came on-screen, sitting at her news desk. She reported that Scott Corbin had been spotted in the Oak Hill area south of Austin. The picture cut to an on-site reporter who interviewed two heavyset African-American women describing a man they had seen at a local shopping center. Their description exactly fit the photograph that had been plastered on TV all day.

"A second sighting occurred in Round Rock," the studio newscaster said, "and another in the Jollyville area. Police are currently investigating each of the sightings. A resident in southeast Austin fired three shots from his deer rifle early this morning at two men fitting the description of Scott Corbin and his accomplice. The men were reportedly hanging around the man's truck. A high school teacher in Dripping Springs reports that Scott Corbin broke into her home at eight P.M. and held her at knifepoint until ten. She says she fought off his repeated attempts to rape her. A sheriff's department spokesperson says that this same woman has reported four break-ins at her home this year, and numerous attempted rapes."

Amanda propped herself up on two pillows and pulled a sheet over her chest. "I hope Sarah is all right."

"She probably took off with him, hoping she might get laid."

"That isn't funny, Marv. She could be in serious danger."

Marv sipped his drink, staring off into space. "People shouldn't stick their noses into other people's business. It always comes back to haunt them."

"What kind of business?"

"Oh, office stuff. Things you don't need to know about."

"There sure is something funny going on at the office. Mr. Shapiro's home being broken into, then Mr. Roman's."

"Shapiro's ex-wife broke into his house . . . I heard him say so."

"What about Mr. Roman's?"

"Kids looking for money to buy drugs. Let's face it, Amanda, the city isn't what it used to be."

Det. Jack Barnaby's frustration grew by the hour. Along with Jim Moyers and Bob Garding, he feared that Sarah would be the next victim—if she was still alive.

Barnaby took a call at headquarters the next morning. He listened intently, then disconnected. "Shit," he said.

"They found her body," Moyers declared.

"Her credit card. She bought gas with it."

"Where?"

"San Antonio."

"When?"

"A few minutes after eight last night."

"Give me the address and I'll get some local officers out there pronto. Maybe somebody will remember her or her car."

Sarah and Scott paid cash in advance and spent a restless night in a small motel a hundred miles west of Kerrville. Corbin explained how he had traded the bicycle he'd found in a garage the night before, then rode to a truck stop near the freeway, wearing his wig and beard. A lone trucker from California had offered him twenty-five dollars to spell him for a few hours, without even asking if Corbin had the proper driver's license. The trucker had seemed desperate to get some sleep. Corbin drove the eighteen-wheeler to a truck stop near Houston, then hitched a ride back to San Antonio with an acquaintance of the California driver's. He had called Sarah from there.

Sarah carried breakfast back to the room from a diner down the road. She again questioned Scott's determination to return to Austin.

"The Chameleon will show himself. He has to want me dead."

"Why, Scott?"

"If he could quietly dispose of me, he could go on killing for years while the whole world continues to look for me. Plus, as long as I'm alive, he's at risk. I'm the only person who knows for sure that I didn't kill those women."

"*I* know it."

He took her hand across the small table. "Thank you." He sipped his coffee. "The killer knows we're together, and that puts you in danger. I won't allow that."

"How could he know?"

"If he's been watching your apartment, he must've seen me come and go."

"I'm frightened to go back, Scott. He'll kill us both."

"I'll drop you off someplace where you can call the police. Ask them to protect you until I find him."

"You mean until he or the police find you and kill you."

Corbin didn't respond right away. Finally he said, "That's a chance I'll have to take."

"If I go back now, they'll arrest me as an accessory or something."

"The charge would never stick. Tell them I kidnapped you."

"They won't believe me."

"They can't prove any different. Tell them I let you go so you could let people know that I'm searching for the real killer, to prove my innocence. If I lure him out, I'll be able to prove that I didn't kill anybody. If not, then . . . well, it won't matter anymore."

An uncomfortable silence followed.

Finally Sarah said, "No."

"No, what?"

"No, I won't go back."

"But you have to. I can't put you in that kind of danger."

Sarah leveled her gaze at him. "I never knew how unalive I was, Scott, until you came into my life. If they had executed you, they would have killed me, too . . . The only difference is, it would have taken a little longer."

Corbin started to say something, but Sarah stopped him with a gesture. She continued, "I'll go any place you want and start a new life with you. Or we can go home and try to prove your innocence. But whatever we decide, we'll do it together or not at all. I will not leave you, Scott. Not now. Not ever."

# Chapter Twenty-eight

Investigating officers from the San Antonio Police Department questioned the Diamond Shamrock clerk who had been on duty the evening before. The clerk was heavyset, male, twenty-three years of age.

"I didn't see nobody."

"How can you say you didn't see anybody? There were probably two hundred people in here on a Friday night." They showed the photographs of Corbin and Sarah Hill again.

"I mean, I didn't see nobody that looked like these pictures. People that pay at the pump don't generally come inside."

"You didn't notice any strange cars, or people who looked as though they might be running from something?"

"No, sir. Like I said, I didn't see nothing or nobody."

Sarah and Scott drove farther west on I-10 Saturday afternoon. They picked up changes of clothes and toiletries along the way, then checked into a small motel where the TV was chained to the dresser.

No matter, as long as cash in advance was accepted for two nights' lodging.

Scott sat in a worn chair next to a small round table while Sarah propped herself up on the bed. They watched satellite-TV news throughout the evening. People continued to report new sightings of the Chameleon in greater Austin. No mention was made of Sarah.

"They don't believe that you were kidnapped," Corbin said, "otherwise they'd be showing your picture as often as mine."

"Maybe they don't even know I've gone anywhere."

"From what you've told me, the police must have been watching your place. They know."

After the news had been off for a while, Sarah asked, "Do you have family back in Tennessee?"

Corbin lowered the TV's volume. "Not living. There was the one sister I told you about—the one the chimney fell on."

"No other brothers or sisters?"

"My mother had something wrong with one of her tubes or something, so she had trouble getting pregnant. It took her forever just to have me. I always figured that's why she treated me so special."

Sarah hesitated, then asked, "Scott, are you still married?"

He almost laughed. "I told you before, I'm divorced."

"Didn't you have children?"

He shifted in the chair, his discomfort visible.

"Well?" she said. "Do you?"

He looked at her for a long moment, then back at the TV. Finally he replied, "A son."

"Is he with his mother?"

"As far as I know."

Piece by piece Sarah garnered the details. When Scott had divorced in Dallas, his wife was granted custody of their two-year-old son, Sean. Corbin was terribly distraught—he adored his son. The divorce occurred because Tanya, Scott's ex-wife, had flaunted extramarital affairs in his face. They had married after a whirlwind romance that included lots of passion and little verbal communication. Sean was born just over nine months after their wedding. Tanya filed for divorce two years later when Scott steadfastly refused to be a party to an open marriage.

Sarah asked what he meant by *open*.

"Tanya would've slept with a posthole digger," Scott said.

"What happened with your son?"

"The court granted me visitation rights, and I drove up to Dallas as often as I was allowed. But sometime between when I was arrested for Rhonda's murder, and then convicted as the Chameleon, Tanya changed Sean's name and moved away. I haven't seen or heard of either since."

In a voice gone husky with emotion, Corbin added, "So yes, Sarah, I have a child. I don't know where he lives and I don't know what name he goes by. My son will be nine years old on December the twenty-eighth, and I'll probably never see him again."

* * *

Following a fast-food lunch in the room on Sunday, Sarah tried again to convince Corbin to start over someplace where nobody ever heard of the Chameleon.

"You could take on a whole new identity."

"Giving up my identity would be like executing *myself,*" he said. "The person I've always been would die." He took a deep breath and slowly released it. "The main reason I won't consider it is that I'm determined to leave my son a good name when I die."

"But his mother changed his name."

"Doesn't matter . . . I'm still his father. I'll be damned if my son is gonna grow up with the world believing that his daddy was a no-good-sonofabitchin' murderer." He slammed his fist against the small table at his side.

Sarah had never seen him so upset. She didn't speak right away. Then she said, "Tell me about your family, Scott. Your dad. I really want to know."

Little by little, he told her. What he had said before was accurate about his dad teaching him that in the end, all a man had to leave was educated, God-loving children and a good name. What Scott hadn't told her was that shortly after his mother died, his father had been accused of embezzling twenty-five thousand dollars from the lumber company he worked for. He had supposedly used the money to pay nursing-home expenses that their medical insurance carrier refused to pay. Blue Cross contended back then that Alzheimer's disease was a psychiatric illness, not organic brain disease, so Scott's mother had not been covered under their policy.

Charged with embezzlement, his dad had been unable to prove his innocence. It came down to his father's word against the employer's—an influential man in the community.

"I always suspected that the owner took the money himself. I know he collected from his theft-insurance policy."

Scott told Sarah that his father was killed the week before he was to go to Brushy Mountain State Prison.

"Right after my mom developed Alzheimer's, he started drinking for the first time in his life, mostly so he could sleep at night. He'd been drinking heavily the day his car flipped on Dead Man's Curve between Johnson City and Bristol. Some people said he committed suicide. Others thought he got killed trying to run away."

"How awful for you. I'm so sorry."

Scott added sadly, "He died with the entire world believing that he was guilty. Or my entire hometown . . . the only world I knew." He sat silent for a moment. "I only went back to Tennessee one time after my parents died."

"What for?"

"I had to find out, so I went to confront the man who owned the lumber company. When I finally found him, he was in a nursing home following a massive stroke. It was even the same nursing home where my mother had spent her last five years. She had died there.

"This man I'm supposed to hate was just lying there all alone," Corbin said, "staring up at nothing, with spit drooling down his chin. He couldn't talk . . . had no idea who I was. I remembered a big, robust blowhard, but what I found was a shriveled old man struggling to stay alive." He shook his head. "Like the rest of us, I suppose." He stopped speaking for a moment, then said, "Sitting there looking at that old man, all I could remember was my dad beside my mother's bed every evening for all the years she was sick, holding her hand and talking softly to her and telling her that everything was going to be all right. Every single day after he got off from work, and every weekend."

Sarah studied Corbin's face, the bewilderment in his eyes. She could almost touch his sense of loss, and she ached inside with his overwhelming frustration and disappointment. After a moment she asked, "Do you believe that your dad was guilty?"

Scott slowly shook his head and raised his eyebrows. "No. But everybody else does."

They didn't leave the motel room on Sunday except when Sarah picked up food. Scott was still sitting up staring at the TV with its sound muted at two A.M.

Sarah tried to read, but couldn't concentrate on the book she'd bought. She said, "I've never known anybody as single-minded as you, Scott. Is it all for your son?"

"Oh, I . . . mostly, yes." He thought for a moment. "I don't have any family to care about me . . . certainly not Tanya, and probably not even my son. Nothing feels as important as proving my innocence."

"Aren't there other things you want?"

"Sure. I'd like to have a home, a wife who really loves me. Go fishing with Sean, grill hamburgers and hot dogs in the backyard. I want to plan vacations and watch movies and eat popcorn and window-shop for furniture. I'd love to write again someday. I was pretty good at it once."

"Could it be pride driving you? Showing the world that you're right?"

He didn't answer right away. Finally he said, "I read a lot in prison. A man named Erik Erikson said we go through different phases as adults. First, when we realize we haven't lived up to our talents and aspirations, which is the midlife crisis. As most everybody knows, that can lead to all sorts of insane behavior. Then there's a later crisis he called integrity versus despair."

"What does that mean?"

"That's when you look not so much at your accomplishments, but whether your life has had meaning . . . has really counted for something. Have I become involved? Do I really care?"

"About what?"

"Something outside yourself. Animals, starving children, whales, the ozone. Something worthwhile and unselfish." He adjusted his position slightly and rotated his head till his neck popped. "I sure haven't lived up to my aspirations so far. As a teenager I thought I was gonna do all sorts of dynamic things when I grew up. Make a difference, you know? So I damn well want the rest of my life to count for something; otherwise, I'd just as well turn myself in and let them execute me now." He slowly shook his head and rubbed the back of his neck. "My life up to now has counted for absolutely nothing."

Sarah read the disenchantment in his face. She reflected on her own situation. What had her life counted for? After several moments, she asked, "Your neck stiff?"

"A little."

"Would you like me to rub it for you?"

"I'd love it."

Scott pulled his chair closer to the bed and Sarah massaged the back of his neck and shoulders. His muscles were as tense as steel cables.

She saw in the mirror over the dresser that Corbin's eyes were not closed. There was a haunting sadness there, as though an idealistic young man from a mountain town in Tennessee had seen more than he had ever bargained for. Sarah was pretty sure she didn't want to know everything he had witnessed. All the places he'd been.

Jack Barnaby asked Bob Garding to join him for breakfast Monday morning at Ma Ferguson's Restaurant near Highland Mall.

Barnaby said, "If she comes back alive, I'm gonna lock her up and press charges for aiding and abetting a murderer."

Garding said, "You can't be sure of that, Jack."

"She went off with that bastard. She lied to me. Women are dying out there and she's been protecting this asshole."

"She's an innocent pawn," Garding argued. "If she is with him, then he kidnapped her."

"She made up a story about having a headache and left the office voluntarily."

"Maybe she left with a headache and Corbin waylaid her in the parking garage."

"She withdrew money from her bank account, Bob. Rented a car and paid cash. She's helping him."

"He could force her to do those things. Threaten her life, or somebody close to her."

"Like who?"

"I don't know, but she would not help this man without a good reason. You don't know Sarah. I'm telling you, he's kidnapped her."

"Oh, my God," Sarah exclaimed, "the police."

She had heard the siren first; then her breath caught when she turned to see flashing lights zooming up directly behind them.

Corbin instinctively lifted his foot from the Corolla's accelerator and checked the speedometer. He spied an exit ramp immediately ahead and moved into the right lane. He was angling off the freeway when the Highway Patrol car flew past and continued in the direction of Kerrville and San Antonio.

Sarah's heart was pounding and her breathing was fast. "Oh, that scared me."

"Me, too." Corbin pulled to a stop at the end of the ramp and sat motionless for several seconds. When a truck blew its horn behind them he moved the car and got back on the freeway.

Sarah tried to moisten her lips with a dry tongue. Her heart was beginning to slow. "That was too close."

Corbin nodded. "We gotta get off the roads. We need a place to stay while things cool down. They probably know our license-tag number by now, so we'll need another car."

"Or another license plate."

He glanced over at her. "What a great idea."

"Thanks."

After a few more miles Sarah said, "Pull off somewhere and find a telephone."

"What for?"

"I just thought of a place where nobody will ever look."

When the idea had first occurred to her, Sarah's impulse was to drive straight to the lake house. On further thought, however, she couldn't risk taking Scott there without knowing for certain that nobody had reserved it since the day Marissa had said it was available. Besides, she knew she could trust Amanda to keep a secret.

Sarah called Amanda from a pay phone. She said that her headache was better, but she wouldn't be in for a few more days due to "personal matters."

"Thank God you're okay, Sarah. I've been so worried. The police were here right before quitting time on Friday, asking all kinds of questions. We thought you had been kidnapped by the Chameleon."

Sarah assured Amanda that she was all right. "With all the stress lately, I needed to get away."

"But . . . why did you leave your car downstairs?"

Sarah searched for a quick reply. "Well, a friend picked me up. Phyllis, my friend from New Orleans. I stayed with her over the weekend."

"Oh, sure, you've mentioned her before."

Sarah said she had to go, but asked if the lake house might still be available. "I really need some time alone."

Amanda checked her computer. "The Stern family went over Friday and Saturday, then left yesterday. It's free until Wednesday afternoon. Would you like to reserve it tonight and tomorrow night?"

"No, I just . . . there's a possibility I could go, but I don't know yet. If I should decide to, I'll schedule it on-line or call you back. And, Amanda, please don't tell anybody that I even inquired about it. All right?"

"Sure. And call if I can do anything for you, Sarah. You've been under a tremendous amount of pressure lately. But don't worry; they're going to catch this man. When they do, you'll feel better in no time. All of us will."

Robert Garding was on the outskirts of Fredericksburg when he pulled his pickup to the side of the road. He sat with the engine idling for several minutes, reflecting on what Jack Barnaby had told him about Sarah's withdrawing money from her savings account and paying cash for a rental car. He knew Sarah well enough to know that she simply would not go off with Scott Corbin of her own free will. If she was with that bastard, he didn't want to imagine what Corbin might have done to force her to go. Or what he'd do when he didn't need her anymore.

Garding quickly swung his truck around and headed east on Highway 290. He could be at Sarah's office in about an hour. She hadn't said she would not be in on Monday. As responsible as Sarah was, if she couldn't make it in, she'd call. Providing she was still alive.

# CHAPTER TWENTY-NINE

Detectives Jack Barnaby and Jim Moyers approached the reception desk and asked if anybody had heard from Sarah.

Amanda said that Sarah had called earlier. "She's fine. She was with her friend Phyllis yesterday. She said she just needs some time to herself now."

"What time did she call?"

"A few minutes after nine."

"Did she say where she was?"

"No, sir, just that she'd be back in a couple of days."

Barnaby turned to see Anthony Shapiro and Marvin Jamison walking toward him. They appeared to be leaving for lunch.

Barnaby asked, "Do either of you know where Sarah might have gone?"

Jamison said, "She called Amanda this morning."

"I already told them that," Amanda said.

Marissa Young joined them at the reception desk, then Cosmo Rivers came along, followed by Tad Roman and Tracy Leigon. Everybody seemed concerned.

Jamison said, "Do you still think Sarah might be with Scott Corbin?"

"We have no direct evidence that she is," Moyers said.

Barnaby added, "Her phone call this morning makes it pretty unlikely." He cleared his throat and asked again, "Do any of you know where she might have gone? It's extremely important that we speak with her as soon as possible."

Nobody did.

Cosmo Rivers asked, "What's new on the serial man? Any new bodies?"

"We're reasonably certain that Corbin is still in Austin," Barnaby replied. He ignored Cosmo's question about new bodies.

Tad Roman asked, "Were you able to determine who the other man was? The one driving the car?"

Moyers answered, "Not yet. Somebody wiped the car clean of fingerprints." He glanced at Amanda, then asked, "Miss Stowe says Sarah may be with her friend, Phyllis. Does anybody know Phyllis's last name or where she lives?"

Marissa Young spoke up. "Sarah told me a few months back that Phyllis had moved to New Orleans, but she never mentioned a last name."

When nobody had anything to add, the detectives left.

Amanda looked at the others nervously, then said, "I hope I didn't do the wrong thing."

Roman said, "What do you mean?"

"Well, I . . . when Sarah called, she asked if anybody was using the lake house this week. I didn't tell the detectives because Sarah said she wanted to be alone. I knew she wouldn't want anybody disturbing her if she decided to go."

Anthony Shapiro scowled at Amanda. "I certainly hope you didn't tell her she could use it." His tone was accusatory.

"No, sir, I just—"

"Because it's occupied," Shapiro said before Amanda could finish her thought. "The Sterns had it all weekend and the Blackwells go in right behind them."

When the others looked at him strangely, Shapiro added, "I checked just minutes ago. I was thinking of using it myself."

Amanda's lips pressed together in a thin line. She did not say anything more.

Scott Corbin climbed out of the water and extended a hand to help Sarah onto the swimming dock. They had taken back roads across from I-10, picked up groceries in Marble Falls, and arrived at Horseshoe Bay in midafternoon. As Sarah had promised there was almost nobody on the lake during the week. They were able to relax for the first time in days, enjoying a leisurely swim.

"I needed that," Sarah said. "The water feels wonderful."

"What a great spot," Corbin said, looking out over the expanse of Lake LBJ.

"I wish we could do this forever." Sarah began toweling her hair dry, then looked up at him. "I never realized how much of my life has been wasted."

He smiled sadly. "Yeah. Mine, too."

* * *

Robert Garding's instinct had been right.

"Yes, sir," Amanda Stowe said, "she did call in. She's taking a couple of days off because of personal reasons."

"Where did she go?"

Amanda shook her head, replying, "She didn't say."

Garding couldn't help noticing that Amanda seemed uncomfortable with his last question. "You're sure?"

"Yes, sir, I'm sure."

"You said she called in this morning around nine. Is that correct?"

Amanda nodded. "Yes, sir."

"Said she wouldn't be in for a few days?"

She nodded again. "That's right."

"But she didn't give you any indication of where she might be going?"

Amanda just looked at him. "She didn't say."

"You're sure about that?"

She shook her pretty head from side to side. "I'm sure, sir. You already asked me that."

This young woman was holding something back and he didn't have time to play games. He had a bad feeling in his gut—a feeling that had guided him through many harrowing experiences in his career. He needed to find Sarah, and find her fast. But he also couldn't piss off the receptionist or she would shut down completely.

Garding thanked Amanda and started to leave. After a couple of steps he casually turned around and smiled his most winning smile. "Miss Stowe, I'm sure you recall that I am a friend of Sarah's."

She nodded. "Yes, sir."

He walked back to her desk, lowered his voice, and looked around as if checking to make sure nobody would overhear. "Sarah would want me to know where she is."

After a moment's hesitation Amanda almost whispered, "She needs some time alone, Mr. Garding. She's been under tremendous pressure lately."

"Oh, I know . . . she told me. But just between you and me, I'm worried about her. Wouldn't you feel better if I at least make sure she's all right?" He winked. "I respect her desire to be alone. I would never intrude."

Amanda held out for a few more minutes, then told him that Sarah had said she might go to the lake house. "She never said for sure."

"Did she sound nervous on the phone?"

"A little."

"Frightened?"

"I don't know, Mr. Garding. I couldn't . . . well, maybe she did. I thought it was because of everything that's been going on."

Garding first got the address of the retreat, then asked if he could use a telephone. Privately.

"Mr. Shapiro isn't in," Amanda said. "I suppose you can use his phone."

Seconds later Garding spoke rapidly to Detective Moyers. "Sarah's almost certainly at their corporate lake house at Horseshoe Bay. Tell Barnaby I've got a bad feeling about it, Jim. Corbin may be with her. I'll meet you there." He gave the address and raced out of the office.

It was late afternoon when Sarah and Scott walked back to the house from the dock. They opened the sliding glass door on the lakefront patio and went inside.

Scott asked, "Did you put anything in the oven?"

"No."

"You sure? Something smells mighty good."

A delectable aroma came from the direction of the kitchen. They looked at each other quizzically and followed their noses.

"What in the—"

"Oh, hello, dear," Marissa Young said, hardly looking up. She was arranging things on the glass-top dining table—three place settings, including china, silverware, and crystal wineglasses. "I know how stressed you've been, Sarah, so I decided to surprise you with a delightful dinner."

Marissa was stylishly dressed in orange Capri pants, heels that emphasized her slender ankles, and a black top with a tastefully low neckline.

Sarah and Scott were dumbfounded. They gestured anxiously behind Marissa's back. With his picture all over TV, how could she not have recognized Corbin? In fact, Marissa had hardly taken notice of Scott.

Sarah felt her pulse racing. She said, "How sweet, Marissa, but . . . I don't understand. What made you come all the way over here?"

"Well, I developed a terrible headache right before

lunch, so I went home. Once I was there I started feeling better, so I just drove on over." She smiled briefly, adding, "Amanda mentioned that you might be coming to the lake."

Marissa talked as she worked, scurrying back and forth between the kitchen and dining area. She ground fresh pepper into a steaming pot on the stove, then tasted the contents with a spoon. She gave an approving look.

Sarah hesitated, then said, "Uh, Marissa, this is my friend, Peter. Peter Buda."

Marissa glanced in Corbin's direction. "Nice to meet you."

"Likewise."

"I hope you enjoy what I've prepared. Why don't you both take a seat?"

"We really should go change," Sarah said.

Scott added, "Yes, our bathing suits are still damp."

"Not to worry, dear, this is a lake house. Mr. Hodge had it furnished accordingly."

Sarah nervously sat while Scott remained standing, trying to think of an excuse to leave before Marissa got a good look at him.

"What a nice surprise," Sarah said halfheartedly. She looked at Corbin, her mind filled with questions. She motioned toward the door with her head.

Marissa took a silver tray from the refrigerator and removed its covering of aluminum foil. Delivering it to the table, she said, "For your appetizer, this is my own variation of sushi . . . I hope you like it. I never cared much for raw fish."

Sarah screamed.

Marissa set an artistically arranged tray of cocktail crackers and marinated human eyeballs on the table. Each eyeball was skewered with a decorative silver toothpick shaped like a saber. Half of the eyes were green, the others, brown. In her opposite hand Marissa cocked a revolver.

Sarah jerked back from the table, screaming hysterically.

Marissa held the gun to Corbin's chest. Looking directly into his face she said sweetly, "Tell me, Scott, dear . . . would you prefer green or brown?"

# Chapter Thirty

Bob Garding cursed the traffic into Marble Falls. He missed the green light at the turnoff to Horseshoe Bay and sat fuming through the longest red light of his life. The instant it changed he blew his horn at the car ahead, then raced around it. He missed having a siren and emergency lights to make people pull the hell over and let him pass. He blew his horn almost constantly, zooming past an RV pulling a boat and trailer. Seconds later he narrowly missed a black Suburban full of shirtless teenagers absolutely flying toward him in the oncoming lane.

Garding tried not to imagine what Corbin was doing to Sarah. The ominous feeling twisting his stomach into knots was growing worse with each second that elapsed. Sarah would never go to the lake house alone. He knew for a fact that she had never been there at all. She had once told him that.

The picture of a girl named Stephanie flashed across Garding's mind. Her lying on a cold steel tray in a dark chamber in the morgue. Stiff. Blind. Her young carcass laid open like the remains of a Thanksgiving turkey. He fought to avoid seeing Sarah's face on Stephanie's mutilated body.

His tires squealed and the engine whined, revving faster and faster as he jammed the accelerator pedal still harder against the floor.

Marissa portioned out eyeball appetizers on each of three Royal Doulton plates. "My favorite is green," she said, "but tiny flecks of yellow add a nice decorative touch."

She hurried to the entertainment console and switched on the FM stereo, dialing past one smooth-jazz and two country stations before settling on a classical station playing Mozart's *Così Fan Tutte.*

The announcer translated the title, "All women do so."

"I just love Mozart," Marissa said. "Don't you?"

It was a rhetorical question. Sarah and Scott sat tightly gagged and bound by gray duct tape to dining room chairs. Both had temporarily exhausted themselves yelling and struggling, and now made unintelligible noises through their noses. A nasty hematoma was developing on Scott's temple where Marissa had struck him with her pistol.

Stirring the pot on the stove once again, Marissa served steaming portions into three matching china bowls.

"Steak-and-kidney pie is an English dish," she said. "The Australians use a lard crust, however, and call it steak-and-kidney puddin'. I prefer the English recipe."

She carried the bowls one by one to the table, conversing as if hosting a garden-club luncheon. "I had thought you were dead, Scott. I am so glad you're not."

She peeled back one edge of the tape from his mouth. "How *did* you manage to survive?"

"They executed the wrong person, you psychotic bitch."

"Well, they certainly did." She showed no hint of taking umbrage.

Corbin growled, "Did you kill those women six years ago?"

When Marissa merely smiled in reply, he demanded through gritted teeth, "And Rhonda Talbot?"

Marissa delicately popped one of the skewered eyeballs into her mouth. She studied Corbin's face as she chewed. She finally swallowed.

"How were you connected to Electronic Business Systems?" Corbin said hoarsely. "How did you wind up at ISI?"

Marissa sipped her glass of wine. While reaching for the bowl of steak-and-kidney pie, she calmly replied, "What better place to work, Scott, dear? Marvin Jamison is knocking down nearly ten thousand dollars a month, then taking his kickbacks as profits in a joint futures-trading account. Long before his divorce, Tony Shapiro exchanged over half of the ISI stock he had coming for options in a foreign corporation's name. He unloads about a hundred shares a week so as not to depress the price. He must have millions in Bermuda. Cosmo Rivers is blackmailing Jamison, then puts that money into an Internet pornography Web site that he created with two partners. Everybody's so busy with his own little chicanery that nobody notices me. I remain squeaky clean, have a great cover, and make the money I need to pursue the hobby I enjoy most." She stopped short. "Oh, goodness, I forgot the liver. Don't you just love a little taste of liver in steak-and-kidney pie? It really should be sautéed fresh, you know . . . liver doesn't freeze well at all."

Marissa turned abruptly and ripped off Sarah's bathing-suit top. When Corbin objected even louder, Marissa pressed the tape back down on his mouth. She took a ten-inch butcher knife from her handbag and drew it lightly around the base of Sarah's neck—the resulting slice was as thin as a paper cut. The necklace of red droplets that formed resembled a string of tiny rubies; then the rubies seemed to melt and trickle down Sarah's chest.

Sarah felt her eyes bulge as though they might spring from their sockets. She thought she would surely either suffocate or die from fright before Marissa killed her. Her overwhelming claustrophobia from being so tightly bound and gagged was almost as bad as the searing pain from Marissa's blade.

Both Sarah and Corbin desperately kicked, bit, shouted, strained—tried everything possible to somehow break loose. Nothing worked. The tape held fast.

"Nice breasts, Sarah," Marissa exclaimed. "Why do you keep them so tightly covered?" She walked to the entertainment console again and raised the volume on the stereo.

"One of the best things about quality construction

is," Marissa declared to Scott when she returned, "it really is soundproof. I love to hear them beg." She ripped the tape from Sarah's mouth. "Scream all you want, dear. Nobody will hear a thing."

Bob Garding raced into Horseshoe Bay Corporation's sales office in Bay Center. A well-dressed couple in their sixties were speaking with the only salesperson in sight, a woman of forty-five wearing an obvious blond wig. The woman had puffy lower lids and spider veins on both cheeks. Garding saw a site map on the wall with an arrow marked with a star. The message below the star was, "You are here."

"Excuse me," he said, breathing hard, "but how do I get to 107 West Cove Street?"

The three gave him a look of admonishment, then continued their conversation.

"Please," he said, "I'm a police officer and I'm in a terrible hurry."

"Oh. You want our Bay Country development at Horseshoe Bay West. What you do is, turn right out of the parking lot and take 2147 west, then . . ."

Garding was out the door before the saleswoman could tell him what kind of day he should have. He raced toward his truck, propelled by an overwhelming sense of doom. Something bad was happening to Sarah. This pervasive discomfort had been growing mile by mile from the moment he'd left Austin. Whatever danger she was in, he knew he had to reach her soon.

Just before opening his truck's door Garding ran his fingers over the reassuring pancake holster inside his khaki trousers. Then he climbed quickly inside and switched on the ignition.

Their wailing siren and flashing bubble light warned drivers out of their way. Jim Moyers absently checked the fastener on his seat belt while Barnaby tested the limits of the unmarked vehicle to the extreme—tires, shocks, suspension, and frame. The big engine screamed as it redlined once again and they careened around a huge truck hauling pink gravel.

Moyers said loudly, "You sure put a lot of faith in what Garding says."

"I've known Bob for fifteen years," Barnaby shouted in return above the whining engine and siren. "When he tells you he's on to something, you'd better listen."

"He never said how he knew she was there."

"Doesn't matter. If he's in that big a hurry, something's going down. The man has an inborn sense about these things. He always did." After a beat Barnaby added, "I just hope Sarah will be alive when we get there."

"Oh, God, no," Sarah screamed. "Please don't."

Marissa traced the butcher knife delicately between Sarah's breasts and down along her abdomen. She drew an oblong shape with the knife's tip beneath the right side of Sarah's rib cage.

"The liver sits exactly here, but plunging the knife in directly would damage it . . . so we simply begin the entry cut over here." She moved the tip of the blade to the area above Sarah's belly button.

Sarah thought she would pass out. She almost wished she could lose consciousness, but knew she'd never awaken if she did. Her world was turning black before her very eyes, and she couldn't move away no matter how hard she tried.

"Oh, but first . . . look at those beautiful eyes. Such a vibrant green, so full of fire. I have always loved your intelligent eyes, Sarah. They remind me of Ireland." Marissa set the longer knife on the dining table and removed a short one from her bag.

Sarah recalled Tracy Leigon's description of what the Chameleon did to his victims. *Her* victims. If Tracy only knew. If *anybody* knew.

Sarah's vocal cords had gone ragged from screaming. She tried to object, but couldn't hear herself above the blare of Ludwig van Beethoven's "Eroica" symphony now overpowering the room.

Robert Garding rounded a curve on two wheels, then hit a straightaway flat-out. Seconds later his pickup leaned precariously as it skidded into the entrance at Horseshoe Bay West.

Jim Moyers checked his global positioning system device, calling out directions to Jack Barnaby. Their adrenaline surged as they sped along the highway at breakneck speeds.

"Take the next right," Moyers shouted. "Six-tenths of a mile and go right again. We're looking for 107."

Scott Corbin felt one section of tape give way ever so slightly on his right ankle. He pushed hard against it with the foot, then the entire leg. While Marissa focused her full attention on Sarah's eyes, Scott's every muscle strained to dislodge the tape. His toes stretched desperately to touch the floor. Something ripped above his left foot. He quickly looked at Marissa—she hadn't noticed. He ground his teeth together, heart slamming against his ribs. His breath was coming in short puffs and grunts. *There!* The first one tore through soundlessly in the music-filled room. Now for the other.

Bob Garding lurched to a stop in front of a beige stucco house with a Spanish-tile roof. He hurriedly double-checked the number on the house: 107. He threw open his pickup's door and jumped to the ground, listening, watching, all senses alert.

With superhuman effort Scott Corbin planted both feet on the floor and lunged headlong toward Marissa's abdomen. His feet were free but his torso and arms remained tightly bound. His neck almost snapped when his head butted against her.

Marissa flew backward, arms flailing, windmilling for balance. She crashed through the sliding glass door onto the patio outside and her knife sailed off into the bushes. Corbin, chair and all, continued to drive forward atop her.

The sound of breaking glass sent Garding's heart into his throat. He pulled his snub-nosed .38 from its holster as he raced around the side of the house.

Two people were scuffling on the patio, shards of

glass all around them. Both had blood on their clothes and skin.

"Halt! Police!"

They ignored Garding's warning.

"Stop where you are."

The woman broke loose and ran inside.

"Stop her," Scott Corbin yelled hoarsely. Heavy gray tape hung from one cheek and one arm. He was struggling to dislodge the tape from around his waist and other arm. "Dammit, stop that woman; she's a murderer."

Garding advanced quickly but cautiously, gripping his revolver in both hands. "Stay right where you are," he shouted.

Marissa ran to where Sarah sat bound to the chair. "Shoot him," Marissa yelled through the smashed door, "he's the Chameleon."

"No," Sarah tried, "it's . . ." But her voice trailed off in a desperate croak.

Garding aimed his gun at Scott Corbin's head. "Facedown on the floor, asshole."

"Dammit," Corbin said, "that woman is the Chameleon. She almost killed Sarah."

Garding winced when he saw the blood trickling down Sarah's bare chest and abdomen. But she was alive. He pulled out a set of handcuffs and slammed Corbin facedown on the cement, continuing to hold the gun at Scott's head.

Marissa started for her own gun across the room, but stopped when Garding glanced back toward her.

Sarah was shaking her head violently from side to side, croaking something unintelligible.

Aware that it would be only a matter of seconds before Sarah would tell, Marissa grabbed the ten-inch knife and held it against Sarah's throat. "Back off or I'll kill her right now."

Corbin shouted from where he lay, "Shoot her, dammit . . . she'll cut Sarah's throat."

Sarah tried to speak, but could not.

Garding looked from Sarah back to Corbin, now struggling to sit up.

In that instant Marissa lunged for her gun and rolled on the floor, firing at Bob Garding.

Two rapid reports followed hers.

Marissa jerked twice, tried to say something, then fell limp. One eye stared up toward the ceiling—a green iris flecked with saffron yellow. The pupil of that eye was fixed and dilated below a perfectly round hole in the center of Marissa's forehead. Her other eye, and the back of her skull, had been blown completely away.

# Chapter Thirty-one

Barnaby and Moyers screeched to a stop beside Garding's white pickup. Climbing out of their car they heard shouts from around the house, followed by rapid gunshots. Each unholstered a Glock 9mm semiautomatic weapon and ran toward the commotion.

Robert Garding attended to Sarah while Moyers and Barnaby quickly checked Corbin's handcuffs, then secured his ankles with flex cuffs. Over his loud objections they stuffed Scott into their vehicle, then called for paramedics and backup from local law enforcement.

Garding helped Sarah onto a sofa and covered her with an afghan. She was desperately trying to tell him something.

"Don't try to talk, Sarah. It's gonna be okay now. It's over."

Jack Barnaby hurried to Garding's side. "You did it, Bob . . . you got the son of a bitch."

"Yeah, but there's something weird here. That dead woman tried to cut Sarah's throat; then she took a shot at me."

"Why?"

"Beats the hell out of me."

Jack Barnaby surveyed the scene again. An acrid smell of spent gunpowder filled the air, one woman lay dead on the floor, and another was dripping blood all over the sofa. He winced when he spotted the tray of marinated eyeballs. An EMS vehicle arrived outside.

"Right now," Barnaby said, "we need to get Sarah to the hospital and Corbin to central booking. We'll sort out the details later."

It was eleven o'clock on a Wednesday morning in Livingston, Texas, when guards led Scott Corbin into the secure visitor's room. The booth for visitations consisted of a locked cage for the offender, separated from the visitor by a thick glass partition. Communication through the glass was via telephone handsets.

Corbin was placed in the enclosure on his side of the glass, and his handcuffs and ankle restraints removed. The guards locked the door behind him, then lurked a respectful distance away.

Sarah stood alongside former detective Robert Garding on the other side of the separation. She took a seat in the visitor's chair and picked up the telephone's handset.

Scott also put a handset to his ear.

Before he could speak, however, Sarah blurted out, "Marissa Young's DNA matched sperm on the victims, Scott."

Corbin thought he must have heard wrong. "Her DNA matched what?"

"The medical examiner called Detective Barnaby

after Marissa's body was taken in. Everybody knew that Marissa had long auburn hair, full breasts, and a perfect little nose. What we didn't know was, she also had a penis and two testicles. She was a man, Scott."

Robert Garding leaned forward and said into the phone, "Maybe I'd better explain. After the ME's examination, a nationwide search of implant manufacturers turned up a Marissa Young who'd had breast augmentation performed in Los Angeles four years ago. The plastic surgeon's records showed she'd had a rhinoplasty and her jaw narrowed at the same time. So far they've kept this information from the media."

Corbin felt his pulse quicken. He held his breath.

"Surprise number two is," Garding said, "before Marissa became Ms. Young, she used to be Mr. Franklyn Russett. His fingerprints were on file from juvenile arrests—everything from animal molestation and torture to breaking and entering and arson.

"Marissa's DNA not only matched semen in the three recent victims, it also matched semen found on two women slashed to death in Los Angeles during the time she, aka Franklyn Russett, was out there having plastic surgery and her beard removed by electrolysis."

"Wait a minute," Corbin said. "Frank Russett was killed over four years ago . . . shot by a prostitute."

Sarah responded. "That's what the newspapers and TV reported."

Garding said, "We found Russett's car in the Colorado River over near Marble Falls four years ago, with bullet holes in the driver's seat, but we never recovered his body. Blood on the seat must've been from the prostitute he killed. We never found her, either."

"So he faked his own death?"

"Sure looks that way. He must've known he needed a radical change when you followed his trail to EBS. After your conviction took the heat off, he took the money from the buyout and bought himself a new identity. The Chameleon pulled the ultimate camouflage and became a whole new person . . . a woman."

"How do you know about—"

"Sarah told me everything you'd uncovered, Scott."

Sarah spoke up excitedly. "One wall in Marissa's bedroom was covered with drawings she had done of eyes, with the victim's name below each pair. Detective Barnaby said it was spooky. This entire wall of eyes watched over her while she slept at night . . . or whatever she did. Detective Moyers found a diary in Marissa's attic describing every gory detail of the murders, along with suitcases full of bloodstained women's clothing. Plus, she—or he—kept a little trophy from each victim, including clothing with Rhonda Talbot's blood on it, Scott, and something from all the other women you were accused of killing."

Corbin was so overwhelmed that he couldn't speak. He blinked back his tears, and placed one hand on the glass opposite Sarah's hand—as close as they could come to touching.

Garding said gravely, "I owe you a big apology,

Corbin. Jack Barnaby and Jim Moyers worked hard to keep this away from reporters while we sorted out the details. They asked me to convey their apologies, too. It's obvious that you're innocent of all charges, and we can prove it. The governor even agreed to spearhead your release. He's in the process of granting a reprieve as we speak. He feels certain that the Board of Pardons and Paroles will recommend a full pardon based on innocence." Garding smiled his crooked smile, adding, "Your conviction will be fully overturned."

Her hand still against the glass, Sarah said, "Your name is going to be cleared, Scott. The nightmare is over. Oh, God, I've missed you. I love you so."

# CHAPTER THIRTY-TWO

Six months later in their two-story home north of Austin, Scott Corbin swiveled his chair around to face Sarah. He held the phone's receiver to one ear, listening intently to what his attorney had to say.

Sarah sat at a matching computer desk across from Scott's, wide-eyed with anticipation. Prior to the phone call both had been hard at work on book manuscripts. Scott's was a work of nonfiction entitled *Wrongful Conviction*. Sarah was on the third chapter of a romance novel—not reading this time, but attempting to write one.

Sarah had resigned her position at ISI after training Amanda Stowe as her replacement, and now worked from home as a part-time consultant for a national banking-software provider. Her remaining time was spent concentrating on her novel, tentatively called *Prisoner of Love,* and on her new husband, Scott Corbin.

When Scott hung up the phone, Sarah asked, "Was that Bob Erwin?"

"Yes."

"Did he meet with the state's attorneys again?"

"Yes."

"Don't keep me in suspense . . . what did he say?"

"The State of Texas upped their settlement offer to twelve million dollars, and they agree to drop all charges against Dr. King."

Sarah came out of her chair and hugged her husband. "Oh, Scott, it's exactly what you wanted."

"There's more."

She drew back and searched his face. He was grinning from ear to ear but his eyes were overflowing with tears.

Sarah said, "About your son?"

He nodded. In a voice gone husky with emotion he said, "Erwin just received a fax from Tanya's lawyer. She's agreed to let Sean visit me this weekend." He wiped his cheeks, adding, "My son is coming to see me, Sarah. He'll be here on Saturday."

They clung to each other, sharing their excitement and their joy. Aside from the day when she and Scott were married, Sarah had never felt so happy or so fulfilled.

Scott nuzzled her neck and squeezed her tight against him. "Every day of my life, Sarah, I thank God that I'm alive . . . if only so I can love you. I love you and my son more than either of you will ever know."

*Exactly the way you're going to love our daughter,* Sarah almost blurted out, but she didn't. She'd wait until after the special dinner she had planned to announce that Scott would soon be the proud father of his very first daughter.

When Sarah's physician had confirmed her pregnancy the day before, he wouldn't venture a guess as to whether it might be a boy or a girl. But she knew. Some things in life you just know. And she knew. Their baby was a girl.

Sarah smiled to herself and said, "I love you with all my heart, Scott Corbin. I feel as though I always have. I know I always will."